It All Comes Down to This

It All Comes Down to This

KAREN ENGLISH

Houghton Mifflin Harcourt
Boston   New York

For information about permission to reproduce selections from this book, write to
trade.permissions@hmco.com or to Permissions, Houghton Mifflin Harcourt Publishing Company,
3 Park Avenue, 19th Floor, New York, New York 10016.

hmhbooks.com

The text was set in Stempel Schneidler Std.

The Library of Congress has cataloged the hardcover edition as follows:
Names: English, Karen, author.
Title: It all comes down to this / by Karen English.
Description: Boston ; New York : Clarion Books, Houghton Mifflin Harcourt,
[2017]. | Summary: "In the summer of 1965, Sophie's family becomes the
first African Americans to move into their upper middle-class neighborhood
in Los Angeles. When riots erupt in nearby Watts, she learns that life and
her own place in it are a lot more complicated than they had seemed."
—Provided by publisher.
Identifiers: LCCN 2016028946
Subjects: | CYAC: Family life—California—Los Angeles—Fiction. | African
Americans—Fiction. | Race relations—Fiction. | Riots—California—Los
Angeles—Fiction. | Los Angeles (Calif.)—History—20th century—Fiction.
| BISAC: JUVENILE FICTION / People & Places / United States / African
American. | JUVENILE FICTION / Social Issues / Prejudice & Racism. |
JUVENILE FICTION / Historical / United States / 20th Century. | JUVENILE
FICTION / Family / General (see also headings under Social Issues). |
JUVENILE FICTION / Social Issues / Friendship. | JUVENILE FICTION / Girls
& Women. | JUVENILE FICTION / Lifestyles / City & Town Life.
Classification: LCC PZ7.E7232 It 2017 | DDC [Fic]—dc23
LC record available at https://lccn.loc.gov/2016028946

ISBN: 978-0-544-83957-1 hardcover
ISBN: 978-0-358-09853-9 paperback

Printed in the United States of America
DOC 10 9 8 7 6 5 4 3 2
4500803801

For my sister, Janice

A special thanks to my editor, Lynne Polvino,
and my agent, Steven Chudney,
for helping to bring this book to life.

CONTENTS

CHAPTER 1
Mrs. Baylor

I SAW MRS. BAYLOR first. I saw her making her way up
Montego Drive as if she was battling a headwind. It was
Monday. She was coming for her interview for the house-
keeping job. I watched her from the den window, and where
Montego Drive curves like a kidney bean, she stopped, with-
drew a hankie from her bra, and mopped her face. Then she
blew a stream of air up at her forehead. I saw how she hauled
herself heavily up the hill and that she resented that the hill was
steep and that she had to worry about having a heart attack or
sweating out her straightened hair. And I saw something else.
She was a woman who was *not* going to like me.

I wasn't going to like her either because she was coming to

take our old housekeeper's place. Shirley was young and pretty and she'd taught my sister, Lily, how to put a smudged brown line in the crease above her eyes and white shadow just beneath her brow. And that Lily needn't fret about her size-nine shoes because she'd heard that Jackie Kennedy wore a ten.

Shirley kept up with celebrity news, too. She told us little-known facts that she had the inside scoop on. But she had boyfriends who came to visit her in the night. My mother didn't like the idea of boyfriends slipping in and out at all hours.

She had to let Shirley go. Lily sulked. I cried.

I left the window, slipped back into my room, and closed the door behind me just as the doorbell rang. Then I walked from one end of my room to the other thinking about stuff: How Lily would be leaving soon for college and I'd be left behind in a lonely house where my mother and father didn't really care for each other, as far as I could see.

I touched one post of my four-poster bed. I ran my hands over the books on my shelf, looking with pride at the dioramas I'd made of scenes from my favorite stories. I decided to ignore the lady who was now crossing the threshold into our home.

I was picking up *Anne of Green Gables*—I'd just started it —when my mother called me. "Sophia, come down here. I have someone I want you to meet."

In my bare feet, I walked as slowly as possible down the hall to the arched doorway that led to our living room. I listened to every creak beneath my steps. When I reached our foyer, I stood next to the entry hall table, lingering there. I drummed my fingers on my mother's briefcase. It was full of all her club stuff and charity stuff and art gallery stuff. When my mother wasn't digging around in her briefcase, that's where she usually kept it—on the entry hall table. I waited there until she called me again.

In the shaft of sunlight spilling from the arched window above our front door, my mother stood next to the piano, resting her forearm on it like a lounge singer. The sun was her spotlight. She had a Dorothy Dandridge kind of beauty. My sister once told me that was how she got our father.

Now my mother gave me the once-over and introduced the new housekeeper. She had been desperate to hire someone quickly.

Mrs. Baylor smiled and turned. Two gold-trimmed teeth glinted in the corners of her smile. She lowered her head but kept her eyes glued on me. "And who's this young lady?" she said in a singsongy way.

"Sophie," I said.

"Sophia," my mother corrected.

"Ah like Sophia Loren," Mrs. Baylor said, her smile growing wider.

She dabbed at her forehead with her balled-up tissue and I noticed an odd scar on her wrist. Triangular, with a slightly raised border and a smooth shining center. I looked at it for a second, then quickly looked away. It was impolite to stare at a person's disfigurement.

Yep. She wasn't going to like me. I could stand on my head and blow bubbles out of my ears, and she wouldn't be impressed. She smiled and smiled at me now, but I didn't believe in that smile for a second.

One evening a week or so later, I went into the kitchen to get a handful of Oreos to eat in front of *Gidget*. My best friend, Jennifer, was over and *Gidget* was our favorite TV show. My mother was off at her art gallery organizing a new exhibit, Lily was out with her friends, and my father was probably at his office. Mrs. Baylor was sitting at the table sipping coffee with a pile of laundry in a basket on the floor next to her. She seemed to be taking a little rest before tackling it.

Let me explain about Jennifer. See, we moved to Montego Drive in the spring. Before that, we lived on Sixth Avenue near Adams.

We were the first colored family on this block, and for the first few weeks we were very aware of our "coloredness" every time we stepped out the front door. Everybody ignored us, but we knew we were annoying them big time just by being colored and living so close.

The kids who rode by on their bikes or on their skates glanced over with curiosity—but they kept going. The first Saturday in our new house I could see a bunch of girls down the street jumping rope, but they were acting as if I wasn't there. I decided to mosey on down. Put my face in front of them and see what happened.

They probably expected me to keep walking, but I stopped. The two girls turning the rope kept it going and the jumper kept jumping—making a point of ignoring me.

"Can I jump?" I asked one turner, noticing she had on a top with a satin fish that was really a pocket. I wished I had that shirt.

"No," she said without looking at me.

"Why?"

"We have enough people," she said.

"It doesn't matter how many jump."

"We have enough," the other turner said.

I spun on my heels and made myself believe that they said no because they really did have enough people. That could be it. But deep down, I knew it wasn't the truth.

Then a week after we moved in, Jennifer popped up on my porch looking shy but friendly. She lived directly across the street in a two-story house that looked just like a *Father Knows Best* house. I always wanted to live in a *Father Knows Best* house. She had red hair and a nose that I call short and she calls pug. She invited me over and we discovered we had *everything* in common. She was twelve, soon to be thirteen, and going into the ninth grade because she had skipped a grade, and I was twelve, soon to be thirteen, and going into the ninth grade because I had skipped a grade. We both loved the Beatles—especially Paul, if we had to choose—and we were still in undershirts, though we both had started our journey toward brassieres. And we loved to read. Me, only real stuff, no fantasy. Definitely no talking animals.

We were going to be like Kim and Ursula from our favorite movie, *Bye Bye Birdie*. And to seal our friendship, when school started, we'd have to skip class—at least once. We were going to meet at the flagpole in front of *my* school at lunchtime—I didn't know how she was going to get there from her private girls' school across town—and then walk on down to that café next to the Leimert Theater, where we were going to order coffee and a Danish and then buy tickets for the double feature. We planned to wait until they were showing something with Doris Day.

Jennifer didn't have to have a housekeeper. She had a grand-mother who lived with her. The grandmother had come all the way from England. She did all the stuff a housekeeper usually did, because Jennifer had a working mother, just like me. Jennifer's school year ended way before mine did. By the time I got out for the summer, she'd already been to England and back with her mother and grandmother. She returned with an idea to have some fun with the people on our block she suspected of being prejudiced.

One afternoon, she pointed out the houses on the block where she thought colored people weren't allowed (unless they were the day workers or the handymen). She'd heard her mother discussing this with her grandmother a while back, though she didn't say how they knew.

I looked at the houses. They seemed quiet and normal.

Jennifer wanted to pull a joke on the prejudiced people in those houses. She came up with a fake fundraiser. The scheme was to present a collection for poor kids in China, just so we could see their reaction to me standing there beside Jennifer.

With our plan all set, we went from one prejudiced house to another, ready to talk about our fake fundraiser. We were soon disappointed. Only Mrs. Cantrell was home. She was an older woman—divorced, Jennifer thought—with her mouth set in a permanent downturn, as if she was suspicious of everything and everyone.

Jennifer had an order form pad from when her school had sold wrapping paper and her mother was the head of the PTA. "We're not taking anyone's money. We're just taking orders for wrapping paper," she had explained to me earlier.

So, when Mrs. Prejudiced Cantrell opened her door, Jennifer began her spiel about poor kids in China and her school's fundraiser. *Summer school* fundraiser. She had to correct herself because it was July. So would Mrs. Cantrell please donate?

There was a long, suspicious-sounding sigh, then an "Oh, I guess so . . ." Mrs. Cantrell disappeared into her house and came back with a five-dollar bill, fresh from her pocketbook, I imagined. She looked at me and pursed her lips with distaste. Jennifer filled out the form for one roll of birthday wrap and handed Mrs. Cantrell the carbon copy. "We're not taking money until we deliver your order," she said. Mrs. Cantrell stuck the five dollars in her apron pocket and sighed again.

"Thank you so much," Jennifer said, turning away and starting down the porch stairs with me in tow. "Oh, I forgot," she added just before Mrs. Cantrell could close her door. "Half of your donation goes to civil rights for colored people in the South. So they can get their rights. They're going to be really happy with your contribution."

I looked at Jennifer with eyes round with shock. My mouth was ready to drop open! Then I had to bite my tongue to keep from laughing. I glanced over at her as we walked on to the next house and saw her beaming with pleasure.

Since no one else was home, there were no more opportunities for our scheme. But I knew I had a friend in Jennifer.

• • •

I could feel Mrs. Baylor's eyes following me around as I went about the business of getting the Oreos and a napkin to wrap them in. Finally, she took a long drag off her cigarette and squinted at the smoke curling off it. "You want to know something?" she said, her voice startling me as it broke through the uneasy silence. "I'm goin' to tell you something that's goin' to shock you, but I'm goin' to tell you anyway, 'cause you need to hear it. And you can tell your mama if you want to, but it's the truth." (She said "truth" like *trood.*) She was probably counting on me *not* to say anything at all to my mother.

I folded the napkin around the cookies and shoved them into my pocket and waited for the truth she was about to tell me.

"You know, with your light skin and that long braid you got hangin' down your back . . . If you ever went to Africa, they'd kill you. It wouldn't be right, but they would."

I stood there speechless.

"Yeah," she went on. "They don't like no light-skin Negroes in *Africa.* Just in case you thinkin' you special because of your color."

I frowned because I didn't think I was special because of my color. I hardly ever remembered my light color.

"That's right. You might not believe me, but they hate light-skin Negroes in Africa." She said the word in three distinct syllables: *Ah-fri-cah.*

I stood there waiting to be released from this lecture. I wanted to tell her the word was *skinned,* not *skin.* I wanted to, but then I thought she might get a notion to spit in my food. She might get a notion to spit in my food for a solid week.

She'd think I was a showoff and that I wasn't respectful, and that I was precocious. Some people didn't like precocious kids. And that's what I was, according to my fourth grade teacher, way back when I was nine. In fact, she was the first person to use that word about me. She'd had my parents come in to discuss skipping me to sixth grade. "Sophia is precocious. Her writing is way beyond her years, in fact. She has an extensive vocabulary and a keen use of language." My mind stopped on the word *keen.* How sharp it sounded.

My parents smiled in a way that signaled she needn't go on. They already knew all of this about me.

"But she's a little withdrawn, as well, I should mention. Maybe a little too self-contained."

They frowned, and that visit led to this: "Do you like school, Sophia?" my father had asked.

"Mostly," I said.

"Well, what do you like about it?"

"Reading biographies."

A pause here where my mother and father looked at each other, then at me.

"Do you like being with friends?"

I had to stop and think because I had only one friend back then, and she was more of an acquaintance. Millicent. We had the same love of reading at every opportunity, so we sometimes ate lunch together. We would just sit on the bench and read while others played around us.

My mother was appalled at the news of just one friend. She had many, many friends. Lily had many, many friends. My mother looked at me as if I had suddenly grown horns, as though I had turned into someone who wasn't her child at all. How could I disappoint her like that?

I waited for Mrs. Baylor's final words. But she seemed to be done. She wanted me to be sad, so I bowed my head a little. I could have told her I hardly ever think of being light, but she wouldn't have believed me. As I walked quietly out of the room, she took what seemed to be a long, satisfying drag on her cigarette. She'd gotten me told.

As Lily had explained it, we were light skinned on purpose. Light-skinned people deliberately married other light-skinned people so they'd have light-skinned children. ("I'm not doing that. It's *pathetic*," Lily had said, and I believed her.) And they were the ones who'd gotten most of the opportunities. White people had made sure of this.

Lily always had profound things to say. Things that made you think and think with your eyes squinted; things that made you see the world in a whole new way.

So I knew then that Mrs. Baylor would probably prefer working for Jennifer's family over working for a light-skinned family who'd gotten all the opportunities.

I told Jennifer what Mrs. Baylor said as soon as I'd settled in the beanbag chair next to the couch. I handed her some Oreos. "Guess what Mrs. Baylor said to me?"

"What?"

"She said if I went to Africa, they'd kill me for being light skinned."

Jennifer's eyes got big. "They would?"

"She said they don't like light-skinned Negroes in Africa."

"They don't? How come?"

I shrugged. What did I know about Africa?

It occurred to me then that Mrs. Baylor would never tell Jennifer that. We unscrewed our Oreos and raked our bottom teeth across the filling. Then we laughed for no reason at all.

CHAPTER 2
Lily

ILY HAD GIVEN ME a list. She said to me, "This is what you need to do before you get to ninth grade. You know ninth grade is really a preparation for high school. So you need to get rid of the weirdness. You need to not be such a bookworm. You need to have more friends than just the little white girl across the street. And there's more stuff—but you'll have to wait for it."

So now I was waiting for it. It was Saturday and Mrs. Baylor had been with us for a few weeks. She usually left for her weekend on Saturday mornings, but she'd asked my mother if she could work overtime. Her daughter in Jamaica was having some kind of problem and Mrs. Baylor needed to send her some money.

I could hear Lily in the bathroom taking a shower. I was still in bed, reading. In seven weeks' time Lily would be going off to her college in Georgia and I'd be left alone in this house with no one to talk to but myself.

Our house could feel lonely because my mother was busy with her life and my father was busy with his. And then there was me. Lily promised to write, and to call once a month when she got to Georgia, but I knew she'd forget. That she'd get too busy to remember me. And when fall came I'd be off to ninth grade at a new school by myself—because Jennifer went to Marlborough in Hancock Park.

I had no idea what to expect from my new school. Lily had heard from someone that there were only a few colored kids there and nobody talked to them and they had to huddle together at lunchtime while people ignored them. That was good to know.

Lily was letting the water run and run and it had already been twenty minutes. Earlier, at the breakfast table, our mother had mentioned the business with the long showers. She said, "Lily, you're not the only one who lives in this house. There are other people who'd like a hot shower besides you, and—" My mother stopped midlecture because just then Lily pushed back her chair, stood up, and quietly walked out of the room—not even clearing her bowl from the table. My mother went on eating her half grapefruit with her special serrated spoon, and I looked back at Mrs. Baylor and caught her with her head bowed and smiling to herself.

My mother was on a diet. That's why she was eating half a grapefruit and drinking a can of Metrecal for breakfast. She was always on a diet. But it never lasted. It wouldn't be long before she'd be sneaking a box of See's Candies into the house and slipping it under the stack of sweaters in her closet—to pick at later while she waited for my father to come home from the Flying Fox. He stopped by there most nights after work to unwind.

While I waited for the shower to shut off, I thought about writing a new novel. I was only in the thinking stage for this one, but it was going to be about my daddy's secret sister. Minerva. She was an outside child. He hadn't even known about her until he was in high school. What a great subject. I came across her picture tucked under the blotter on my father's desk in his home office. Lily knew all about her and explained to me who she was. That's what gave me my great idea.

I listened to the shower going full blast as if Lily had a point to prove. I sank down into the bedcovers, thinking and thinking and occasionally reading a couple of pages of *Anne of Green Gables,* to help put me in a writing mood.

The shower cut off and there was a period of silence. I

waited, breathing softly and listening, debating if I should tell Lily what had happened a few days ago—down at the Bakers'. I risked annoying her, but I wanted her opinion. I'd have to see what her mood was first.

She could be moody. I could usually judge her frame of mind by the way she searched for what she wanted to wear. If her mood was bad, then there'd be a lot of jerking drawers open, rummaging around, and slamming them shut in a violent way. Or there'd be stomping over to the closet we shared and sliding clothes back and forth on the closet rod. If she didn't find something quickly, there'd be accusations about people messing with her stuff. People—meaning *me*.

So I braced myself when the door opened and a cloud of apple-scented steam followed her into the room. She had on her white terry-cloth robe and her hair was making a wet splotch on the back of it. In her hand, her transistor radio was belting out Martha and the Vandellas' "Heat Wave."

She stopped, held the radio like a microphone, and began to sing the words at the top of her lungs, moving around as if she was on a stage. When the song ended she fell back on her bed and yelled, "I love that song!" Then she got up, walked over to me, and said, "You know what I think? I think I'm going to remember this song forever."

Apparently, her friend Lydia had played it over and over at her pool party the week before and Lily had felt pure happiness when everyone began to sing the song at the top of their lungs.

"You know you only feel pure happiness like ten times in your whole life."

"Only ten times?" I asked.

"Okay—maybe twenty times."

As she and her friends sang, Lily said, it was as if the music drifted up into the sky and hovered over all of LA. As though everyone she knew was dancing to Martha and the Vandellas. And they were all in this heat wave together. It was like magic, she told me.

Lydia was Lily's best friend. She lived around the corner on Escalon. Her family had been the first colored family on her block, just like us. Her father was a judge and her mother a lawyer. So she was way more bourgeois than we were. She already had a car. It was a used Corvair, but still, to me it represented freedom and independence.

I thought of those twenty times and soon disputed that "fact." People had to have more than twenty experiences of joy in their whole life. They had to.

"It's never going to be like that again. Because I'm going away and they're going away. Next year, I'll hardly know those people. Or the knowing will change and we'll all be half forgotten in each other's lives because we'll be busy making new lives."

I didn't like the sound of that. I didn't like when she talked about her new life to come. She sat down at her vanity and began to examine her face. Lily liked looking at herself. She liked checking up on her beauty. When we walked down Crenshaw, she looked in the big plate glass windows of the stores along the way over and over.

"I'm going by Marcia Stevens later," she said. "I saw a Help Wanted sign in their window and I'm going down there to check it out. I know I'm only going to be here for another month or so but, hey, why not?"

Marcia Stevens was a boutique in Marlton Square.

"I've never seen any colored people working there," I said.

"So? We don't know for a fact that they don't hire colored."

"They probably won't hire you?"

"I'm going to try anyway."

When we first moved to Montego Drive, the stupidest thing happened. One of the Baker girls walked up when I was sitting on the porch reading and stood there at a safe distance at the end of our walkway. I hadn't yet met them, but from what Jennifer told me, I knew there were three girls in the Baker family and they were the ones who'd locked me out of their rope jumping. I knew this one was the youngest and her two older sisters had probably put her up to it.

I looked at her and waited. Was she going to ask to be my friend? Was she going to introduce herself? Finally, she said, "Why do you have that white girl living with you?"

I didn't know who she was talking about, so I thought it was a joke. "What?"

"That white girl. Why is she living with you?"

Then it became clear. She was talking about my sister. I suppose with her gray eyes and light brown hair, Lily could look white to some *white* people, but she'd never fool anyone *colored*. Any colored person could tell right off she was one of them.

"That's my *sister* and she's not white," I said, and the Baker girl just turned on her heels and trotted back down the street. I guess to make her report to her sisters.

"The one who asked you that question," Jennifer said later, "that's Marcy. They're always putting her up to stuff. Because she's kind of slow."

Slow, I thought, thankful I wasn't slow.

I watched Lily begin to roll her hair on giant rollers.

"I have something to tell you," I said.

"What?" she asked. But just then The Temptations' "My Girl"

was suddenly coming out of her radio. With only half her hair rolled, Lily stood up and started doing the Temptation Walk. She pulled me up next to her and said, "Follow me." Then it was as if she was climbing stairs, slowly, with her head going this way and that, her eyes closed, and I knew she was drifting off to that place where someone was calling her "My Girl." Someone who had to just stop in his tracks and do a slow pivot like Smokey Robinson with his brilliant smile that slid over his mouth and drifted right up to his laughing eyes.

That was going to happen to me one day, I thought. Someone was going to call me "My Girl!" As soon as I got my figure and my mother let me get my hair cut.

The song ended and Lily flopped down on her little bench in front of her vanity and began to scrutinize her highlights.

"So what were you going to tell me?" she asked.

CHAPTER 3
The Bakers

I T HAPPENED a few days ago. If only we hadn't been playing jacks on Jennifer's porch. Weren't we too old for jacks
anyway? If only we hadn't seen kids going down there with
towels around their necks and thongs flip-flopping on their feet.
If only the day hadn't been so still and hot. Jennifer looked past
me and said, "Those kids are walking down to the Bakers' to go
swimming." I turned around and watched them saunter by.

"They have a pool," she said. "I swam in it last summer . . ."
She drifted off, probably remembering what that felt like.

I glanced over at her. She was going to want to go down
there. I remembered vividly the Bakers' brand of meanness when
they wouldn't let me jump rope.

We looked toward their house. The Baker girls—Marcy,

Deidre, and Jilly—didn't go to the school where I'd be going. They went to Saint Mary's. The girls at Saint Mary's wore uniforms and hiked up their pleated skirts as soon as they left school, Jennifer told me. "I heard the nuns make you kneel on the carpet and if your skirt doesn't reach the floor, they say it's too short and send you home." She looked toward their house again. "Let's go ask them if we can swim."

"I don't want to."

"Why?"

"Because they're not going to let me."

"You don't know that."

"Yes, I do. And I don't want to go."

Jennifer bounced the small rubber ball and scooped up five jacks. But it felt like she was going to sulk. I was still on threesies. She continued to sixies, sevensies, and on and on until she'd scooped up every jack. Then she put a super-bored look on her face and said unenthusiastically, "Wanna play another game?"

"Okay," I said. "I'll go with you to the Bakers'."

I trudged home to get into my suit and grab a towel out of the linen closet. I slipped on my Bermudas and T-shirt over my suit. If I was going to be turned away, I didn't want it to be in just my swimsuit with the ruffle at the waist. I went to find Mrs. Baylor to tell her where I was going. She was mopping the kitchen floor. She stopped and put her hand on her hip, waiting.

"I'm going swimming down at the Bakers.'"

"Where do they live?"

"Just down the street."

She sighed. "So they invited you to go swimming down at their house, did they?"

"Jennifer wants to go. She said it'll be okay."

"And you believe that, do you?"

"She said it'll be okay," I repeated.

"Hmmph." She shook her head and kind of chuckled to herself. "You go on, girl. And see what happen to you." She dunked the mop in the bucket and then twisted the water out. "You not a little white girl. You going to see."

I knew I wasn't a little white girl. I knew what I was.

I dragged a bit as we walked down to the Bakers', slowed by the scenarios I pictured. Deidre Baker, the oldest, chasing me out of her backyard with a broom. All the kids laughing at me and pointing.

"Come on," Jennifer said. "Why are you going so slow?"

I picked up my pace.

We could hear the whoops and hollers and splashing as soon as we walked up the driveway to a wrought iron gate standing ajar as if it were personally saying, *Come on in.* Jennifer looked at me and grinned. I didn't feel like grinning.

Jennifer forged ahead and I followed, suddenly feeling my

heart in my mouth. We walked through the gate and the splashing stopped. It was as if a faucet going full blast had suddenly shut off. All went quiet and all eyes turned to me, then to Jennifer, then back to me.

"Hi, Jilly," Jennifer said. Jilly was our age. She came over and stood in front of us. She crossed her arms.

"Can we swim?" Jennifer continued, as though she wasn't noticing anything out of the ordinary.

Jilly looked me up and down. "You know we don't allow colored people in our pool—or our house." Marcy hurried over and joined her. Then Deidre. All three of them crossed their arms and stared at me.

I felt my face grow warm. I swallowed. I wanted to back out of their yard. All the kids in the pool were now treading water and watching intently.

One girl, sitting on the side with her feet in the water, stopped eating her hot dog and held it at her mouth without taking a bite.

The world stopped spinning. I almost stopped breathing. There was still the welcoming scent of chlorine and Coppertone and hot dogs and mustard. I thought I could even smell the Hawaiian Punch. All the happy smells that meant summer and fun. But they were not for me. Not for me.

We stood there with our towels around our necks trying to decide what to do next.

"You can stay, but not her." Deidre pointed her finger at me and kind of jabbed it in my direction as if she might poke it through my chest. Jennifer looked at Deidre's finger and then at me. I stepped back a bit.

Jennifer stared at Deidre as if not quite comprehending what she was saying. "What?" she finally said.

"*You* can stay. Only you."

Jennifer glanced at me and then she slowly turned to go.

"But *you* can stay, I said," Deidre repeated.

Jennifer shook her head. "I'm not staying if Sophie can't."

"No, Jennifer," I said quickly (and I felt I had to do this). "Go on. It's okay. I don't want to swim in their pool anyway." What I meant to say but didn't was: *You're the only friend I have. What if you start thinking I'm getting in the way of your fun? Then you might not want to be my friend anymore.*

"No, I'm not staying," she said firmly.

"I want you to stay. You have to."

"No, I don't either. They're prejudiced." She pointed her finger at Deidre, then waved it at the three of them. "You're all prejudiced."

In response, Deidre put her hands on her hips. Marcy

stepped forward. "So what if we are? We don't care if we're prejudiced. We like being prejudiced."

"How would you like it if people were prejudiced against you, and for no reason?"

"I wouldn't care," Marcy said.

"You would, too."

"No—because I have plenty of other friends."

"You're stupid," Jennifer said. She grabbed my arm. "Let's go."

I shrugged as if I didn't care, not even a little bit. We left through the gate, our towels still around our necks.

"I don't want to go home yet," I said to Jennifer. I didn't want to have to explain the situation to Mrs. Baylor. It felt like a kind of shame that I'd brought on myself. And she might be ready with a *Ha! And you thought you were so special.*

We walked back up the street, past my house, and continued to the end, around the corner, and then down Escalon until we came to the pass-through that ran between the driveways of two houses in the middle of the block. It bordered the Bakers' backyard, with a wall of hedges separating it.

Quietly we crept up the narrow walkway to their hedge. Through an opening in the branches we could see much of the Bakers' yard. Kids were back to splashing and diving for the pennies someone had thrown into the pool, and Deidre—who everyone called Dee Dee—was there with her feet dangling in the water. Then someone splashed her and she jumped up, bursting into laughter.

"I wish I had me a peashooter," Jennifer said.

We both laughed and then clapped our hands over our mouths before someone could hear us.

Deidre jumped into the pool, climbed out, and ran across the cement to a bag of chips on the patio table.

"Oh, too bad she didn't slip and fall," I said.

We almost bent in half with a laughing fit. Jennifer regained her control and shushed me.

We watched as Deidre flopped down on the bench across from Jilly, a leg on either side, and they began to share the bag of chips. Jilly looked pleased with herself. Then Marcy climbed out of the pool and made Deidre scoot over so they could all share the bench and the chips. Everything had returned to normal. It was as if nothing had happened. Jennifer and I showing up was barely a hiccup in their afternoon activities, and they were back to their usual summer fun.

Suddenly, Jilly was up and jumping into the pool, diving down and then resurfacing, her dark-blond hair floating on the water behind her. She rubbed the droplets out of her eyes while laughing and calling to one of the other kids

We grew tired of the spectacle and turned to go. I had

expected to feel much worse than I did. It was just the way it was. Anyway, I could imagine beating up each and every one of those kids. I could imagine beating them and beating them and beating them. Even the boys.

We walked back up the street. Jennifer went into her house and I just hung out in the backyard until I heard the garage door go up and my mother's car pull in. She was probably coming from her gallery. Mrs. Baylor was running the vacuum in the living room and singing "Amazing Grace." As I hurried past, she shut it off and said, "I thought you were going swimming down to your little friend's house. What happened?" She seemed to regard me suspiciously. Could she know? Why was she looking at me like that?

"I did go down there," I said, not really lying.

"Why your hair not wet?"

"I wore a cap."

She cocked her head. "They don't ever keep your hair dry."

"Mine does," I said.

"Only if you wear a shammy around your hairline. Did you wear a shammy?"

The lies were piling up and making me feel funny. I didn't think of myself as a liar. "No," I said, and hurried past. She seemed to think about this for a second. Then she turned the vacuum cleaner back on and returned to her song. Which made me feel extra guilty, since I was reminded that God was watching me and I really didn't want to be a wretch, like the lyrics said.

Lily sat there for a moment. She put the radio down and swiv-eled on her bench to look at me with her head cocked and her eyes narrowed. I felt a storm brewing. "You didn't say anything to those little girls?"

"No."

"Then what did you do?"

"Came home," I said.

"Did you tell Mom?"

"No."

"Don't tell her."

"Why?"

"Because I'm going to take care of those little bitches."

I looked over at her and waited, but she'd already gone back to rolling her hair on the big plastic rollers. She had something in mind. I felt a flutter in my stomach. Then I heard our front door open and close. I made it to the den window just in time to see my father leave. Just in time to see him skip down the front steps, pluck the morning paper off the hibiscus bush, look at it for a moment, and then toss it back toward the front porch. He headed for his car.

The way he eased his Chrysler 300 out of the driveway and

turned its nose toward Olympiad reminded me of a long, sleek, twin-finned creature slipping away. Where was he going on a Saturday? Earlier, I'd heard my mother grabbing her datebook and briefcase and heading out that same door, her heels clicking on the entry-hall tiles. Everyone was always *going*.

CHAPTER 4
The Rest of Saturday

LATER MY SISTER was gone, too. Off to her interview. She planned to walk all the way there, come back with a job, and shock everybody. When she'd told our mother about her plan, our mother had said, "They won't hire you. They don't hire colored there." Lily told her she was going to try anyway. Lily said that because she is brave, and unlike me, she doesn't let anything stand in her way. *Nothing.*

So then it was just me and Mrs. Baylor. I pictured her sitting in the breakfast nook, legs up on the padded bench, flipping through a Hollywood gossip magazine and sipping coffee out of one of my mother's china cups. I stayed in the bedroom, thinking about Jennifer's call an hour or two after the pool party incident. One

of the kids who'd been there had given her a report on what happened after we left.

First, Linda Cruz made it clear that she was Spanish and not
Mexican and she couldn't have colored people at her house either. So I'd better not come walking up to her front door because
her father would just turn me around and send me on my way.

Then Jilly Baker had said that Linda looked more Mexican
than Spanish, and Linda said that was because she'd been at the
beach a lot and her color wasn't her real color.

"What's wrong with Mexican?" I'd asked.

"Beats me," Jennifer said.

"I mean you get to speak Spanish *and* English," I went on.
"Wish *I* could speak two languages."

It was crazy. Well, they were pretty dark, the Cruz kids. But
why did that always have to be a bad thing?

I thought to go over to Jennifer's to see if she felt like walking down
to the library with me. But then I remembered she had to go to her
little cousin's birthday party. She was probably already gone.

I headed to the kitchen, not sure what I was going to want
once I got there. When I reached the hall, I heard Mrs. Baylor's radio and felt disappointed. I was hoping she'd be dusting or something in another part of the house by then.

I paused in the dining room. The small pull-down door that

connected the built-in buffet in the dining room to the kitchen counter had not been closed all the way. Through the opening, I could see Mrs. Baylor. She wasn't kicked back at the kitchen table sipping coffee. She was standing at the ironing board, pressing one of my father's dress shirts. Every once in a while, she stopped to dip her hand in a small bowl and sprinkle water over the shirt. Occasionally, she reached for her smoldering cigarette resting in a Mason jar lid on the counter behind her. She'd take a long drag, lifting her chin and closing her eyes. Then, to avoid blowing smoke on Daddy's clean shirt, she'd draw her lips to the side to exhale.

A Pepsodent toothpaste jingle was playing and Mrs. Baylor was nodding her head to the beat of it. She sprinkled, she ironed a bit, she reached back to get her cigarette, she took a puff, she blew it out over her shoulder, then she started all over.

"It's not polite to spy on folks," she said, making me jump back, startled. "What are you doing peeking through that little opening?" She sang this to me in her Jamaican way, then picked up her cigarette again. "Get in here and get whatever you want to get and then go on with you."

I closed the little door and stepped into the kitchen. She continued ironing as if I wasn't there. I got a glass down from the cabinet and set it on the table.

"I just want a glass of juice," I said, though I didn't really.

She shrugged. "You don't need permission from me."

Suddenly I was self-conscious about the way I'd opened the cabinet; the way I'd reached for a glass, then opened the refrigerator and got out the pitcher of juice.

"You make sure you put that back," she said.

I was already going to put the pitcher back. Why wouldn't I? That's why I was nervous. She was always watching and measuring and waiting for me to make a mistake.

"You don't have home training?" Mrs. Baylor set the iron down firmly and stood with one hand on her hip. "You don't know how to address a person?"

I poured my juice. "Address?" I asked quietly.

Mrs. Baylor shook her head slowly, tsking at the same time. "You don't know how to say 'Good afternoon, Mrs. Baylor' or 'How you doin'?'"

"Good afternoon," I said, knowing it was too late and Mrs. Baylor probably wanted it to be too late.

"Where's your sister? I suppose she be in her bed getting her beauty rest."

"Lily left to see about a job."

"Oh?" Mrs. Baylor lifted an eyebrow skeptically.

"At Marcia Stevens."

"The boutique?"

I nodded. She seemed disappointed.

"They don't hire Negroes at that place."

I said nothing.

"What? She thinking she going to pass for white now?"

I continued my silence.

She flashed her gold-trimmed teeth and smacked her thigh. "That's it, isn't it? I am right about that." She sighed and slowly shook her head. "I am not surprised. I'm not surprised about Miss Lily."

I didn't like Mrs. Baylor calling my sister *Miss* Lily. Lily was just Lily. She never tried to be *Miss* anything.

The phone rang. Mrs. Baylor answered it and I could tell it was my mother because Mrs. Baylor stopped to search for something in the freezer. I slipped out with my glass of juice.

Once in my room, I sat down on the window seat and pulled the curtain back. I held my breath and listened. Soon I could hear the washing machine.

I was alone. Just me and Mrs. Baylor—and Oscar, who probably needed to be walked. I decided to take him for a stroll around the neighborhood.

The Cruz boys, Anthony and Marcus, were in their front yard throwing a baseball back and forth. I thought I could get past them without being noticed, but then I heard, "That's sure an ugly dog."

It was Anthony Cruz. I ignored him. If I weren't a girl, he'd probably have liked to come over and give me a push or confront me with our faces only inches apart so I could feel his hot breath while he talked bad. But then I realized I was kind of going overboard in imagining too much of a confrontation. He wasn't necessarily saying it meanly. He was more astonished.

"That's the way bulldogs look," I said.

Anthony caught the ball in his glove. He turned to me. "Why'd you get that kind of dog?"

"It was mainly my sister's idea." Lily had read up on bulldogs and didn't like that they had such a sad history of being used for bullbaiting and all. She started begging for one. She loved their little old man faces and their sad, wary expressions. Daddy finally broke down and gave Oscar to Lily for her fifteenth birthday. Now we all loved Oscar. Daddy didn't like the name at first, but Lily insisted. She said Oscar was a bulldog's name and she had her heart set on naming him that.

Anthony nodded.

I had to pull at the leash because Oscar had other things to do, it seemed, and he didn't want to stop. I'd seen Anthony Cruz before. Jennifer had pointed him out. He was cute, and Jennifer had a seventy percent crush on him, she admitted. Jennifer had a one hundred percent crush on Paul McCartney, so Anthony was kind of up there. I knew he lived on our street, but I'd never really thought about him. I checked out him and his brother now. Yes. They still looked Mexican to me even though their sister insisted they were all Spanish.

"Can I pet him?" Anthony asked, surprising me.

I hesitated, not knowing if he was being sincere. "Okay," I said finally.

Anthony stepped forward with his hand all ready to pet Oscar, but for some reason Oscar didn't want any part of him. He actually bared his teeth and began to make this low, scary growl in his throat. He pulled at the leash in Anthony's direction and I had to really hold on tight.

"Whoa," Anthony said. "I get the hint."

I laughed. That sounded so funny and grown-up and kind and perceptive, I started liking Anthony Cruz right then and there. But then I tried to stop, because I knew Jennifer already had a crush on him.

"I know what happened at the Bakers' yesterday," he said. "My sister told me."

I looked at him closely to see if his face would reveal how he felt about it. I couldn't tell. "Yeah. Well . . ." I suddenly felt self-conscious. I turned to go, yanking on the leash to pull Oscar after me and feeling Anthony Cruz's eyes on my back. Maybe he would remember this—me walking my dog past him and his brother throwing a baseball back and forth—one day far into the future, after we were married. It would be a story to tell our children. I had to stop myself then, and remember that Jennifer had a seventy percent crush on him. He was off-limits, *crushwise.*

I continued on my way, planning to go up Presidio to get back home instead of my own street so he wouldn't think I was walking back and forth in front of his house hoping he'd talk to me again. If I were Lily, I'd have just the right quip for him. I'd be able to say something smart—something that would lasso him in and make him mine. But then I'd have to explain all that to Jennifer, and she might not take it well.

Mrs. Baylor was just leaving as I was coming up the walkway with Oscar. She had her purse over her arm and her son was waiting in the driveway in an idling Volkswagen. I peered into the car to get a good look at him in the shadowed interior. I wanted to see "Mr. Nigel Nigel Nigel," as Lily called him. Mrs. Baylor had been in our house only a few weeks, but we'd heard her bragging to our mother about her beloved son, Nigel, a zillion times.

"I've got an appointment and you don't need to know where," she said. "I'll be back in an hour or two. You got your piano lesson at three and your mama said you need to practice, especially with the recital coming up. Now I'm off. You better do your practicing."

The recital. I didn't want to be in it. I hated piano lessons.

I hated to practice. Plus, Jennifer had told me that this time Jilly Baker was going to be in it. She was a really good piano player, and now her teacher and my teacher, Mrs. Virgil, were going to join their recitals together. I didn't even want to think about it. Or Mrs. Virgil. I didn't care for her. Not as a person all by herself, but as a person in relation to *me*. She was a spitter. Almost everything she said came out on a spray of spit. She probably knew it and it was okay by her. Some spit even got on the piano keys. Then I'd have to play those keys and think, *When are you leaving so I can run and wash my hands?* It was torture.

I didn't care for her moles, either. How on earth had she gotten that many moles? They were of all sizes, all over her face. Some were big, some were just black dots, but there were so many, I sometimes couldn't concentrate when she was talking to me because I was busy looking at them and wondering if she was completely aware of them and how she washed her face. Was she careful not to rub too hard and maybe rub one away? Then I imagined how that might sting.

Oh, the misery of piano lessons.

I checked Jennifer's driveway. No car. Her mother had probably taken her to lunch at a restaurant after her appointment. When I was out with my mother at the department store and waiting for her to get her face powder mixed to just the right shade and it was going on and on, I would say, "Mom, can we get something to eat at Sutton's?" Sutton's is a cafeteria down the street from the department store, with trays that you slide down a steel counter to select just what you want for your entrée and side dish. And the desserts. So many desserts to choose from! And there's a treasure chest by the door where you can reach in and pluck out a little souvenir. For free.

But every time I asked if we could go there, after waiting through all the mixing of powder and the selection of stockings in just the right shade, where she'd slip her hand into the samples and turn them this way and that—after I waited all this out without complaining—she'd look at me and say, "We have food at home."

I'd think, *How come Jennifer's mother takes her to Sutton's after shopping?* How come the one time I'd been there it was with Jennifer's mom? What was wrong with my family? We never did things like Jennifer's family.

When I asked Lily about this, she explained that our mother grew up poor in North Carolina, one of nine kids. And when you grow up poor, certain worries about money just stick with you.

I went into our empty house.

The piano looked just like it was waiting for me to sit down and start practicing "Für Elise." I turned my back on it and sauntered down the hall and into my daddy's office, where I wasn't supposed to be. I stood there leaning against the closed door, my heart beating with excitement and the dread of being discovered.

No. Daddy was off somewhere and Mrs. Baylor was at an appointment and my mother was at her gallery.

I looked around, then scooted over to his desk, plopped down into his plush desk chair, and spun until I got sick of it. The room swam for a few moments after I stopped, but I soon got my equilibrium back. I opened some drawers, closed them, then lifted the corner of the blotter to look at the picture of my aunt Minerva, the subject of my new book, *The Outside Child*. Lily had overheard our parents discussing her once, and she'd filled me in.

It seems Grandpa Willis had Aunt Minerva with this other woman, not Grandma Nell. This woman lived in the next county over from him and Grandma Nell, and Daddy didn't even know about Minerva until he was in high school.

I'd come across the picture of her under the ink blotter on Daddy's desk the last time I'd sneaked into his office. I'd asked about the picture only because it had been hidden.

"That's Daddy's sister," Lily had told me.

"I didn't know he had a sister."

"That's because Grandma Nell isn't her mother. Her mother is this woman Grandpa Willis" — she paused — "had a thing with."

I knew what she was talking about. There was a time when I didn't know anything. But now I knew just what Lily meant.

I found the photo again under the blotter and slipped it into my shirt pocket. I wanted to look at it and look at it—later, when it was just me and the picture and I wasn't worried about anyone discovering me with it.

Next, I picked up my daddy's letter opener and ran my finger across its sharp tip. Then I started hooking paper clips together into a chain. I'd have to remember to unhook them before I left the room. After I got sick of making the paper clip chain, I checked the rest of the drawers looking for something else revealing. The top one was sticking a little, so I left it alone. Probably nothing but a pile of boring-looking business papers.

I opened the top middle drawer. Nothing interesting. I was just about to close it when I spotted the corner of an envelope under the desk organizer. I pulled it out and stared at it. It was a letter, still sealed in a pink envelope. Paula Morrisy was the name of the sender. The return address was in Leimert Park. Who was Paula Morrisy and why was her unopened letter hidden under the desk organizer? A client, probably. But . . . something felt as if she wasn't a client. A thank you note? No. It was shaped like a letter. I wondered if I should show it to Lily. Just show it to her. Maybe we could open it—to see what it was, exactly.

Then I had a better idea. I would read it *after* my daddy

opened it himself—now that I knew where it was. That was such a good plan, I couldn't help smiling to myself.

It smelled of perfume, I noticed. Something sweet. Too sweet. I didn't like the fragrance. I stared at the name above the return address for a few moments longer. Then I slipped the letter back into its hiding place, making sure a corner was still showing, just the way I'd found it.

I opened the bottom drawer—the file drawer. They weren't client files; they were for family, stuff like birth certificates and house insurance and life insurance and repair bills and receipts for major items like our refrigerator and television and washing machine. I picked up a file labeled Personal and opened it.

My parents' birth certificates were on top. They were listed as colored and their parents were listed as colored, too. And my father's father's occupation was barber. His family, the LaBranches, lived in Gueydan, a town in Vermilion Parish in Louisiana. Their language was listed as well: French. "Creole," my mother had explained. Not the French of France. I liked looking at everyone's birth certificates—especially my parents'. Everything was so *summed up* about them on those pieces of paper.

I'd never met my grandpa Willis or my daddy's poor, cheated-on mother, Grandma Nell. They died before I was born.

Just then I heard the front door open and close. I touched the picture in the pocket of my pedal pushers and stood up at the sound of Mrs. Baylor's approaching steps. She must have forgotten something. She went into her room and rummaged around in there for a bit while I tried to decide if I could slip out of Daddy's office quietly. But then she was shuffling down the hall and opening the door and giving me a hard look.

"Now what do you think you doin'? I bet your daddy has told you a million times to stay out of his office. So explain yourself, if you please."

"I was looking for carbon paper," I lied, and I didn't even know where that lie came from—it just tumbled out of my mouth easily. Was I turning into a liar?

"What you be wantin' carbon paper for?"

"For my book—to have an extra copy as I'm writing."

She was silent as she slowly tilted her head to the side. "You telling the truth?"

"Yes," I said weakly.

She watched me some more and seemed to be waiting. "Well, go on," she finally said. "Get your carbon, if that's what you came for."

I looked through the rest of the desk drawers, knowing there was no carbon paper in any of them. I stood up and shrugged. "I guess he doesn't have any," I said.

"Now, let me ask you something," she began. She squinted at me. "Something I want to know."

"Yes?"

"I been watching you. And that sister of yours—the one who thinks she's queen of England. Now I seen she got some colored friends. But what about you? Why you don't have any colored friends?"

I stood there, confused. It was like when she told me the Africans would kill me if I ever went to Africa. I couldn't think of anything to say then, either.

"I didn't have that many friends at my old school," I finally said. "I had acquaintances, but just a few. There were lots of colored kids at my old school but I just wasn't one of the popular ones. Not many people liked me."

"And how that happen?"

"I don't really know. I guess people thought of me as too bookish. I guess."

"Hmm," she said.

I couldn't tell what she thought of this. "I haven't had a chance to meet anyone at my new school because it hasn't started yet."

"There going to be some Negroes at this new school?"

"Probably not that many."

"You try and make you some friends of your own kind. Then you all can understand each other."

I didn't get it. I understood Jennifer perfectly well, and she understood me. "Okay," I said. Though I didn't know how I'd go about doing that, actually.

"Hmm." It was a quick, short sound. "I'm not surprised you don't have but one friend."

I felt my face grow warm. Mrs. Baylor watched me as I closed the bottom desk drawer and left the room. I wanted to put away my picture of Minerva.

We lived in a split-level house with the den, my daddy's home office, and Mrs. Baylor's room and bath on the upper level. Lily's and my room and bath and our parents' room and bath were on the main level—as well as the living room, dining room, and kitchen. Split level didn't seem like anything you'd see in a movie or read about in a book. That's why I wished I lived in a house like Jennifer's. A house that looked like it could be in a book or a movie. Two stories, with a staircase you could see from the front door.

I skipped down the few steps leading to the foyer and crossed the hall toward my room. I shut the door behind me and pulled the picture out of my pocket. For a while, I just stared at it and smiled. *I have* this, I thought. Little Minerva, with my daddy's faintly square jaw—but on her, the squareness was softer. Little Minerva, in her cheap-looking dress. The picture was black and white—I guess they didn't have color photographs then. I imagined her dress to be a pale, listless yellow from too many washings. It was sleeveless, with ruffles at the shoulder and a thin black velvet ribbon under the collar tied in a bow.

There she was, sitting with one forearm on the table, her other hand cupping her chin—and a shy smile revealing tiny baby teeth that looked like little white kernels of corn. Big brown eyes, but nearly lashless. Her hair was carelessly gathered up and tied with a bow that drooped sadly. You could tell her mother —whoever she was—had tried. That this was meant to be a picture that would make her seem loved and cared for. Poor little Minerva, the *outside child,* raised by her mother alone.

This is what Lily had told me: One day, Minerva's mother brought little Minerva to the house to show her to our grandmother. Grandma Nell had her stand at the end of the walkway and take off the girl's bonnet so she could scrutinize her and decide that she was indeed Grandpa Willis's outside child. She had Minerva's mother take her around the back so Rosie, their housekeeper, could give the girl a glass of lemonade. I don't know what Grandpa Willis told Grandma Nell—but they stayed together.

Lily recounted this dramatic scene for me just as she'd heard our father recount it to our mother. I thought about it over and over until I felt I knew this little girl. I knew her heart.

Then I thought of something else. What if my daddy had

one of those kinds of children? I frowned and pictured a lady bringing the little outside child over to show my mother. Then I put that thought out of my head and slipped the picture under my pajamas in my top dresser drawer. Over the next few days, I thought about it like a secret. Sometimes I took the picture out and just looked at Minerva, imagining the sadness surrounding her existence.

I was going to climb into her brain and heart and write what was there. I was going to put away that other stupid novel I was writing, about two teenage French sleuths, Fleur and Lizeth (what was I thinking?), and begin my new novel about Minerva.

I thought of my plot. I was going to make it so that everybody knew how she came about and no one wanted to be friends with her because she was a symbol of disgrace. Through no fault of her own, of course, since she didn't make herself. I'd write about the cruelty of the parents who wouldn't let their children play with her. And how kids would whisper about her behind their hands. And just generally about the sadness of everything. I was going to make it *really* sad. Poor little Minerva. I almost had myself in tears. Yet—there was a flutter of excitement in my stomach.

The doorbell rang. Mrs. Virgil, with all her moles and her

music and her juicy mouth, was on the porch waiting for me to let her in.

She nodded at me, said my name like a question—"Sophie?" —then bustled past with her handbag over her arm. She stopped in the middle of the living room, looked back at me as she placed her bag on the coffee table, and said, "Let's start with the proper way to sit at the piano." She crossed her arms and waited. "Show me how I told you to sit on the piano bench," she instructed right off. "Did you practice?"

I sat down slowly. "Yes," I said, because right after my last lesson, I did practice—for a minute or two.

"Why do you need the right posture at the piano?"

"For comfort?" I guessed.

She looked at me then and her mouth shrank to a grim line as she drew her lips in.

She shook her head slowly from side to side. "What else?"

It came to me miraculously. "To avoid injury?" I asked.

"Okay. Let's see. Show me."

I pulled the bench forward, then stopped as I heard her loud sigh. "That's too far forward and you're too far back on the bench. Sit on the edge like I told you. Engage those core muscles."

I did as she said. Except for the engaging part, because I didn't exactly know what she meant by core muscles.

"How should you rest your fingers on the keys?" she fired at me.

I looked at my hands and centered them according to the two black keys in the middle of the keyboard.

She tapped my forearms with a pencil that was suddenly in her hand. I raised them a bit. She rested the pencil on one of my arms and it slid off. She cocked her head and looked at me. Then she shook her head again—slowly. "That pencil would have stayed put if your arm had been horizontal."

I raised my elbows a bit more.

"Too late." She sat on the bench beside me. I wanted to get up, but I was trapped.

She turned to me while I stared straight ahead. "You know what your problem is?"

I shook my head.

She looked around. "You're spoiled."

"What?"

"You heard me. You won't get anywhere being so spoiled."

I didn't like being called spoiled. She had no reason to say that. I did nearly everything I was supposed to do—well, most of the time. So I was the opposite of spoiled.

Then she asked, "How are you in school? Do you pay attention? Do your work?"

Now I was insulted. Of course I paid attention and did my work. Schoolwork was easy for me. I kept those thoughts to myself.

"I think you're just spoiled."

I wiped my cheek. I couldn't wait for the lesson to be over.

CHAPTER 5
She Got It!

I GOT IT," Lily said. She sat on the end of her bed. "I got it." She shook her head with disbelief.

I put my book down. I'd been reading since Mrs. Virgil left. And thinking about the new book I was going to write. And putting off starting it. I could begin with Minerva's mother telling her she was an outside child or maybe her just finding out, or maybe some kids telling her in a mean way. There were so many ways to go. I thought about the look on Minerva's face. I thought of her walking by her father's house and seeing his "real" children (my father's little brothers) playing in the front yard.

"I got it," Lily said again in a near whisper.

"You got hired?"

"They don't know I'm colored," Lily went on. "Mrs. Singer,

the owner, had spoken to someone who was supposed to come for an interview. Someone who was the neighbor of someone who goes to Mrs. Singer's cousin's temple. Someone Jewish. But she didn't remember the person's name. I guess that person just changed her mind and didn't show up. Somehow she thought *I* was her. Can you *believe it?* What luck!"

Lily sat up a little straighter. "They think I'm the Jewish person." Her eyes widened at the thought. She leaned over to check herself in the vanity mirror. She pushed her hair back, swiveling her head from side to side, but kept her eyes focused on her face.

"You don't look Jewish, to me," I said, thinking of Melissa Miller in sixth grade. Melissa was olive skinned with long lashes and straight dark eyebrows like Audrey Hepburn's. When I thought *Jewish,* she was the person who came to mind. Melissa with her cheeks dusted with fine, pale brown hairs that could be seen only in the light of the sun. I was fascinated by this and searched for the same tiny hairs on my own face. But mine was smooth and bald as an apple.

"You could get into trouble," I added.

Lily looked at me for a couple of beats. "Yeah," she said slowly. "I could."

"And what if your friends come in to see you?"

"It's a free country. White people can have colored friends." She piled her hair on top of her head and lifted her chin. She squinted at her reflection and took a long, thoughtful breath. "I might lighten my hair some more. You know what? The owner, Mrs. Singer—she even asked which temple I attend. I only know the one on La Cienega Boulevard, Temple Beth Am. So I told her that and she seemed pleased."

I gasped. "You shouldn't have done that, Lily."

"Why not? I can just read up on some stuff, learn about the religion, I guess."

"You can't pretend to be a religion you're not."

"Why not?"

"I think that would be a sin."

"Oh, you're so serious." She trotted over and gave me one of her triumphant hugs.

"Don't be silly." She turned toward the mirror again and ran both hands through her hair. She angled her face this way and that. "I think if you look at me really fast, I could look Jewish."

But what did Jewish look like? I thought about Melissa Miller again. She looked way different from Michael Foxman, who was also Jewish and had red hair and red eyelashes. He was in love with Melissa Miller. In sixth grade he told me glumly, as we stood in line in front of the auditorium door, waiting to go in for Friday square dancing, that I was plain.

It was startling to me. To be summed up like that. "Now, Melissa is pretty," he went on. A few days later, I studied her while we washed paintbrushes in the janitor's room. I studied her and all that made her pretty because I agreed with Michael Foxman. He had a keen eye.

We were also in the janitor's room rinsing paintbrushes the next Friday when Melissa told me how a woman got pregnant. It was the grossest thing I'd ever heard, and I didn't believe it for a second. Grandma Nanny, my mother's mother who lived in North Carolina, had nine children! She would have never done such a thing nine times, nor my mother *two times*. I was pretty certain of that. I didn't take this new information to my mother or even to Lily. I just continued to feel comfortable in the way I saw things. I knew Melissa was wrong.

Of course, she turned out to be right.

"Maybe I'll even start wearing a Star of David," Lily said.

"If you do that, that's like making fun of a person's religion. Like you're just *using* the religion."

"You're so serious," she said again. "How'd you get so serious? I'm only joking."

I didn't believe her. It would be like the time Lily pretended to be Catholic because this boy she liked was Catholic and she thought maybe she could see him if she went to his church. She dragged me with her.

Lily did everything just like the Catholics, especially when she spotted him walking up the church's steps between his mother and father behind us. She'd read up on what to do, so when I tried to pull open that big, tall, heavy door to the actual church part, she yanked me back to do the sign of the cross with the holy water. Then she stepped ahead of me to lead the way. I watched her kneel on one leg at the end of the pew, and she nodded for me to do the same. She crossed her chest with such a solemn look on her face, I thought she might be suddenly sincere.

When it came time for Communion—when you had to stand and go to the place up front to kneel and receive the wafer —Lily stood, bowed her head, and, with her hands clasped at her chest, walked up the aisle in a line with all the other real Catholics. I held my breath. She knelt down as if there was nothing wrong with it, then opened her mouth to get that wafer put on her tongue like everyone else. Then she stood and walked back, making her face look just like that of an angel, which got my heart beating fast with fear. My sister would surely be going to hell for making fun of someone else's religion—all to make a boy notice her.

And now she would be making fun of the Jewish religion by pretending to be Jewish and saying she was a member of Temple Beth Am on La Cienega. And she didn't seem the least bit worried about it.

"I'm not going to pretend to be Jewish," she said later. "I'm just not going to say I'm not."

CHAPTER 6
Mrs. Baylor's Room

THE MANSFIELDS WERE coming for dinner. We had them over once a year. I'd learned they were coming when our mother started fussing about the menu the week before. Then at the breakfast table (one of the few times we all sat together) she suddenly changed her mind and asked Daddy if he thought baked chicken and asparagus and stuffed potatoes would be good.

He was reading the newspaper. "Fine by me," he said from behind it. Then she asked him if lamb would be better. That's when he lowered the paper and stared at her. She stared back. "Lamb is fine, Nina," he said.

Lily was annoyed. They were coming the evening of the Fourth of July and that meant Lily would have to cut short her fun at the beach with her friends and get back in time for dinner. Though it didn't matter to me, I wasn't sure why we were having them to dinner on a holiday.

The Mansfields were bringing their daughter, Robin. I didn't like her. And their son, Dale. He had been Lily's escort to the cotillion last year. Robin's eyes were blue like a robin's egg, and she was quite taken with her own "good hair." Her long braid ended with a finger-size curl that looked like spun silk. Mine ended in a clump of sagebrush. She pointed this out to me once. "Your mother has to straighten your hair," she said, her eyes darting around my hairline. "My mother just has to put water and Wildroot Cream Oil on mine." Then she smiled as if it was all she could do to keep from laughing at the frizz at the end of my braid.

That was when I was ten, when her mother first brought her over so we could get acquainted.

"You want to play with Barbies?" she had asked, eyeing my Barbie dream house on the table in the corner beside my bed.

I looked at it as if I'd forgotten it was there. "Oh, I don't play with that anymore. It's for babies," I said, delighting in her look of disappointment. "Let's go outside and play with Oscar." I was counting on her being timid around Oscar, too afraid he'd jump or slobber on her to enjoy herself.

· · ·

So they were coming. The Mansfields. With that stuck-up Robin. Dale Mansfield was at Dartmouth now. He was a distant memory to Lily. Though I'd heard her badmouthing him to Lydia.

"Who'd be willing to do all that? He'd already been an escort twice. His junior year and senior year."

I was sitting in the dining room with the door open, supposedly reading. Lily and Lydia were out on the patio passing a cigarette back and forth between them. It was an early evening in May, and the cotillion experience was long behind her, but Lily was sharing, with her new friend, the travails of her past life. Our mother wasn't at home—nor our father. And Shirley didn't care if Lily smoked.

"My mother arranged the whole thing. She said he was from a good family."

"What does that even mean?" Lydia asked. "Probably money. Oh, and his father is a doctor."

"Surgeon," Lily said. "There's a difference." Apparently a surgeon was of a higher status than a doctor. People looked up to doctors, but they looked up to surgeons more.

They were quiet for a bit. I waited.

Finally, Lily said, "What? Did she think she was picking out a future husband for me?" I heard her take a long, angry drag on the cigarette—and that drag was full of defiance and bravado.

When I got old enough, I planned to smoke my cigarettes in just that way. They both sat quietly, as if they were thinking this over.

"Bet his dad would buy you guys a house."

"I don't want a house," Lily said. "I'm not even in college yet. I just wanted to choose my own escort. He couldn't even dance."

"Not even the waltz?" Lydia asked.

"I'm not talking about cotillion dances. I'm talking about real dancing. He doesn't even have rhythm."

"How can he be colored and not have rhythm?"

"Believe me — I now know it's possible."

I heard Lily flick the cigarette butt across the yard in expert fashion. She'd probably been practicing. But I knew she'd be out there later, looking for that butt before our mother could come across it. Then I heard her light up another, and all they had for me after that was the sound of them passing the cigarette back and forth.

"Good family," Lily said after a while with disgust.

Now she was looking for her necklace — the blue topaz one set in a gold heart on a gold chain. The necklace Daddy had given her for her sixteenth birthday.

"Did you take it?" she asked me.

I was searching in the closet for something to wear. Something that wouldn't make me look like a baby. "No, I didn't take it. I don't even like necklaces." I sighed. I had such a limited wardrobe.

Lily turned her jewelry box over on the top of her dresser and ran her fingers through the pile. "I know I put it in here," she muttered to herself. "I wore it to my birthday dinner at the Coconut Grove. Remember? I put it here—right in this jewelry box. I remember clearly."

"Maybe it fell behind the dresser."

"Oh? So it just walked out of my jewelry box and hurled itself off the dresser. Is that what you're saying?"

I didn't like it when Lily said things like that to me. When she accused me of being ridiculous. Now she was irritated. The drawer-opening-and-slamming-shut phase was just starting up.

"Are you sure you didn't *borrow* it?" she said over her shoulder, squinting at me suspiciously.

"I didn't borrow it. I haven't *seen* it."

She began to pull out dresser drawers and dump the contents on the floor.

"Why do you want to find it so much when you don't even really like Dale?"

"It's not that I don't like him. He's just not my type." She squatted and started going through all the stuff on the floor, then stopped and frowned. "I just want my necklace, the one Daddy gave me on my birthday! It's my necklace. I want it."

I didn't get it. She was always saying snide things about our father. Like the other day when she told me our mother should sing that song to him, "Guess Who I Saw Today," which was about a woman running across her husband and another woman in a small, dimly lit café.

Lily hinted all the time that our father was untrue. That he was arrogant—her word—and thought he was above it all. She said our mother should spend all his money or at least buy everything she wants because he's such a jerk. And that every man has the capacity to be a jerk.

I didn't believe this. I didn't believe that all men could be jerks.

Now she was on the floor looking for the necklace she once said he probably had his secretary buy.

Suddenly she stopped, sat back, and placed both hands on her thighs. "I bet you Mrs. Baylor took it," she said.

"Mrs. Baylor?"

"Yeah. She probably took it to give to her daughter, the one who's still in Jamaica. I feel it. Anyway, she doesn't like me and it would be just like her to take something of mine."

"I don't think so, Lily."

"Come on. It makes sense. She wants me to suffer."

"Why would she think *that* would make you suffer?"

"I don't know. I can't climb into her brain. But you must

know she hates us." Lily wiped her tears away with the fingertips of both hands. "Help me check her room."

"We can't go in there."

"Oh yeah, we can, too. She's gone home for the weekend. Maybe she left it hidden someplace."

"Wouldn't she take it with her?"

"Maybe. But let's look anyway."

It felt funny sneaking into the room that had once belonged to our beloved Shirley. Shirley, who made us tacos. And who let me read my stories to her and let me start from the beginning whenever I added a new part so she could get the full flavor.

As Shirley stood at the stove, stirring a pot of stew or whatever, she'd squint with real concentration when I read to her. And make comments when I finished. Such as: "That's real good, but I don't think you can write about little white girls."

She was referring to my Fleur and Lizeth story.

"Why not?"

"'Cause you're not white."

"But it's just make-believe."

"Can't you come up with something about colored girls? Don't they have a story?"

That was before I'd discovered little Minerva.

We knew this room well—and just the thought that it was

now Mrs. Baylor's room made it seem strange. It even had a different smell—a tired sweetness, like cologne over sweat. I looked around. She'd placed a folded brown afghan at the foot of her narrow bed and a doily on the nightstand. The nightstand held her Bible and a framed photo of all her children. There was her Mason jar of water on the floor beside the bed. I picked it up and looked at it. I smelled it to see if it was alcohol.

"Just water," I said. Lily glanced over her shoulder at me, but her mind was on her necklace. I envisioned Mrs. Baylor taking a long swig from that jar in the middle of the night. Lily crossed the room and picked up Mrs. Baylor's Bible from the nightstand. For some strange reason, she flipped through the pages.

"You should put that back."

"Why?"

"That's her Bible."

My sister looked at me and slowly shook her head. She replaced the Bible. I picked up the framed photo. "These are her sons. This one is in the Marines," I said, placing my finger on the guy in the military uniform. "He's in Vietnam. I heard her tell Mom." I pointed to the other young man in the picture. "And this is the one she's always bragging about."

"*Mr. Nigel Nigel Nigel*—the shining star?" Lily said.

"I saw him in person."

She took the picture from me, stared at it for a few moments. "When?" She gave it back.

"Saturday. Before you came back from your interview."

She opened her mouth as if she wanted to ask something about him, but then she just drew in her lips.

Mrs. Baylor's son was at the University of California Berkeley and she was quite proud to tell us and then repeat it at every opportunity.

"He was valedictorian of his graduating class," I said.

"Yes," she said. "We're reminded of that every time we turn around."

Lily took the picture out of my hand again and stared at it some more. She seemed to drift off. But then she shook herself out of it, put the picture back on the nightstand, and started in on the dresser drawers—carefully pulling each one open, then gently sliding her hands between and beneath the folded clothing.

I picked up the Mason jar lid, which was also on the nightstand.

"This is what she uses for an ashtray."

My sister wasn't listening. She was checking the bottom drawer when I suddenly thought of something disturbing. "What if she put a hair on each drawer?" I said.

"What?"

"You know, to see if someone's opened it to go into her things. She could have put a hair on each drawer, and if the hair is gone, she knows that means the drawer's been opened."

Lily shook her head. "Honestly, Sophie, how do you think of stuff like that? I swear."

I swallowed hard. I was getting nervous.

Next, Lily lifted a corner of the mattress and raked her arm along the box springs, reaching in between all the way up to her armpit. She stood and straightened the bedspread, then stepped back and examined it. "It looks the same, doesn't it?" she asked, before dropping to her knees and peering under the bed.

"Check the nightstand drawers," she told me.

I didn't want to check the nightstand drawers. I opened the top one. It was a mess in there.

Lily looked over, watching me. "Move stuff around, look under stuff. You search like a man."

"A man?"

"Yeah, you know how Mom complains about the way Daddy looks for stuff? Like in the kitchen cabinet—he never moves anything, never looks behind the cans and jars and boxes of pasta."

I really didn't want to put my hand in there among the scraps of paper and pens and pencils and stray peppermints and gum wrappers. There was a metal container of thick-looking hair grease and lipstick the color of wine.

I held up the lipstick. "She wears this when she gets dressed up."

Lily rolled her eyes. "I don't need to know that."

There was another photograph of Nigel on the dresser. But in this one he was wearing a cap and gown. I stepped over for a closer look and said, "That must be his high school graduation picture."

Lily closed the bottom dresser drawer and reached out for it. "Let me see that." She raised her chin, and I knew that look. It was her *I don't really care* look. All a pretense, I bet.

I handed it over. She glanced at it, then stood up. She took it to the bed and sat down. She stared at it, then put her forefinger on her mouth, and I could see her chest rise and fall in shallow breaths. I moved over next to her to see what she was seeing. He had laughing eyes—like Smoky Robinson's and as if there was a joke going on inside his head. He was dark—as dark as an African—and had a lovely smile, white, white teeth against his dark skin. I reached for the picture to return it to the dresser, but Lily held on to it for an extra second.

"Just kidding," she said, standing up. "Not my type."

"Then give it to me," I said.

"Yeah, yeah. *Here.*"

We heard the toilet flush then—in Mrs. Baylor's bathroom at the end of the hall.

We froze. That couldn't be Mrs. Baylor in the bathroom because she was supposed to be gone—on her weekend! I quickly returned the picture to the dresser.

We heard water running and then the bathroom door was opening. We stood side by side, facing the doorway as if it was about to admit a firing squad into the room. But maybe she'd turn right and head down the three steps to the kitchen. Or maybe she'd turn left and head for the steps leading to the foyer.

But no, she was coming. We could hear her approach, and any second Mrs. Baylor was going to come through the door. What could we say that would explain why we were in there? I glanced at Lily. She was standing ramrod straight, barely breathing. She was afraid. I could feel it. I could feel her mind racing as she tried to come up with something.

Mrs. Baylor came through the door and stopped short. She stood there looking at us, her head slowly tilting to the side, her eyebrows sinking into a deep furrow. "What are you doing in *here?* In *this* place. You tell me that."

I looked to Lily, waiting for her to speak. She appeared to have no plans to do anything of the sort.

"Perhaps you didn't hear me. I said, 'What the hell are you doing in my room?'"

Lily looked down and said quietly, "I was looking for something."

"And what was that, might I ask?" Mrs. Baylor put her hands on her hips. "You thought I was gone, didn't you? You thought I was already on my way home. Well, Miss Lily, your mama asked me to stay to cook for her company. So I am here to cook for the company." She looked triumphant. "Surprise!"

I jumped in. "We weren't looking for anything, Mrs. Baylor. Lily's just saying that. We were curious. We just wanted to see what your room looked like." I glanced over at my sister. She appeared surly and defiant under Mrs. Baylor's glare. Mrs. Baylor glanced at me as if I was of no importance. She was directing everything she said at Lily.

"I plan to tell your mama that you all were snoopin' around in my business. Puttin' your nose where it don't belong."

I kept my eyes fixed on a spot on the rug.

"You can go now, and don't you let me catch you doing this again. As long as I'm working in this house, this room is off-limits. You got that?"

"Yes, Mrs. Baylor," I said. "We're very, very sorry."

Mrs. Baylor stared at Lily, waiting for her apology.

"Sorry," Lily said.

"You don't sound sorry. I don't hear no sorrow in your voice." She stepped aside from the door so we could leave. "You sound like you think you got a right to be just anywhere you please, Miss Queen of England. Well, you got no right to be in here."

"I *am* sorry. We won't ever do this again," Lily said in a flat-sounding voice, as if she was just saying words from a script.

As soon as we were back in the bedroom, she sat down hard on her bed. "I know she has my necklace."

"You don't know—"

"Yeah, I do," she said, cutting me off.

But when I moved the dresser away from the wall, we saw it there on the floor. Mrs. Baylor *didn't* have the necklace.

Lily glossed over her surprise and shame. "I moved the dresser and didn't see anything," she said.

"You didn't move it far enough." I dropped it in her hand. "Here's your precious necklace. You get to wear it, after all."

"I'm not wearing it. I've changed my mind."

CHAPTER 7
The Mansfields

L ILY WORE the tiny gold posts that Lydia had used when she'd pierced Lily's ears in her bathroom in the spring. After Lily told me how easy it was, I wanted to get mine pierced, too.

"You weren't scared?" I asked.

"Maybe a little."

"You think Mom will give me permission to get mine done?"

"Don't be silly, Sophie. You don't ask permission for something like that. You just do it. You'll get put on punishment. Something short, most likely. But you'll have pierced ears."

• • •

I finished dressing first and was on my way to the living room when Lily said, "Hold up."

I stopped with my hand on the door.

"I'm going to signal you every time Dovie Mansfield brags about something." She winked. "It'll be fun."

"How are you going to signal me?"

"Watch what I do with my fingers. You'll see."

I started to leave, then stopped again. "Why do we have to have them to dinner anyway?" I was thinking of Robin.

"So they'll invite us to their grand end-of-the-summer barbecue."

"I don't get it."

"This dinner will be fresh in Dovie Mansfield's mind when she makes up her guest list."

"That seems like so much trouble."

"I agree."

Our mother, dressed in green silk flowing pants and a gold boat-neck blouse, assessed Lily coolly when she made her appearance in white capris and a brown sleeveless knit top. But the Mansfields were already there, so she had to put on her hostess face and ignore Lily's casual clothes for the time being.

I checked Robin. She'd shot up past me and now had breasts.

Not fair—she looked more like a teenager than I did. I was only a month and a half away from thirteen. But then I remembered that she was six months older, so there.

She'd gotten her hair cut into a thick, blunt flip that swung easily when she moved her head. She'd be swinging her hair around all night, I predicted.

She looked me up and down and gathered her lips together against a giggle.

"You remember Robin, Sophie," my mother said. "I guess it's been a while since you two have seen each other." Robin had been away at Los Olivares Academy up in Ojai. I was sure Mrs. Mansfield was all the time giving my mother an earful about the boarding school: the cost, the exclusivity, the wilderness excursions designed to build self-confidence (Robin seemed to have gotten a big dose of that), the three international trips. Robin wouldn't begin to experience those until her junior year, so we were saved from having to hear about them, at least.

"Where's Bob?" Dr. Mansfield asked. He was a heavy man with plump fingers and a double chin. His stomach fell over his belt and he kept trying to discreetly hike up his pants.

Mom was taking Dovie Mansfield's coat and I caught her checking the label before hanging it in the hall closet. "Oh, he's back there in his home office," she said, indicating the closed door down the upper hall. "On an important call. He'll be out in a minute." She held out her hands palms up, and nodded toward our living room.

Lily looked down the hall at the closed door and her expression hardened.

Mom led the way and indicated that the Mansfields should take the couch in front of the hors d'oeuvres on the coffee table. Robin squeezed in. Dale, who'd been hanging back near the front door, now followed behind. Robin gazed at the food without interest. Not once had she really, really looked at me since the snide once-over. It was as if she was trying to let me know that I was irrelevant. I was determined not to look at her and her swinging flip either, since she thought she was so superior. I looked everywhere but at her.

Mrs. Mansfield rubbed her hands together. "This is great, Nina."

"Don't give me the credit. Our housekeeper made them."

"Lucky you."

Dale found a chair in the corner and sat down. He wasn't really bad looking. He just looked . . . soft. And he had our dog Oscar's sad eyes, as if he'd given up on trying to please. He smiled over at me where I'd taken a chair across from him. I smiled back. He glanced at Lily, who was pointedly ignoring the poor guy. I felt sorry for him. Lily had perched herself on the piano bench and looked prepared to be amused.

Now that Lily and I had discussed Dr. Mansfield, I had a new way of looking at him. He wasn't a handsome man, but he had a way of carrying himself as if he were—like my father. I compared him with Dale, and then Dale with his birdlike mother with the long thin nose and hair so dark and dull looking, I bet it was dyed.

Lily said that it doesn't matter what you look like when you're a surgeon. You're still going to get plenty of women fawning over you. In fact, she bet Dr. Mansfield had lots of women. She could tell just by looking at him.

I wanted to know how she could do that and she said she had her ways.

"Haven't you noticed how he raises his eyebrows so that they go up in the middle—all debonair-like?" she asked. "That makes him look like a man who believes that everything will naturally go his way. Men like that cheat on their wives. They think, 'Why should only one woman get to love me? I am so great, I need to spread it around.'"

"Do you think Daddy thinks like that?"

She looked at me and said nothing.

The Mansfields weren't close family friends—they were

convenient family friends. It was all about people noticing who got invited where. It was so crazy.

I glanced over at Dr. Mansfield to see if he looked like a ladies' man. Then I peered at Dovie Mansfield popping a shrimp on a cracker into her mouth and chewing slowly while Nancy Wilson played in the background on the stereo. Robin had been listlessly working on her shrimp, which she nibbled and then replaced on her napkin for a minute or so before taking another nibble. It was as if she was just going through the motions.

Daddy finally came in, rubbing his hands together and putting on his big company smile. "So what do we have here?" My mother didn't like what he was wearing either (casual tan pants and an open-collar white shirt). I could tell by her appraising look.

Dale and his father stood and shook hands with Daddy. Dale returned to his seat while the men backslapped each other and said jovial things back and forth.

"Ahhh . . ." my mother said, settling in her chair. "Finally, the busy man is off the phone." She looked at my father and he lost his smile for a second.

"We just picked up Dale from Dartmouth this morning," Dovie Mansfield said.

For a moment I had a picture of them driving all the way there and back, but then I knew she meant they picked him up at the airport.

Dale ducked his head, probably embarrassed, and Lily pretended to scratch her chin with her forefinger. One finger . . . That was it. Lily was signaling brag number one: the mention of Dartmouth. I tried not to smile.

Our mother's voice was full of sympathy when she said, "Oh my . . . you must be tired, Dale."

Daddy was handing Dr. Mansfield a drink—something brown, which meant strong liquor.

He turned to Dale. "So how's college treating you?"

"He's loving it," Mrs. Mansfield answered for him. "In fact, he's on his way to getting out in three years instead of four. He insisted on taking two additional courses during the first summer session." She grinned demurely at Dale. "He is *so* ambitious."

Lily looked at me and rolled her eyes, making me nearly burst out laughing. Then she ran two fingers through her hair to signal brag number two. I had to bite my tongue to keep a straight face.

Meanwhile, Dr. Mansfield took a swig of his drink, set it down, then leaned back and formed a church steeple with his fingers. He didn't contribute to the conversation. He just looked thoughtful. He was doing that to look like an authority figure, I realized. My pediatrician did the same thing with his fingers when he was sitting behind his desk getting ready to tell my mother something about my allergies or what booster shots I needed.

"And—*drumroll*," Dovie Mansfield went on, looking around. "Dale made the dean's list!"

Lily caught my eye and began tapping her mouth with three fingers. She kept tapping until I laughed out loud and everyone turned to look at me. There was a moment of awkward silence. I coughed to show that they'd heard a cough, not a laugh. Still, Mrs. Mansfield frowned at me and looked puzzled. After a moment she turned toward my mother, but Robin's eyes lingered on me suspiciously. Then she looked down at her hands in her lap and smiled faintly.

"These are delicious," Dovie Mansfield said, finishing off another hors d'oeuvre. This time she plucked the shrimp off the cracker, ate it separately, and then popped the cracker into her mouth. She turned to Dr. Mansfield. "Remember that wonderful seafood place down the beach from our summer house? Didn't they have the best shrimp?" She reached for another one.

Dr. Mansfield looked over at her as if he'd been deep in thought about something else. "Yeah, sure," he said. I saw my sister look at me slyly and tap the space between her eyebrows slowly four times. I was fascinated. She was right.

At dinner, Mrs. Mansfield gave a detailed account of the AKA North Atlantic Regional Conference in Atlanta: who was there, the activities, the pink and green merchandise you could buy (mugs, headbands, knitted gloves, and on and on). The AKA was a popular colored sorority. It was big on on the Howard campus in D.C., where Mrs. Mansfield had gone. But Spelman, where our mother went, didn't allow sororities. They probably thought that being at an all-girls college was enough sisterhood for anybody.

Lily ran her hand over her hair, wiggling all five of her fingers ever so slightly for my benefit. Dovie Mansfield knew our mother wasn't an AKA. She was just rubbing it in. But even if they'd had sororities at Spelman, my mother would have never pledged. She'd never felt she fit in with girls from the city in college. She was a poor sharecropper's daughter who happened to be very smart. So smart that her high school teachers had raised money to provide her with a college scholarship. She wouldn't have wanted to chance a rejection.

"Why didn't you attend, Nina? You would have loved it."

My mother smiled and said simply, "I'm not an AKA, Dovie. I thought you knew that. And anyway, this is my busy time with the Links. And I'm now president of the Wives of the Bench and Bar—you know, it's the club for colored judges' and lawyers' wives. It's very time-consuming." She shrugged. And that seemed to shut Dovie up.

Lily smirked at me, but I could tell she was proud of our mother for subtly brushing off Mrs. Mansfield's attempt to one-up her.

Our father suddenly piped up with, "So, Dale, what's your sport?"

Dale stopped cutting his lamb off the bone and put his utensils down. He cleared his throat and glanced at his father. "I'm a lacrosse fan, sir, and I used to play it." He checked his father again, who stared at him without expression.

Daddy said, "Oh. Well. I really know nothing about lacrosse. Isn't that like baseball only with a different kind of bat?"

"You're thinking of cricket," Dale said.

Dr. Mansfield buttered his roll and took a bite out of it. It seemed that he'd decided to have no part in the conversation.

Mrs. Mansfield spoke up then. "Oh, Dale was an excellent lacrosse player in high school. Excellent." She looked quickly to Dr. Mansfield (giving me the impression that this had once been a touchy topic — Dale playing such a foreign kind of sport).

"So, Lily — you're going to Spelman in the fall," Mrs. Mansfield tried again.

"Yes," Lily answered.

"Where else did you apply?" Her closed mouth twitched as if she was about to hear something that would satisfy her.

"Just a couple of the UCs. UCLA and UC Berkeley. Oh, and Brown."

"And did you get in?"

"Yes, I got into all three of them."

"My, my," Mrs. Mansfield said, looking a little let down for some reason. I sneaked a glance at Robin. She rolled her eyes as if it was no big thing. She planned to be accepted by all the schools she applied to as well. What was the big deal?

Then silence—except for the clinking of forks against plates.

"But I bet you're excited about leaving home and going off to Atlanta, right?" Dovie Mansfield asked after a bit.

I waited for Lily to answer and took a sip of water to make the knot suddenly forming in my throat go away. She was really leaving. Then there'd be no one to tell me what to do—or how to think about things when I was going along thinking the wrong way.

How could she say, "Yes, I'm excited," and smile so politely?

"Let me tell you something," Mrs. Mansfield said, as if it was only the two of them sitting there at the table. "You go to Spelman and you'll make friends you'll have for years. You go to one of those big universities, and you'll be just a student ID number." Mrs. Mansfield even got some color in her cheeks as she was explaining this.

I was the only one who knew for a fact that Lily didn't want to go to Spelman, the college for Negro women. Her first choice was UC Berkeley, but she'd settled on Spelman to please our mother.

"That's where I'm sending Robin," Dovie Mansfield said.

"I'm not going to a Negro college," Robin stated evenly.

Lily looked at her quickly as if a tiny bit surprised.

Mrs. Mansfield didn't miss a beat. "We can discuss that later," she said, looking at everyone but her daughter.

"Just so you know," Robin added.

Mrs. Mansfield stared at Robin meaningfully, but Robin went on eating her stuffed potato as if she had merely stated neutral information.

Mrs. Mansfield recovered quickly, suddenly turning to me —showing the uneven application of her foundation, which made me think of my mother getting hers specially mixed. "I have someone for you to meet, Sophie. The child of a colleague of Dr. Mansfield's at the hospital. He has a daughter just your age. They're fresh from London. She's smart like you and she's new here and would love to have a friend. It would be nice if she and Robin could get to know each other, but Robin's leaving to go back to boarding school soon and . . ." She let her voice drift off.

I smiled, not knowing what else to do.

"You'll meet her at our barbecue in a few weeks." She nodded and winked. I wondered what the wink was for. I was still thinking about it when the dinner concluded and the grownups went into the living room and Mrs. Baylor cleared the table and started the cleanup. Robin, Lily, Dale, and I went up to the den to watch television.

Robin sat with her arms crossed, staring at the blank screen as the TV warmed up. It was clear she thought she was enduring the last hour of an extremely boring evening.

I looked at her and immediately hated her flip all over again. And the white headband, too, while I was at it. I hated her Wildroot Cream Oiled hair. And the way she made sure her eyes never met mine for more than a few seconds; the way she had no questions about my life or revelations about hers. Well, I could be quiet, too. I could out-quiet her. *Let's just see who can be the queen of quiet,* I thought.

Then, out of Dale, came the most astonishing words. "My parents are the phoniest people I know. I mean, could they be any phonier?"

Lily and I turned to him at the same time, surprised.

"What do you mean?" Lily asked, and I knew that she was just trying to goad information out of him. We knew exactly what he meant.

"My mother all the time bragging about me." He looked at Lily. "Do you know what that feels like?" It was a question not meant to be answered. Even I knew that.

"Your mother's proud of you," Lily said. I thought maybe she was trying to be nice to Dale after badmouthing him to Lydia.

"It wasn't my idea to be a debutante escort three times. It was hers," he said, still referring to his mother.

Robin smiled and gazed out the big picture window at the dark sky. Lily and I looked at each other. We'd been too hard on poor Dale. He seemed so relaxed now. He sat forward, his forearms on his thighs, his hands hanging loosely between them, with a different air about him completely. "I'm not going back," he declared.

"To Dartmouth?"

"Yeah."

Lily raised an eyebrow, as if seeing him from a new perspective. "So what are you going to do?"

"I enlisted."

"What?" Lily exclaimed, her eyes wide with disbelief.

"I enlisted. In the Marines. I leave for boot camp next week. Camp Pendleton, near San Diego."

Lily looked flabbergasted. "Why on earth did you do that? *Why?*"

Dale seemed cool and confident. "Because I wanted to. *I* wanted to. *Me.* And it's *my* life."

Robin sighed audibly and rolled her eyes. She caught Lily's attention, who frowned as she looked Robin up and down. Robin leaned forward, retrieved an *Ebony* off the coffee table, and began to flip through it.

"When are you going to tell your parents what you've done?"

"I guess I'll tell them before I leave."

Lily shook her head slowly. "I can't believe you did that." She almost sounded as if he'd betrayed *her*. "People are trying to stay *out* of Vietnam. Not join up."

Dale chuckled. "The world's not going to end."

"But your parents have plans for you."

"They'll have to make an adjustment. Anyway, I'm not going back."

Robin yawned as if she'd heard all this one time too many.

"You know how many guys would love to have a student deferment? And you're just throwing it away."

The opening credits for *Lassie* had begun and he turned to look at them—probably just to end the discussion.

"Anyway, I don't fit in at Dartmouth," he said a little later, surprising us again. His mouth was set in a slight pout.

"Why?" Lily asked.

"Because he doesn't fit in anywhere," Robin explained.

Lily and I both turned to give her a hard look. I saw her swallow—which showed she wasn't so sure of herself, after all.

"Why are you being so mean? What is your *problem*?" Lily asked.

"I don't have a problem," Robin said, raising her chin a little.

"Oh, you have a problem, all right."

"You know what?" Dale said. "My mother cried for two days when I didn't get into Harvard. That's a big secret. That I applied and didn't get in." He turned back to the TV. End of discussion. Robin Mansfield continued to flip through the magazine pages as if she couldn't wait for the evening to be over.

Later, while she was rolling her hair before going to bed, Lily said, "Did you notice how Daddy jumped up when the phone rang right in the middle of dinner? Why didn't he just let Mrs. Baylor get it? I can't wait to get out of here."

I looked up from *Footlights for Jean*, which was about a young girl who got to be an apprentice at a playhouse. Lily's words felt like a slap. *She's eager,* I thought. *She's eager to leave.*

CHAPTER 8
Transfiguration

I TOLD MY MOTHER what happened and that I refused to stay and swim at the Bakers' and that I called the Baker girls prejudiced. She didn't believe me. She wants to hear it from you," Jennifer said.

We were sitting on her back porch steps. I could hear her grandmother moving around in the kitchen, preparing Jennifer's lunch, which Jennifer would soon eat at the kitchen table. Jennifer's family ate dinner together in the dining room, just like families on TV. Plus, Jennifer had to ask if she could be excused before she got up and left the table. But she never had to do dishes, because her grandmother did them—probably happily. She made Jennifer's bed and laid out her school clothes, as well. It was as if Jennifer had loving care from all around—and being an only child, she didn't have to share it with anybody.

My father was rarely home for dinner, and half the time my mother was away at one of her meetings or at her art gallery. Often Lily ate in our room or the den while yapping on the phone and I sat at the kitchen table by myself. I didn't like that or dislike it. It was just the way it was.

Shirley used to sit across from me when she saw me sitting there alone. She'd drink her coffee, which she'd spiked with some of my father's brown liquor from the cabinet over the refrigerator. (I'd seen her do it before and it seemed to put her in a good mood.) She'd ask me about my day—all the things that happened at school. Then she'd give me lots of advice on what I needed to do to be popular and hip. "You need to stand up straight, for one thing. You dip a little. Like a turtle peeking out of its shell. Move like you have confidence, girl! Like you're too cool." She'd sip her coffee and give me a wink, and I'd think she didn't know just how far I was from being too cool.

Mrs. Baylor, on the other hand, would only give me a quick glance on her way up to her room with her mug of coffee and her cigarette. Then there'd be quiet behind her closed door and I'd picture her slowly thumbing through the *Los Angeles Sentinel,* our Negro newspaper. Reading the articles—passing judgment on them in her mind. Approving or disapproving of the opinions in the opinions section.

A couple of years ago, I read about those girls who were killed in a bombing at a church in Alabama in my father's copy of the *Los Angeles Sentinel*. I looked at their faces and imagined them getting ready for church, getting their hair done—and I had to think these things on my own because my mother and father shook their heads at the news accounts on TV, but they didn't say much of anything. I knew it was bad, but we each kept the bad to ourselves.

I waited for Jennifer to finish her grumbling because I wanted her take on my new book. Finally, I had my chance.

"What happened to *The Odd Cases of Fleur and Lizeth*?" Jennifer asked.

"I'm writing something else now. It's called *The Outside Child*."

She scratched her chin and looked like she was gearing herself up for punishment—another long chapter she'd have to endure, and then I'd be badgering her about what she thought.

"What's it about?" she asked. She grabbed her Hula-Hoop and started swirling it around her waist—hands free—with her eyes closed.

"It's about a child that a man has with a woman who is not his wife."

Jennifer's eyes popped open. "You mean an *illegitimate* child?"

Oh yeah. Another word for an outside child was *illegitimate*.

"If the mother and father aren't married to each other, that's what's called illegitimate," Jennifer went on.

"I know what *illegitimate* means," I said, momentarily happy that I wasn't one of those children.

"So the setting is going to be a long time ago. And it's going to be really bad to be an outside child. Twice as bad as it is today. And she doesn't even know she's an outside child. She always wonders why some children are not allowed to play with her and why people whisper about her."

Jennifer didn't say anything. She was back to Hula-Hooping slowly with her eyes closed. Then she opened them. "You know what?" she said excitedly. "There should be this picture—a fake picture—of her father on the mantle over the fireplace. Um, um —you know how when you buy a frame and it comes with a picture? The mother can use that picture and say it's her father."

"Yeah," I said slowly. "But those frames come with pictures of white people, and the outside child is not white. She's colored."

"Okay. Then let it be just this person the mother once knew —some old friend. She can pretend that guy is the girl's father.

And she can make up all kinds of fake stuff about him. Have the girl really believe it."

"Yeah," I said slowly. That was actually a good idea.

We got permission to walk to the library on Fifty-Fourth Street. We both needed something new to read. I was nearing the final third of *Footlights for Jean* and Jennifer was almost finished with *Black Beauty*. I wanted to be ready with a new book the moment I'd finished the last page.

"When we get back, my mother will probably be home and then you can tell her what happened," Jennifer said. "You can tell her I really stuck up for you."

We'd reached the bottom of the hill where Escalon, Presidio, and Montego Drives came together like the spokes of a wheel. That's where we spotted Jilly and her sister Marcy (the dimwitted one) and another girl we didn't know. "Let's hide and throw rocks at them," Jennifer said.

"No, let's beat 'em up," I said, feeling confident for a moment. There had been too many on the Bakers' side when I'd gone down to their house to swim, but now there were just three of them—and the third person looked like a scrawny little cousin or something.

Jennifer led the way across the street. She stopped in front of the three girls and I joined her. But I changed my mind about beating them up. I didn't know how to beat up anyone. I wouldn't even know where to begin.

"Hey," she said.

Jilly, who was the biggest of the three, stepped forward as if to say, *I'll handle this.*

Jennifer stepped forward, as well. "You and your whole family are prejudiced," she said.

"How come you didn't say that last year when you were swimming in our pool?"

"I didn't know you were prejudiced back then. And now that I know, you can't come to my house."

"We don't want to come to your house," Marcy piped up. "Anyway, we're the ones with the swimming pool. Everybody wants to come to *our* house. *Everybody.* No one wants to go to your house. Don't you know that?"

"And we can't help it if colored people steal and start fights," Jilly added.

My mouth dropped open a little. I'd never stolen anything in my life. And I'd never started a fight.

The only thing left for Jennifer to do would be to punch her in the face. But of course, she couldn't do that. It wasn't her battle. It was my battle. Yet, I was letting Jennifer do all the talking.

The cousin started snickering. They moved past us and she

turned and pointed, then glided one forefinger over the other as if to say, *Shame on you!*

"I should have smacked that girl," I said, looking back at them and feeling sorry, for two seconds, that I'd missed the opportunity.

"It was three against two," Jennifer said.

"Two and a half against two."

"Yeah, you don't want to beat up a half."

We were quiet as we turned down Fifty-Fourth toward the library. "I hate those girls," Jennifer said then.

"And I've never stolen anything in my life." I gritted my teeth at the injustice of being accused of something I'd never even done.

We were passing Transfiguration. "Me and Lily went to that church because this boy she liked once goes there."

"What was it like?"

"Like a regular church."

We stopped and gazed up at the tiled roof, then down at the tall heavy doors that looked like they'd been taken from a mission. I'd studied California history in fourth grade. I was fascinated with California missions and how the priests did such nice things for the Indians, civilizing them and all. According to my teacher.

But then, it seemed as if the Indians had been helpful to the settlers as well, so I didn't see why they needed civilizing. And something told me that they probably liked their own ways and religion just as much as the priests liked theirs. Why were people always trying to *change* other people, anyway?

"Let's go in," Jennifer said.

"I don't feel like it." I was eager to get to the library.

"I want to look inside."

She started up the steps and I followed her. I owed her this, since she'd tried to take up for me while I'd just stood there watching. I pointed out the sponge in the bowl of water on a stand inside the door.

"You wet your fingers on the sponge and then touch your forehead and shoulders and chest."

"I already knew that."

"How?"

"We're Episcopalian—the Church of England," Jennifer said. "Episcopalians make the sign of the cross as well."

"My mother's Methodist, so I think that makes us all Methodist. But not my father. He never goes to church. He doesn't want to miss football, probably. Which I think must be a sin." I thought about that for a minute. "My mother's church is on Adams, near the Children's Home Society, where Lily did her volunteer work last summer before the cotillion. All the debutantes had to do some charity work."

"How'd she like it?"

"She said she was kind of disappointed that there were no children. She thought she'd be able to see real orphans, but apparently the orphans were kept somewhere else. That big white house is just for offices."

We pulled open another set of tall doors and went into the main part of the church.

Jennifer looked around. "The people you see in this kind of church are usually old. Have you noticed?" she whispered. "I mean, when they show church scenes in movies."

"Old women," I observed. "They don't show old men."

"Because the women are more holy," Jennifer said. We tiptoed up the aisle. Sure enough, three old ladies were kneeling in polished pews, holding rosaries with somber looks on their faces. I envied them their holiness. I looked at the stained glass windows all around us depicting several holy scenes.

I showed Jennifer how to almost kneel before we found seats in one of the back pews. "The right knee goes almost to the floor, but not all the way," I told her. I had noticed this over and over while I was in this church with Lily. Jennifer and I looked at the prayer books, but we didn't pick them up because that wouldn't have felt right. We did stuff a few donation envelopes in our pockets, though. There were a bunch, so I thought it would be okay.

At one point we saw a woman get up, kneel slightly at the end of the pew, cross herself, then go to the array of little cups of candles near the altar. She put some change in a basket on a shelf above the candles. She took a match from a small dish on the table and lit it from one of the flames. Then she touched it to the wick of another candle.

"She's lighting the candle for a wish," I explained to Jennifer. "If you want God to do something, you make a wish and light a candle. But you have to donate some money first. For charity."

"How much?"

"I'm not sure."

Jennifer stared at the glowing candles, probably thinking of all the wishes that had been made there.

I motioned toward the little doors along the wall at the back of the church. "Those are closets for telling the priests your sins. You go in there and kneel down and tell all the sins you committed during the past week."

"But what if you don't have any sins?"

"Everyone has sins. Otherwise you'd be an angel—they don't have sins."

"I don't have *any* sins," Jennifer said. "I'm serious. I try really hard *not* to get sins."

I glanced up at the stained glass depictions of Jesus all around and then at the statue in the front of the church. His hands were turned palms forward as if he were giving or receiving something. I'd seen this Jesus with the long, flowing brown hair at my mother's church, too. They looked exactly the same.

When I glanced over at Jennifer, she was doing that "om" thing. Making that meditation sound with her eyes closed. She'd picked that up somewhere and now she did it from time to time. "Jennifer, cut that out. That's not for church."

She giggled and snapped out of it.

"You know what I wonder?" I whispered to her.

"What?"

"How come they make Jesus look like that?"

"What do you mean? That's the way he looks."

"When I was little, my Sunday school teacher said that in the Bible it describes Jesus as having 'skin like copper, hair like lamb's wool.' So why don't they make him with 'skin like copper and hair like lamb's wool'?" I asked.

"Because that's not the way he looks," Jennifer whispered.

"But what about the Bible?"

She shrugged. "I don't remember reading that."

"Well, have you read the whole Bible?"

"No, but if it was in there, everybody would know about it," she said.

I thought about this. It didn't make sense to me, but for some reason I let it go.

"Can we light a candle?" Jennifer whispered.

I looked over at them—at the few already lit and glowing. "I suppose so."

I had four quarters. Daddy had given me money for no reason. Sometimes he did that, probably so I would remember him as being a good father when I grew up and left home.

"Do you have any money?" I asked.

"A quarter," she said, digging it out of the pocket of her pedal pushers.

"We'll both put in a quarter, and then we can wish for something together," I said.

"What should we wish for?" she asked.

I thought about Lily leaving for Georgia in August. I could wish that she would stay and go to a college close to home, that we could share our room until one of us got married. But that would benefit only me, which wasn't fair, since Jennifer was putting in a quarter, too.

"I know what we can wish for," Jennifer said.

"What?"

"That Marcy Baker will be bitten by a dog with rabies and have to get thirteen shots in her stomach." We both giggled over that one. And then the giggles grew, until one of the old ladies looked up at us with a frown. She brought one gloved finger to her lips, which were scrunched and hard looking and made me vow that when I grew old, I would make sure that I smiled all the time.

"Look at that old woman," I said to Jennifer, nodding in the woman's direction. "If the wind changed, her face would freeze like that."

"How do you know when the wind changes?"

I had to think about that. I didn't know. I shrugged, then said, "I suppose we have to wish for something good and not bad."

She squinted, considering this. "It's hard to think of something good."

"That we make all As in ninth grade," I whispered.

"That we grow breasts and get out of our undershirts."

"No, not that!" I said quickly. "We can't wish that in *church*."

"Okay, all As."

I put our quarters in the basket and she lit the candle. Then we both closed our eyes and wished for good grades.

We made it to the library and realized immediately that we didn't feel like being there. But it was lucky that we at least went through the front door to look at the community bulletin board. It was always full of the same kinds of things: old, used items for sale; tutoring requests or tutoring offers; quilting classes; gardening classes, and on and on . . . But this time there was a flyer posted that was of interest. The community center was hosting a play called *That Talk,* sponsored by the drama club (the one for adults), but it was for the youth. Youth ages thirteen to seventeen.

That's what caught my attention. *Thirteen* to seventeen. We were twelve—very nearly thirteen. My birthday was in September and Jennifer's was in October. If you rounded up, we were thirteen!

"We did this play at my school. Last year," Jennifer said, full of excitement. "Oh, I love this play! I couldn't be in it because it was open only to seniors. Oh my gosh—I can't believe it! We have to do this! It's kind of an adaptation of another play called *The School for Scandal.* The setting is in a school, but also in an attic. Olivia is this girl who opens the play with the line, um . . . 'I am missing. But I haven't gone anywhere.'"

My ears perked up.

"It's got villains and everything. We have to try out. Oh, we have to," Jennifer went on. "I mean we *have* to." She pulled me by the arm toward the circulation desk. "Let's see if there are scripts. Come on."

The librarian pointed to a stack of mimeographed sheets at

the end of the counter. "Tryouts—first week of August," she announced. I felt the most wonderful warmth wash over me. Outside of writing, acting was what I was born to do! Actually . . . I
was born to do so many things.

"Good," Jennifer said. "I'll be back from sleep-away camp by
then."

I'd forgotten about sleep-away camp. Jennifer had been
mentioning it here and there since June. I guess I was just putting
her upcoming absence out of my mind. I didn't like the thought
of being on my own after she left.

I skimmed the first couple of pages and decided I liked the
play already. I could tell from the names and the plot summary.

Sixteen-year-old Olivia has pretended to run away from
home. She's actually hiding in the wardrobe in the attic. While
she is "gone," she explains her reasons for taking this "vacation."
As she mentions each person who has wronged her, the audience
sees a scene revealing a slice of their lives. During these scenes,
we see and hear Olivia's comments and we also hear about Olivia
from each character's point of view. At the end, Olivia returns and
it is as if she'd never gone away.

*Olivia: I am missing but I haven't gone anywhere. Finally,
my mother has checked my diary and has read exactly what I
planted for her to read. Now she thinks she knows everything.*

It was those first three lines that grabbed me. I knew that part was written for *me*. And no one had better get in my way.

Jennifer wanted the villain role. She said she was born to be Julie, the English teacher's pet and Olivia's number one tormentor.

My stomach suddenly had butterflies. "I've got to be Olivia."

"Yay-yah," Jennifer said. (This was her new way of saying *yeah*.) "Give me five."

We slapped palms and left the library thumbing through our scripts.

"Tryouts are kind of far off, but I'm taking the script with me to sleep-away camp, anyway."

"Let's go home and read our scripts tonight—to get an overview—and read them together tomorrow."

With our plan agreed upon, we decided to go by the community center on our way back to Montego Drive. Just to get a feel for the stage—because as far as we were concerned, we were going to be on that stage performing in a few weeks. After Jennifer came back from sleep-away camp.

"Remember, when we try out, we have to act like teenagers and not mention our real ages," Jennifer said as we walked down Fifty-Fourth toward Angeles Vista.

"How do we act like teenagers?"

"By being mostly quiet and kind of above it all. If we don't say a lot, people will think we're mature."

Mature . . . I liked that word because then we could refer to certain boys as "immature," and feel pretty mature while saying it.

We pushed through the doors of the community center and found ourselves in the multipurpose room, where only a few kids were hanging out. Three boys who lived around the corner on Orinda were at the carom table, which is like pool but with small wooden disks instead of balls. Anthony Cruz and some boys I'd never seen before were playing doubles Ping-Pong. I glanced at Jennifer. She wasn't looking at him, but I knew she'd seen him. She shook the hair out of her face and took a few steps into the room.

The foosball table stood ignored. Some older girls were sitting off to the side watching the happenings listlessly. At first, they barely glanced at us.

"There's Anthony Cruz," I said in a low voice.

"Who cares?" Jennifer said.

"Don't you still like him?"

"Maybe I do, maybe I don't." She shook the hair out of her face again. She sure was doing a lot of that since we'd arrived, and I was beginning to find it annoying.

At one end of the room was the stage. I felt a pull in that direction.

"Let's get up on the stage," I whispered.

"What for?" Jennifer asked. She was obviously waiting for Anthony Cruz to notice her. She flung her hair out of her face *again* and looked around. One of the girls whispered to her friend and they both glanced over at us and laughed. Then she said something to the friend sitting on the other side of her and they both turned to give us the once-over with bored, heavy-lidded eyes.

Then they turned away as if to say, *Yeah, no competition.*

"Let's explore first," Jennifer said. She led the way by the Ping-Pong table and looked over her shoulder at Anthony. "Hi, Anthony," she said.

He glanced at her quickly and then back at the ball coming his way. "Hey."

She smiled with crazy triumph for no reason at all, as far as I could see. Then we wandered out to the patio and through another door to a study hall, and then into a kitchen. We peeked into every nook and cranny. Going around ignored, unseen, and overlooked was right up our alley. We inspected the cabinets. Cold cereal and Wonder Bread. In the refrigerator, we found eggs and milk and a pink box of glazed doughnuts. My mouth watered. Jennifer sniffed the milk.

"Still good," she announced. "Wonder if they have any cookies."

"Come on. Let's go up on the stage," I urged.

We slipped out of the kitchen and retraced our steps back to the multipurpose room. The stage curtains were drawn. We climbed the steps on the side and scooted behind them. It was dark, with the exception of a thin band of light where the curtain didn't quite touch the floor. We sat cross-legged on the floor and squinted at our scripts as we angled them toward the light under the curtain.

"I'm supposed to be missing," I said, "but I'm actually hiding in a wardrobe in the attic."

"They should have found you easily, now that I think about it." Jennifer commented.

"It's a play, not real life," I said, annoyed.

"All I know is I want to be Julie, because she's so mean. But in real life I'm not mean—at all. Get it?"

"I get it exactly," I said. And I did. I just couldn't explain it. Once again my stomach was full of butterflies. We read some more and it was the most glorious, absorbing thing. Finally, Jennifer closed her script and got herself into some kind of yoga position. Legs crossed, eyes closed, and her hands with palms up resting on her thighs, thumb and forefinger touching. I closed my script, too. I shut my eyes, got into that same position, and tried to think only: *Om.*

CHAPTER 9
Marcia Stevens

ON SATURDAY I woke up excited. Jennifer's mom was taking us shopping and then on to Sutton's, the cafeteria located down the street from May Company Department Store. The great thing about Sutton's was that everything was laid out—right in front of you. All you had to do was slide your tray along a steel counter and select what you wanted from all the main dishes and desserts and drinks. It was heaven.

So I was excited about that, and also that I was going to get the role of Olivia in the play. The sweet Olivia. Just as I reached for the script on my nightstand, I heard my mother out in the hall going on and on about her datebook.

"Have you seen Mom's datebook?" Lily asked me. She was

slipping into her work outfit—a yellow sheath and some white flats. Her hair was still in rollers.

"No," I said.

"She's walking around accusing people."

People meant *us*. Every once in a while our mother misplaced her datebook. It was where she kept all of her appointments and phone numbers. When she misplaced it, she blamed everyone in the house (except Mrs. Baylor—if Mom blamed her, she kept it to herself).

"I left it right here," I heard her screaming. Well, not screaming. But just a few decibels below a scream. "Right here on this entry hall table. And now it's gone." She appeared in our doorway. "Look for my datebook," she said in a voice full of grit and resolve.

That meant pretending you were searching for it with the determination of a dog missing a bone: scoping under beds, poking around in closets, checking the dirty clothes hamper, the buffet drawers in the dining room. As a joke, Lily would even check the medicine cabinets. Just so we could say, "We've looked *everywhere!*"

On this occasion, our mother found it just where she'd left it—on the floor next to her side of the bed—making me wonder why she didn't look there first.

She slinked away like a cat.

"Daddy didn't get home until after two," Lily said matter-of-factly.

"Was he playing poker with his friends?" I asked. Sometimes he called home to tell our mother not to wait up for him because he'd be playing poker with his buddies.

"Something like that."

"I am sure that I want to be Olivia," I announced as soon as Jennifer opened her door.

She grinned. "And I'm doubly sure I want to be Julie."

We beamed at each other for still not wanting to compete for the same role.

Jennifer looked back toward her house and dropped her voice. "Listen, you have to tell my mother how much I took up for you when we went to the Bakers'."

"Why?"

"She wants to hear exactly what happened, but from you. I guess she wants to be sure that I did take up for you, a lot."

So I told Jennifer's mother what had happened and how Jennifer really stuck up for me. The whole time I was talking, Mrs. Abbott cocked her head to the side and back a bit as if she was trying to see whether I was telling the truth about Jennifer or exaggerating. She sighed a long sigh that seemed to go on forever. Then I did exaggerate a little. I told Mrs. Abbott that Jennifer had been getting ready to leave with me, but I'd begged and begged her to stay and have fun. And she'd absolutely refused.

Mrs. Abbott turned to look at her daughter and really scrutinize her. Jennifer kept her eyes on me. "Is that true, Jennifer?" her mom asked, and Jennifer nodded so slowly and somberly, she looked completely believable. "Yes, Mummy, and I refused."

Mrs. Abbott glanced from Jennifer to me and back to Jennifer again. "If this should ever happen in the future, you make them understand that they wouldn't like to be treated that way and that we're all human beings created equal. Is that clear?"

"Yes."

"Next time, let it be an opportunity to teach them about how God created us all equal."

First of all, I knew Jennifer was not going to bother trying to teach the Baker girls anything, and I probably wouldn't either. But here's the thing. My mind had practically stopped on the word *Mummy.* I liked the ring of *Mummy* so much that I wondered for just a second if I could get away with calling *my* mother Mummy.

Soon we were off to Sutton's by way of May Company for a little shopping. Mrs. Abbott let us ride in the front seat next to her so Jennifer could turn the knob up and down the dial until she landed on KFWB. Lucky break—the Beach Boys were singing "California Girls," and we sang along with them because, after all, we were California girls. Extra lucky for us—right after that, with no commercial breaks, the Beatles' "Help" came on.

"I saw them on Ed Sullivan," Jennifer said.

"Me, too."

We sang "Help" all the way to the shopping center.

At May Company, we followed Jennifer's mom around the shoe department while she picked up one shoe after another, turning it this way and that. She was looking for the perfect pillbox hat for church, as well. This was almost as boring as watching my mother get her face powder mixed. After a while Jennifer draped herself on the counter in the hat department, moaning.

"Mummy, can me and Sophie go to SavOn's and look at the magazines? We need to check the styles so we can get wardrobes together for ninth grade. We want to see if the fall teen magazines are out."

I could tell Mrs. Abbott kind of wanted to be rid of us as well so she could do some serious shopping, unburdened by Jennifer's whining. She looked at her watch. "Meet me in the juniors' section in one hour."

We turned toward the back exit.

"One hour!" she called to us as we hurried out the door.

We were free! To check out the makeup and the cheap costume jewelry and the candy aisle, and to find the teen magazines to slowly pore over and discuss. Although seeing some fall stuff in the store already made me realize that I did not like the push of things. Why couldn't life linger . . . and then move on when a person was ready? I did not like this rush to the end of summer, when Lily would be leaving me.

We were walking past Prides, a small coffee shop wedged between SavOn's and Von's Supermarket, when I looked in the big plate glass window and saw my father. He was sitting at one of the small café tables. With a woman. I stopped. I wasn't close enough for him to notice me. Besides, he appeared to be deep in conversation.

Jennifer, who had walked on, soon realized I wasn't at her side. She stopped and turned back. "Come on. What are you doing? What are you looking at?"

I was looking at my father leaning forward and saying something to that woman who was *not* my mother—something that was making her smile. I was looking at him putting his hand on top of hers. Then she put her other hand on his. He reached out to touch her cheek.

My stomach dropped.

That wasn't his secretary, Mrs. Mosely. She was short and stout and way too old. Maybe fifty. This was someone with a heart-shaped face. And a slim figure; I could tell, even though she was seated. I could tell by her slender arms in her sleeveless shift and her wrist full of bangles. It was that Paula person. Something told me. I was certain. That was her.

"Come on!" Jennifer said. "Now we have less than an hour!" She started toward me.

My father was leaning back, laughing. I stood there stunned, my stomach queasy.

"I'm coming! I'm coming!" I hurried toward her with my mouth suddenly dry and my heart beating out of my chest.

"Well, hurry up!" Jennifer said, and then she examined me and frowned. "Why are you looking like that?"

"Like what?"

"I can't explain it." She studied my face. "Like you have a stomachache or something."

"I do have a stomachache," I said. "Maybe the cereal I ate for breakfast was too old."

She snorted. "I've never heard of cereal being too old."

Nothing seemed good then. We checked the eye shadows and lipsticks, swiping the back of our hands with samples of apricot ice and pink blush. We held gold-plated hoops to our ears and tried on bracelets. Jennifer critiqued me, and I critiqued her. Then we checked the latest issues of *Ingenue* and *Mademoiselle* and *Seventeen* and decided we'd get box-pleated skirts in tartan plaid —green—for the first day of school. Even if it was hot. They wore uniforms at Jennifer's school, but they had free dress the first week.

We made it back to May Company on time and found Mrs. Abbott in the juniors' department, where she held up items of clothing for Jennifer's approval or disapproval. To most, Jennifer slowly shook her head.

I stood to the side. From time to time, I felt tears at the ready that could, if I let my guard down for one second, spill over and roll down my cheeks.

I wanted to go home. But there was still lunch to get through, with no appetite whatsoever. Jennifer had weaseled the trip to Sutton's out of her mother as a treat for me since that awful thing had happened to me at the Bakers'. We only had to walk down the street and enter through the cafeteria's big welcoming doors, with its famous treasure chest just inside.

I followed Jennifer and her mom into the restaurant. The place had lost its allure. Mrs. Abbott led the way to a booth and staked it out by setting down her purchases there. Then we got plates and utensils and trays to push along the stainless steel counter as we decided what we wanted. It was simple for me. I got whatever Jennifer got. She was pleased, thinking we were on the exact same wavelength.

I watched her eat her macaroni and cheese and fried chicken and green beans and coconut cake while I pushed my food around my plate between tiny bites.

"Are you okay?" Mrs. Abbott asked me.

"She said her stomach is bothering her," Jennifer offered.

"Do we need to get you home?"

"No, I'm okay. I'm just not real hungry."

When we had finished, Jennifer led the way to the treasure chest. Even that had lost its appeal. Jennifer wanted a glitter pen. The last time she had come, another girl had gotten the last one.

Now she looked back at me. "I saw a bunch this time. You get one and I'll get one, and then we can write each other notes in glitter."

"Okay," I said.

She frowned. "What's wrong?"

"Nothing."

She plucked out a purple glitter pen. "Get a purple one, too," she urged.

I looked into the chest. Among the whistles on colorful coiled plastic key chains, small blue rubber footballs, Frisbees, yo-yos, bubbles, and glow jewelry, I saw green and red and blue glitter pens. Where were the purple ones? The hostess, who also oversaw the treasure chest to make sure kids took just one prize and not a handful, had turned away to speak to a man in a suit who looked like he could be the manager.

She came back to her duties just as I finally spotted a purple glitter pen and was retrieving it from the mound of treasures.

She narrowed her eyes at me. "How many prizes did you get?"

I held up my pen. "Just this," I said.

She turned to Jennifer. "Did this girl get one treasure or more than one?"

She must not have realized that Jennifer and I were together. "She got just the one," Jennifer said, seemingly puzzled.

"Are you sure?"

"Yes."

By then Jennifer's mom was coming over to see what the problem was. The lady must have put Jennifer and her mother together. She leaned close in, but I heard her say to Mrs. Abbott, "I think that little colored girl got an extra prize."

"What makes you think that?"

"Well," she said with a smile, as if she and Mrs. Abbott were secret friends, "you know how they are. They'll steal at the drop of a pin."

I saw Mrs. Abbott grow red. "No, I *don't* know how they are. I can assure you, this girl would never steal anything." She looped her arms with mine and Jennifer's and marched us out of the restaurant. I wanted so badly to glance back at the hostess, just to see the look on her face—but I didn't. I hurried to keep up with Jennifer and her mom.

"Forget what that silly woman said." Mrs. Abbott looked

down at me. "Just put it out of your mind. What an idiot," she added under her breath as if she were talking only to herself.

"Can we go by Marcia Stevens to see Sophie's sister?" We were in the parking lot behind May Company, standing beside the car.

"We can see her another time," I said quickly.

Mrs. Abbott looked at me. She smiled as if she thought this was something I really wanted to do, but I was just being polite. And, probably to try to make up for all the bad stuff that had happened to me lately, she drew in a big breath and said, "Okay. Let's go see Sophie's sister. Why not?"

My heart sank.

Before I knew it, we were pulling into a parking space behind Marcia Stevens, and Jennifer was jumping out of the car before her mom could even turn off the ignition.

"Calm down, Jennifer," Mrs. Abbott said. "This is Lily's place of work. Don't go running in there expecting her to drop everything to tend to you. Let's take our time, and wait for her to come over to us — when she has a moment."

Jennifer turned to me and rolled her eyes out of her mother's line of vision.

A bell chimed overhead as Mrs. Abbott pushed through the door. We looked around for Lily. She was nowhere to be seen. I felt relieved. My heart was beating almost loudly enough for someone to hear. I stood just inside the door, trying to will Lily to go on a coffee break or to get off early or *something.*

Mrs. Abbott's attention was drawn to a stack of lightweight crew-neck sweaters. "These are such lovely colors," she said, running her hand over the pale lavender one at the top of the stack. "Look, Jennifer. What do you think?"

Jennifer glanced over her shoulder. She shrugged. "It's okay. I guess." Her mind was probably on Lily. Where was she?

I recognized the owner of Marcia Stevens from my sister's description of her: kind of old—at least in her forties—blond hair with dark roots, and lipstick applied slightly above the top lip line, like Lucille Ball. Happily, she was busy ringing up a purchase.

Then we saw Lily coming out of the stockroom with four or five off-the-shoulder summer blouses in soft green. She was heading to the register. She spotted us and stopped. I could tell that she was momentarily flustered. She smiled and waved, but it was not an eager wave. It was a halfhearted one that she was trying to make look friendly and eager.

She went over to Mrs. Singer, who was now in the middle of a conversation with Phyllis, the other sales girl.

Lily said something to her while gesturing toward us. Mrs. Singer, obviously more engaged in what she was saying to

Phyllis, glanced at us standing by the entrance and she, too, gave a little wave.

Finally, Lily hurried over to us. "What are you guys doing here?" she said, and then smiled to blunt some of the panic in her voice. "I mean, this is a real surprise."

Jennifer beamed. "It was my idea," she said.

Lily looked over her shoulder. Mrs. Singer was now dealing with another customer—leaning forward and draping a scarf around the woman's neck and then cooing over the effect it added to the top the woman was wearing.

"Oh, great," Lily said, but her tone revealed her distraction. Jennifer's mom looked at Lily closely. "We're going to get out of here," she said. "Don't want to interrupt your work and get you in hot water." She started ushering Jennifer and me toward the door as we said our goodbyes.

It felt so good to be out of that store. We climbed into the car and headed home.

I needed to think. I needed to sit on my bed and ponder what I'd seen. I needed to understand the look on my father's face when he'd put his hand on that woman's hand.

I thought about him all Sunday. I sneaked looks at him at breakfast while he read the newspaper. He laughed at a *Family Circus* cartoon (we all loved *Family Circus* cartoons), and that seemed like a special betrayal—that he was able to laugh with us as if everything was just fine. He leaned toward my mother and shared it with her. She laughed, too. And I thought, *Mom, don't laugh with that liar—that fake person.*

The cartoon was the one where PJ asks his father if he can test his knee reflex. It shows PJ innocently holding a real hammer. It *was* funny, and I could have laughed if I'd wanted to. But I decided not to. How could my father just sit there at the breakfast table with the rest of us and be so false?

At one point, just before he moseyed to the den to watch Sunday news shows, he looked at me and said, "Why so quiet, Sweet Pea? Something wrong?" And that was guilt talking, because my father almost never asked about me. That woman had to be that Paula person, the one who'd written the letter. He must have read it by now. I planned to check on my next visit to his precious office.

CHAPTER 10
Don't Pass This Way

EARLY ON MONDAY MORNING I heard loud scraping coming from the front of the house. Lily groaned, turned over onto her stomach, and put the pillow over her head. "What's that noise?" she said in a muffled voice.

I was reading at the time. I got up, trudged into the den, looked out the window, and came almost face to face with *Mr. Nigel, Nigel, Nigel* scraping old paint off the windowsills. He was up on a ladder outside, scraping away.

I returned to the bedroom. "It's Mrs. Baylor's son. The one in the cap and gown. The *Nigel, Nigel, Nigel* guy. He's getting ready to paint some windowsills in front of the house," I said. Those sills were all cracked and splintered. Our mother had been asking our father to do it for ages, but he didn't do things like that. He just sat in cafés with strange women.

I looked at Lily, who now had the blanket pulled over her head. I thought about telling her what I'd seen when I was with Jennifer on Saturday. But I decided not to. I'd keep the secret to myself. For now.

I reached for the script and flipped to the first page of dialogue. I flipped more pages, happy to see Olivia on almost every one. I needed to memorize all of it.

Lily pulled herself up and then sat for a bit with her face in her hands. She threw the covers off and swung her legs over the side of the bed. Then she got up. I followed her into the den. She peeked out the window, near the one Nigel was working on. "That's him," she said. "*Mr. Nigel, Nigel, Nigel.*" She yawned—a really big fake yawn.

He was darker than Mrs. Baylor—darker than a burnt sienna crayon. And he was tall and muscular in his work pants and white T-shirt. He climbed down from the ladder and scooted it over a bit and wiped the sweat off his forehead with the back of his hand.

"He should have one of those things tennis players wear on their heads to catch the sweat," I said to Lily.

"Yeah. He should."

I thought of my sister's guy friends. This past spring she'd had a boyfriend. James. They met in drama class and started going around together. He was light skinned with curly hair so everyone said they made a cute couple. I wondered if that was the reason he dated her—mostly. And if *her* reason had more to do with senior prom than liking James, because after the prom had come and gone, we saw less and less of him until the day we realized he had faded away.

It was a Sunday morning at the breakfast table, and our mother had said, "Where's James these days? Why's he making himself so scarce?" Even Daddy looked up from his coffee and newspaper as if he had been wondering, too. Which was strange, because Daddy was usually not interested in things like our friends or what was going on in our lives.

"We broke up," Lily said. She dropped her eyes, trying to show sadness, but I knew the truth. I'd listened to her while she was on the phone with Lydia. She was just tired of him. *The guy has no conversation. Just cars and football. I want someone who can teach me something I don't know. Something new.*

I turned back to the window. *Mr. Nigel, Nigel, Nigel* was climbing back up the ladder to do more scraping. "Do you think he's cute?" I asked, and I actually saw my sister flinch. She bit her lip and didn't answer, just headed downstairs to our bathroom. A minute later, the shower was going full blast.

I climbed back into bed. I reached under it for my three-ring binder, placed the binder on my lap, and stared at it. Then I opened it and read: *Little Minerva looked at the picture on the mantle. It was a picture of her daddy. He was so handsome and brave. Her mama had told her all about his courage in the big war and how he'd been awarded seven medals.* I crossed out "seven" and replaced it with "ten."

Minerva felt someone behind her.

"He was the greatest man who ever lived," she heard her mother say.

"What made him so great?" Minerva asked.

"He loved his family—you and me—more than anything. He was totally devoted to us."

A few days ago I'd had a brilliant idea. I would make Minerva's father really alive but somewhere far away. And I would make him have amnesia. Yes, *amnesia.* And he would be in a hospital somewhere and people—the nurses and doctors—would all the time be trying to find out who he was. He would tell them that he couldn't remember anything *except* the name Minerva. Yes, he would know all about Minerva. And he'd have a way more interesting life than her father in real life, Grandpa Willis —the barber.

But for now, I'd have to put it aside so I could learn my lines. I couldn't concentrate on two projects at once. I would get back to Minerva's story after I got the role. There was all the time in the world to write it. I stood up and put the binder on my bookshelf.

Then I stepped back and looked at it and sighed. *I'm not abandoning you, Minerva. I promise.*

Lily emerged from the bathroom for a moment to get the telephone. Then I heard the bathroom window slide open. Soon she'd be on the phone with Lydia and smoking out the window. My sister hid a pack in the cabinet under the sink, toward the back.

I got dressed quickly, then dashed outside with my script just in time to see Jennifer leaving for dance class with her grandmother. Shoot. I'd have to wait until she got back.

Mrs. Baylor's son looked down at me from his ladder and smiled. "Hey," he said. His smile was full of very, very even white teeth and he had a perfect dimple in his right cheek. A very, very deep dimple that hadn't shown up much in his picture with the cap and gown.

"I'm Nathan. You might know me as Nigel, if my mother's mentioned me."

I wanted to say, *She's only mentioned you a million times.* "Hi," I said. "I'm Sophie."

"Sophie," he said. "A black girl named Sophie."

My mind stopped on the word *black*. How easily he'd said it! It could almost be a bad word. Calling someone black might bring on a fight. But his ease filled me with a secret pleasure, as if he was allowing me into his very special club. Of black people.

"Yes. But my mother calls me Sophia."

"That's better," he said.

I stood there for a moment, watching him and waiting for him to say something more. But he just winked and went back to scraping with his little scraping tool. Behind me I could hear my mother in the kitchen getting her breakfast. Lily and my mother really hadn't been getting along lately. Nowadays, my sister did everything in her power to sidestep her. If they crossed paths, Mom might smell smoke in her hair or tell Lily her pants were too tight or ask why she put all those blond streaks in her hair. She might say that she looked like a streetwalker. Our mother had plenty of criticism for Lily. She called her spoiled and ungrateful and told her she'd never had to pick tobacco in the hot sun and then sit down at the end of the row and wait for her sister in the next row to catch up so she wouldn't wind up doing more than her part. She never had to go without shoes in the summer or share bathwater with her siblings.

Then Lily would ask how that was her fault, and our mother would say she was being disrespectful, and Lily would ask how that was being disrespectful, then our mother would say even that question was disrespectful. And then I would go outside so I wouldn't have to hear them anymore, because nobody was going to win.

I took my script back to the bedroom and started studying it. "Sophie, let's take Oscar for a walk," Lily said out of the blue. She'd brought her Cheerios into the room and was now drinking the milk straight out of the bowl. She wiped her mouth with her hand. I looked at her suspiciously. When was the last time she'd wanted to walk Oscar—with *me?* I put away *That Talk.*

"You go get him and I'll meet you out front," she said.

After I slipped the leash over Oscar's head and laughed at how fast he was wagging his tail, I led him around to the front of the house, where Lily was waiting for me and making a show of *not* looking at Mrs. Baylor's son. I noticed Mrs. Baylor's son was *not* looking at my sister, either.

Before we could start our walk, I heard the Helms Bakery truck's horn behind us. "Let's get doughnuts," I said, moving to the curb to wave at the truck.

Lily reached into her pocket and pulled out a dollar.

The Helms truck came down our street on Mondays. If you stood at the curb, the driver would pull up right in front of you. Then he'd hop out, scoot around to the side, slide open the side doors, and let you step inside. That's where all the long drawers were—drawers the width of the truck. You'd point and he'd pull open the drawer, and there would be rows and rows of doughnuts. The next drawer would hold cupcakes of every kind, or cinnamon rolls and sticky buns.

My mouth watered as the Helms driver stopped next to us and jumped out of his seat. He dashed around to the sliding doors and opened them to reveal the "magic" drawers. I pointed at the top one and he slid it open.

"I want a jelly doughnut. Lemon," I said.

"Make that two," Lily said. "And one bear claw."

He dropped the doughnuts and bear claw into a white bag, using a square of waxed paper. Lily paid him and deposited the change in her pocket.

We were set. We continued walking, with Oscar tugging at the leash and our little bag of pastries to eat on the way.

"Who's the bear claw for?" I asked. But Lily didn't answer because just then her attention was elsewhere.

On the other side of the street, Deidre Baker—the one who'd almost jabbed me in the chest with her forefinger as if it were the barrel of a gun while her sister smugly delivered the news about "no colored allowed"—was making her way up the hill toward Olympiad.

She spotted us and slowed.

Lily slowed, too.

Deidre was probably going over to her friend Carla's. Carla

lived on Olympiad in the big white house with the pillars. It sat where Montego Drive ended.

Lily stopped and stood there, waiting as Deidre neared.

I saw a change come over Deidre's face: a craftiness. I knew that she was trying to decide what to do. Perhaps she should turn around and walk home or go another way to Carla's. But then a look of grit seemed to replace all doubt. Without looking at us directly, she took in a big, deep breath. She lifted her chin and kept on coming. Apparently the sight of the empty street in front and behind her was now of no consequence. That's how much she thought the world belonged to *her*.

When she was opposite our house, Lily gave Oscar a tug, crossed over, and stood facing her.

They stared each other down for a few seconds, with Deidre pulling herself up to her full height—as if that was going to protect her.

Finally, Lily said, "Did you tell my sister that she couldn't come to your house because no colored people are allowed?"

I'd actually never seen anyone go pale before, but it was as if all the color drained out of Deidre's plump little cherub face. You could see that she was considering brushing past, but Lily stood in the way. She seemed to add to her calculation the empty street, and the fact that we lived ten houses up from hers so there could be other occasions like this.

Lily didn't wait for a response. "Who do you think you are, you little *peckerwood*? Who the hell do you think you are?"

My eyes grew big. I couldn't help a little giggle. Lily had said she'd take care of the Baker girls, but I never could picture how that would happen and I never felt so, so . . . I didn't know a word for it. *Gleeful.*

"Let me tell you something, *little girl!* You want to get to Olympiad? You'd better take Presidio from now on because we're not going to allow you or your sisters to walk by our house even if you're on the other side of the street! I see you walk by my house, I'ma sic this dog on your behind."

My mouth dropped open. It was thrilling to hear this delicious threat coming out of my big sister's mouth. It was also thrilling to see Deidre Baker's lower lip begin to quiver. She attempted to brush by us.

"Hold up, hotshot!" my sister said. "Where do you think you're going?"

Deidre had a moment of courage. "I'm going to tell my father what you said."

"Tell him! Tell him to come on up here. And tell him my daddy's got something for him." She lowered her voice. "And you know what I mean."

Deidre's eyes widened. "We can call the police."

Lily had an answer for that as well. "Listen here, little girl.

My father's a prosecutor. You know what that is? He puts away criminals. He knows all the police around here and they *love* him!" (That wasn't true. Daddy was a defense attorney. The police didn't love him.)

Only then did it seem to occur to Deidre that she'd better follow my sister's rules. The order was immediately in place. She turned and started down the hill to go the long way around to Olympiad.

I'd never heard Lily sound like that. I was amazed that she had it in her. That she could talk so rough and loud, with one hand on her hip, the forefinger of the other hand jabbing the air in Deidre's direction, as if any second she was going to spear her forehead with it.

I felt a sense of pure joy wash over me. I felt like dancing right there on the sidewalk. I was in warmth and light. I felt like high-fiving my sister. I watched Deidre go all the way back down Montego Drive to take Presidio—the long way around up to Olympiad—and I felt vindicated.

"Can we do that—not allow her to walk by our house?" I asked.

Lily cackled. "As long as *she* believes we can do it, that's all that matters. And you know what? She'll remember this the rest of her stupid life."

• • •

We walked Oscar only around the corner and back. So I began to suspect that this was my sister's way of getting out and
being seen by Nigel. He was in the open garage, searching
through our father's toolbox when we returned. She stopped
and watched him for a bit. Then she handed me Oscar's leash
and said, "Take Oscar around the back and give him some fresh
water." I ignored her and stayed put; miraculously, she didn't
seem to notice. She clearly had other things on her mind as she
walked over to Mrs. Baylor's son with the small white bag in her
hand.

Nigel looked up from his rummaging and seemed caught a
bit off-guard. "You know if your dad has some more sandpaper?"
he asked.

"I don't know about tools and sandpaper and paint and
paintbrushes and . . ."

She smiled.

"Got it." He stood up, leaned back on our mother's car, and
crossed his arms. He looked at my sister but said nothing. Then
he smiled as if he knew his smile was his best feature.

"Got you something," Lily said. She handed him the bag
with the bear claw. He peeked inside. He took out the claw,
held it up, and squinted at it. Then he looked at her and said, "I
don't know, girl. You're kind of scary. You sure this is okay
to eat?"

She tried not to laugh, but gave in. I could tell he liked her laughing at his joke.

Finally, she said, "Give it back, then."

Instead he took a big bite. "Mmm, mmm." He licked icing off his fingers.

"So you're Nigel. I've heard sooo much about you."

"That's my good Jamaican name, but I use my middle name. Nathan. More American-friendly."

"Yeah. That *is* a bit more American-friendly, *Nigel.*"

Then it was his turn to laugh. I could tell Lily liked making him laugh, too. And I could tell she was nervous. Her hand went to her hip. But then she crossed her arms and her weight shifted to one leg as she looked up the street toward Olympiad. She brushed a lock of hair behind her ear and then brought it out to twist and twist it. It was as if she didn't know what to do with herself.

"So my mama's been bragging about me?"

"We've heard *all* about you, Nigel. *Everything,*" Lily said, her eyes twinkling.

He smiled. "Now I'm worried."

She laughed again, then looked at me. "Take Oscar to the backyard. And give him some water." I couldn't get away with not doing it this time because she watched until I did as she said.

I got Oscar all situated, then went into the den to turn on

the TV. Through the open window I could still hear their voices, but I couldn't make out the words. While I waited for the television to warm up, I looked out the window—just in time to see Nigel walk my sister up the porch steps and whisper something in her ear.

Then he stepped back and looked at her. Lily blushed and looked away, then back again. I left the window just as she was coming through the door. I hurried down the three steps, crossed the foyer, and followed her into our room.

"Do you like him?" I asked straight out once I'd closed the door behind me. "I saw him whisper something in your ear. What did he say?"

I thought she would tell me to mind my own business, but she just said flatly, "He said, 'I like you, too.' Just like that."

"And do you like him?" I asked.

"He's okay," she answered, turning away to check herself in the mirror.

But I knew better.

Nathan was packed up and gone by the time Lily left for work. Then it was just me and Mrs. Baylor in the quiet house. I grabbed my script from my nightstand, cast a guilty look at the binder on the shelf, and climbed onto my bed to sit cross-legged. I placed the script on my lap and opened it. Again, I felt butterflies in my stomach.

CHAPTER 11
The Beginning

T HE VERY NEXT DAY, my sister, in big sunglasses and a long white gauzy skirt, took a stack of her magazines and a glass of lemonade outside to the patio lounge. She was working on a tan—smearing Coppertone all over her face and arms and aiming her face at the sun. She thought her new color would look good with the blond highlights she'd put in her hair. She'd worry about her legs later, I supposed.

Mrs. Baylor's son had finished every windowsill on the front and sides of the house and had now moved to the back. Which was precisely why Lily was there, I suspected. As they say, "Even Ray Charles could see that." Nathan painted, and she pretended not to notice him.

There was no clever repartee while he worked. He was

businesslike that way. But I knew she was just waiting for some continuance of the declaration he'd made on the front porch the day before. So while she waited, she read her magazines in his vicinity, being very obvious, even to me.

It was funny to watch: Lily trying to seem all casual, as if she was not trying to be pretty in his company. Pretending she was just reading her magazines deeply and without a thought to the person painting windowsills in the hot summer sun behind her.

At one point I decided to wander outside and sit on the stone steps just beyond our dining room's French doors. She looked back at me and I knew she wanted me gone, but I just picked up Oscar's ball and threw it across the lawn. He went tearing after it as if there was nothing else in the world but that old rubber ball.

Nathan glanced over his shoulder at me and smiled his big beautiful smile. I waved at him, and then felt kind of emboldened. I got up and went over to the ladder.

Shielding my eyes, I looked up at him.

"You like painting houses?"

He looked down at me and smiled again. "I've never painted a whole house, Sophia."

"But do you like this?" I pressed, pleased that he called me Sophia.

Lily sighed loud enough for us to hear. It felt like a signal. I ignored her.

"Yeah, I like painting. I like the rhythm of it," he told me. He glanced at Lily.

She was listening and flipping through her magazine. It sounded like annoyed flipping. I knew she wanted me back in the house.

I looked toward the dining room window, suddenly feeling my mother's presence. Sure enough, she was standing there, taking in the whole scene: Nathan on his ladder, me nearby questioning him, Lily on the chaise. I saw her nostrils flare slightly.

Then she was poking her head out the door. "Lily, can I speak to you for a minute?"

Lily looked up at our mother standing in the shadow of the doorway. She rolled her eyes and put her magazine face-down on her lap as if she was mentally gearing herself up for irritation. Then she closed it, placed it on the little table next to her that held her lemonade, and pulled herself up. She headed for the dining room door.

My mother stood there waiting with her hands on her hips.

Jennifer had asked me once, "How come colored women always put their hands on their hips?"

"They don't always do that," I'd said.

"Uh-huh . . . In *Gone with the Wind* that maid, the one with the high voice, does it. And so does Kingfish's wife on that show

that came on a long time ago, *Amos 'n' Andy,* and also in this movie
I saw, *Imitation of Life.* That white-looking girl's mother."

"I don't know," I said skeptically.

But now I saw my mother with both hands on her hips, as if
she was going to let Lily have it doubly.

I followed them inside and went into the kitchen for a glass
of water, where I came upon Mrs. Baylor seated at the table folding towels. The argument starting up in the living room was loud
enough to hear.

"Lily, I didn't hire that boy for your amusement," my mother
said right off.

Mrs. Baylor's folding slowed. She leaned forward toward
the dining room ever so slightly. But she didn't need to. We could
hear them clearly.

"What are you talking about?" Lily said.

"I know what you're doing."

"What am I doing, Mom?"

"Putting yourself on display. Trying to make that boy whom
I hired to take care of some projects around here—projects your
father never has time for—you're trying to make him notice you."

I didn't like hearing the word *father.* I felt a prick of anger.

My mother might as well have slapped my sister—to have
her scheme pointed out like that.

"Why are you always accusing me of things? Anyway, why would I want to do that?"

Her protest sounded weak, even to my ears.

I noticed Mrs. Baylor was taking a long time folding and smoothing.

"Good question. Why would you? What would be the point, after all?"

Mrs. Baylor pulled another towel out of the basket. She shook it out with a quick, angry-sounding snap.

"What's that supposed to mean?"

"You just want to toy with him."

"I don't know what you're talking about." Lily's voice rose and took on a hurt tone. "I could have been in my bathing suit, sunning, but I wasn't! I'm in a skirt down to my ankles, just reading my magazines. And enjoying the outdoors."

"You just leave that boy alone. He's here to work, not to be distracted by you."

"I *am* leaving him alone. I'm just reading my *magazines.*"

"You're trying to toy with him. Make him like you and then sashay on your merry way."

I looked at Mrs. Baylor. She had drawn her lips in while she smoothed and smoothed the folded towel.

"I'm doing no such thing. Why would you say that about me?"

To my ears she sounded genuinely hurt. I took my glass outside. I didn't really want the water, but I was stuck with it. While slipping past my mother and sister, I chanced a look. Lily was flushed and near tears. My mother looked cold. They didn't notice me.

Once outside, I realized Mrs. Baylor's son could hear them too. He was painting, but he was listening. I sat on the top step and put my glass down.

"I know you, Lily. I used to do that myself when I was young and silly."

"I'm not *you*," Lily said, sounding as if she was about to make herself hysterical—on purpose. She started down the hall toward our room. "I'm not you!" she said again before she slammed the door behind her.

I glanced up at Mrs. Baylor's son. *Nathan.* His expression revealed nothing as he went back and forth along the windowsill with his paintbrush. He didn't fool me, though. I knew where his attention was focused. And Mrs. Baylor's. She was probably in the kitchen folding towels and spitting kittens. I'd read that somewhere: *spitting kittens.* It meant being really, really mad.

Finally, our mother left for one of her meetings. As soon as the door closed behind her, Lily marched past me and out to the lounge chair to retrieve her magazines. She gathered them up and then stood there a moment, gazing off at the hills behind our house. She looked like she was trying to calm herself.

I was surprised to see Nathan coming around the house carrying a can of turpentine. He stopped short and stared at Lily. He looked kind of embarrassed, and as he passed her on his way to get his tarp to put away in his car, he did a strange thing. The strangest thing I'd ever seen. He took her hand—just for a half second. Lily jumped because she hadn't heard him approach. He took her hand for the tiniest moment and then let it go. She turned around and stared at him as he went about the business of gathering his equipment and things—packing up. It was as if some secret communication had passed between them.

I knew Lily. I knew he'd taken her breath away, and now she was confused. I knew she didn't know what to think. It was one of those rare moments when my sister found herself flustered and at a loss.

Then he was gone.

CHAPTER 12
Tennis

I HEARD A VOICE from far away. It was Lily telling me to wake up. "Wake up, wake up, wake up." I opened my eyes to see her standing over me. I was sleepy, having stayed up late the night before memorizing my lines for the play. "Get up, Sophie. I've got the day off and Daddy's working in his home office today. We can get the car. And I'm in a good mood! We're starting on your well-roundedness immediately. I'm going to teach you how to play tennis."

"Huh? Tennis?"

"Yes. It's a good day for a lesson."

"But I'd planned to work on my part in the play."

"What play is that again?"

"*That Talk.*"

"So you're trying out for a role?"

"The role of Olivia. She's the main character."

Lily looked at me and sighed. "Sophie, Sophie, Sophie." She laughed. "You're wasting your time. They're not going to give you that role."

"Yes, they are. Because I'm going to be better than anyone else."

"Don't count on it." She disappeared into the bathroom. The sound of the shower soon followed.

"Today I'm in a park kind of mood," she sang behind the closed door.

What on earth was a park kind of mood?

Lily managed to wrangle the car from our lying, cheating father. Even though it was a Wednesday. The night before, he'd mentioned he'd be working in his home office this morning, and Lily was probably thinking, *Why should the car sit in the driveway all day, looking useless with its big fins and silver grill, anyway?* Lily loved driving the car, though she usually tried to get it on Sundays, when he spent all day sprawled on the sofa watching sports and messing up the newspaper. That drove my mother crazy. "If you could just refold the paper and stack it on the coffee table. If you could just do that for me if it's not too much trouble." But it was too much apparently, because it always looked as if he'd tossed the whole thing at the ceiling and let it rain down wherever. *Mom,* I wanted to say, *the Sunday paper is the least of your troubles.*

We drove to Ladera Park, with Lily in her big sunglasses singing at the top of her lungs, "Sitting in the park—waiting on you-ou-ou-ou," and probably thinking about Nathan.

By the time we pulled up, it was late morning and three of the four courts were taken. College kids, I imagined—home for the summer. On the first court a Barbie look-alike had a pail of balls and was practicing her serve—one ball after the other.

"We've lucked out, Sophie," Lily said. "The last court is free."

I felt a tiny bit self-conscious as we carried our rackets and basket of balls to the empty court. We were the only colored people around. Some might have been confused about Lily, but with my tinge of color and crinkly hair, there'd be no question about me.

Jennifer once asked me what it felt like—to be Negro. I said I couldn't really explain it. Just that you remembered what you were all the time. *All* the time. From the time you got up in the morning until you went to bed at night. But you really remembered it when you were the only Negro around.

Like now.

We hauled our rackets and basket of balls past the first

court—puffing up our chests and walking extra-straight and tall to show we belonged here like everyone else—past the second court and the third, to the last court.

Lily began to serve balls to the other side immediately, reaching up and elongating her already long legs as she came up on tiptoe. She started to hit the balls as if she was mad. *Whack, whack, whack.* "Look at my feet," she ordered. "See how I stay away from the line? You can't even touch it a little bit until after you hit the ball. And right now you're just aiming to get it in that space on the other side of the net." She pointed. "Watch me." She smacked the ball and it hit the ground just where she intended it to go.

At the same time a car pulled up at the curb. I recognized it from having seen it parked in the Bakers' driveway. Jilly jumped out and then Deidre. I waited for Marcy, but it was their mother who got out next from behind the wheel, and it took some time because she was slow and heavy.

Lily glanced at them and served the next ball. I felt a small uneasy stir in my stomach, remembering what she had said to Deidre. In contrast, Lily seemed perfectly at ease, as if she'd forgotten the whole exchange.

She turned to me. "Now, get over there and gather up the balls, and let's see if you can do something like what I just did."

Again, I glanced at the Baker girls. They were surveying the courts. Lily checked them as well and said, "Get going, Sophie."

I dashed to the other side of the net and gathered up the balls. I dropped them in the basket and returned to her side. I picked one up, made sure my feet were away from the line, but my attempt to hit it the way Lily did was a failure. The ball smashed into the net, not over it.

"Again," Lily said, tossing me another ball, then picking at her thumbnail. She glanced at the Baker girls and their mother, who were now passing the first court, then the second court. Lily kept her eye on them. "Keep at it," she said to me. They walked right by the third court and came straight to ours. I saw that Mrs. Baker had a tight little cap of auburn curls, as if she'd just taken the rollers out and hadn't yet combed her hair.

I couldn't tell if she knew what Lily had said to Deidre. I felt a bubble of fear and it grew as I checked Lily. But I saw only defiance on Lily's face. The Baker girls and their mother settled on the bench next to our court. "Are you going to be much longer?" Mrs. Baker called out.

Lily turned away, ignoring her. Following suit, I ignored her as well.

"I said, are you going to be much longer?" She called out again, but with a tiny edge in her voice. Lily said nothing. As soon as Mrs. Baker realized Lily was ignoring her, her expression hardened. I looked at Lily, trying to determine what she would do next. She glanced at Deidre and raised an eyebrow, almost smiling. Deidre looked away, and that's when I realized she hadn't told. She hadn't told her mother what Lily had said because she must have believed that my father *did* "have something" for her father if he dared to come up to our house for a confrontation.

Mrs. Baker pulled some knitting out of a bag, but it remained on her lap as she watched us with a stern look. She whispered to Jilly, and Jilly got up and trotted over to us.

Lily tossed me a ball.

I swatted at it and it went right into the net. There was giggling from the bench. I dismissed that. Something about Lily ignoring them gave me courage. She tossed me another ball.

"My mother wants to know how much longer you're going to be?" Jilly asked with her eyes slightly squinted.

Lily turned around and gazed at Jilly for a few seconds. She cocked her head and looked skyward. "Oh, not long," she said, giving Jilly a wide pageant smile. Jilly met the smile with a flustered look. I stared from one to the other. Jilly held Lily's gaze for a moment, then turned on her heels and headed back to the bench. She said something to her mother, and the three of them turned toward Lily as if to keep an eye on her and to make clear that they would be monitoring the situation and perhaps protesting if it turned out to be longer than "not long."

Then Lily caught my eye and made a motion with her chin. I

trotted over. She reached into her pants pocket and took out two quarters. She put them in my hand. "Go to the store and get us some water. I don't plan to *ever* leave this court."

"Can you do that?"

"Watch me."

I started off reluctantly. I didn't want to miss anything. I looked back over my shoulder and stopped. Mrs. Baker was suddenly standing up and placing her knitting on the bench beside her.

"Excuse me," she called out. "My daughters happen to have a lesson in ten minutes. Just how long are you going to *be?*" I waited to see how Lily would handle this.

Lily turned toward Mrs. Baker and sauntered over to her, getting into her space a little bit. She was the taller of the two. "Excuse me?" she said in a tone that was slightly challenging. She stared Mrs. Baker down as if to say, *Oh no, you don't!* Mrs. Baker took a step back.

Lily smiled and looked her up and down. And that's when I realized Mrs. Baker's whiteness was of no use to her in this particular situation—facing my sister and having to look up as she decided whether to repeat herself. There was almost no one around but the people on the other courts, and they were thinking only of their games.

My sister had the edge.

Mrs. Baker settled her mouth into a sneer and then said,

"My daughters have their tennis lesson in . . ." She looked at her watch. "Actually seven minutes."

"And why would that concern me?" Lily asked.

Mrs. Baker seemed momentarily flustered. "*Because* you are taking up this court not with a *real* game but just hitting tennis balls this way and that." Now the two Baker girls grinned.

"And your point is?"

"These courts are for *games,* not practicing serves."

Lily looked around. "Is that posted somewhere?"

"It's just standard information."

Deidre piped up then. "Yeah, everybody knows that."

Lily turned to her and laughed. "Really? Does everybody know that? Are you sure?"

"That's right," Mrs. Baker said, crossing her arms.

"Well, before I answer your question, I have a question for you." Lily looked off at the other courts. She fiddled with the strings of her racket, straightening them the way players do on TV. Finally, she said, "How did you happen to choose to come to our court, anyway? I'm just curious." She said this with a quick little shrug, her eyes still on the strings of her racket as she straightened them. "Just wondering," she added.

Mrs. Baker gave Lily a long look. Lily held her gaze with a tiny smile on her face. "I mean, you walked by the first court where that blond girl was *practicing her serve.* You walked by the second court. You walked by the third court, and came directly to this court. What were you thinking? How did you make that decision?"

Mrs. Baker said nothing. She continued to meet Lily's gaze —maybe hoping to intimidate her

"That's what I thought," Lily said. She laughed, sauntered over to the serving line, picked up a ball, gazed at it, tossed it in the air, and whacked it with a flat thud smack in the center of the racket.

"I think I'm going to be here for a while," she called to Mrs. Baker. "But you're welcome to stay and watch." She turned to me. "Go get that water. It's hot out here."

We laughed all the way to 31 Flavors. At first Mrs. Baker had seemed determined to wait us out, but when Lily and I settled in a shady area of the court to rest and sip our water, she packed up her knitting in a huff and marched off with her daughters.

"Isn't that park a public park? Don't our parents pay taxes? And what kind of lie was that? Her daughters have a tennis lesson scheduled. How can you schedule a lesson at a public park? What the hell," Lily said. She started laughing again, and that made me laugh, too. "How about that funny little hairdo she had? I should have poured my water over those little curls. Wouldn't that have been hilarious?"

I imagined it and burst out laughing again.

The air of the ice cream shop felt cool against my hot skin. The big tubs of pastel-colored ice cream looked thrilling. I couldn't wait to taste the sweet creaminess of butter pecan. I looked around, and there was Nathan. In the far corner. Nathan —and a girl—sitting at one of the small, round tables. She was petite and brown skinned. She was wearing a high ponytail and headband. Very pretty.

I nudged Lily. "There's Nathan." She followed my pointing finger, and her lips parted a little bit. She swallowed, reached for a numbered ticket from a little red dispenser on the glass case, and turned her back to him. She put both palms on the case and peered in at the ice cream. "Mmm, maybe I'll try pistachio for a change," she said, tapping the glass over the big tub of pistachio.

"Me, too," I said.

She smiled and glanced at the small wrought iron tables and chairs just outside the door.

"Let's sit outside after we get our cones."

As soon as we exited the shop, I headed for an empty table and pulled out the chair facing the parking lot. She pulled out the one facing the shop. We ate silently for a few minutes, still drained from the heat.

"They came to our court because we were the only colored," I said, then twirled my ice cream against my tongue.

Lily looked past me into the shop and shrugged.

"They didn't want us to play," I added.

"Not if it meant they'd have to wait."

Two little girls in pink polka-dot sundresses toddled by, holding on to their mother's hands.

"Twins," we said at the same time, and then did a high-five. "You owe me a Coke," we said in unison. Lily started to laugh. I liked that she was having fun with me. Maybe she'd miss me, after all, when she went off to Georgia.

"That must be his girlfriend," she said.

"Whose girlfriend?"

"Nathan's." She stood up.

"What's wrong?" I said.

"Nothing. I'm just ready to go."

I looked over my shoulder into the shop. Yes, the girl was pretty, with her serious brown eyes behind horn-rimmed glasses. They were deep in conversation. She laughed at something he said, then shook her head from side to side.

"Quit staring," Lily said. "Let's go."

"She's pretty," I said.

Lily sniffed.

We passed a lazy, quiet hour with Lily reading *The House of Mirth* on the patio chaise and me in our room poring over my script, then I put it aside and decided to take Oscar for a walk. The house had its usual empty feeling. My father had commandeered his car as soon as we got back as if he had somewhere important to go, and my mother was off to her gallery.

Oscar perked up when the patio door slammed behind me. I could barely get his collar on because he kept licking my hand. By the time I had him on the leash, he was pulling toward the backyard gate.

Lily had been reading *The House of Mirth* all week. I asked her if I could read it after she was finished, but she told me it was probably too grown-up for me and I wouldn't like it. I told her I would and she couldn't know what I would like or not like.

To annoy her, I looked over and said, "Are you upset that you saw Mrs. Baylor's son with that girl?" Oscar sniffed around my tennis shoes.

"I'm reading," she said. And I knew she was not going to get into it.

I was heading back up Montego Drive toward home when Nathan pulled up alongside me in his Volkswagen. He leaned over and rolled down the passenger window.

"Hey," he said.

Oscar pulled at the leash. I pulled back.

"Anybody home? I need to get my second tarp. I accidentally

left it in your backyard." He flashed his winning smile. "Thought I'd only need one for this other job I'm doing today, but it's bigger than I thought."

"Lily's there," I said.

"Great." He started to pull away.

"Wait a minute," I said, even as I questioned myself about what I was going to do. "Um, we saw you at Thirty-One Flavors."

He looked puzzled. "When?"

"Just a little while ago."

"Who's we?"

"Me and Lily."

He looked off for a second. He sighed. "Oh." He ran his hand over his head. "Well."

"Is that your girlfriend?"

"She was."

"So you're just friends now?"

He drummed his steering wheel with his forefingers and bit his lower lip as if he was suddenly in deep thought. Coming out of it, he said, "Well, I'd better go get my tarp." And he drove off up the hill.

When I got back to the house, I led Oscar straight to the backyard. Nathan was squatting over his tarp, folding it into a neat square. Lily, with her eyes fixed on her book, was busy ignoring him. I pulled a dog biscuit out of my pocket and held it out so Oscar could jump up on his short little legs to try to get it. I had to remember to jerk my hand away from his sharp teeth. He looked so funny, I had to laugh.

Nathan smiled up at me. He got the tarp into a neat package and stood. He walked over to Lily, holding the folded tarp pressed against his chest.

"Hey," he said.

"Oh, hey." She glanced at him, then went back to her book.

He reached out and took it from her hands. She sighed and watched him read the title.

"*The House of Mirth,*" he said. "Sad ending, but let me not give it away. I'll say no more."

"So, in other words, you've read it."

He nodded and saluted her, then turned to go, but Oscar darted over to him. Nathan squatted to scratch his neck. "Nice dog," he said. Then he was gone.

I went into the house, through the living room, out the front door, and straight to Jennifer's. She opened the door and stepped out. We sat down on her porch.

"My sister likes Mrs. Baylor's son," I told her.

"Wow!" Her eyes lit up. She rubbed her palms together. "How do you know?"

"I can tell. And it's true love. I know that already."

"Give me the details," Jennifer said. "And I'll tell you if it's true love or not."

I told her what I had observed: Lily was always flustered around him but trying to pretend she wasn't. She didn't even know him but she got jealous when she saw him with another girl. And she tried to be around him but acted as if she wasn't trying to be around him.

Jennifer grinned, thrilled. "She's falling in love! What's your mom going to say?"

"My mother's not going to know."

"Would she mind?"

"*Yeah,* she'd mind."

"Why? You told me he's at UC Berkeley. He's gotta be smart to go to UC Berkeley."

"That's not enough for my mother. And . . ." I didn't want to tell Jennifer the other reason. It felt shameful and embarrassing—something white people wouldn't understand. But I blurted it out anyway. "He's dark skinned."

Jennifer frowned. "So?"

"It's hard to explain." It was the kind of thing that nobody talked about openly. It felt like I was letting her in on a secret. "See, light-skinned colored people almost always marry light-skinned colored people on purpose. So they'll have light-skinned kids."

"Why?

"I can't explain it. Nobody admits it, but I've seen it—a lot. And Lily told me about a Negro college that makes you send your picture when you apply, and if you're darker than a paper bag, you don't get in." It embarrassed me to say this and I wished I hadn't.

Jennifer dropped her mouth open and her eyes got big. "Really?" She looked down and we sat there in silence for a moment.

I changed the subject. "Wonder who else is trying out for Olivia."

She smiled slyly. "I found out."

"Who?"

"Guess."

"Don't make me guess."

"Deidre and her friend Carla."

My heart sank. I expected to have competition, but knowing who it was made it more real. There were probably going to be a lot of folks trying out for Olivia. But that part was mine. It was mine already. It had to be.

"Don't worry. I bet you'll get it," Jennifer said.

I wondered. I looked over at her to see if I could read her face, but Jennifer had turned her attention to a mosquito bite on her ankle. She slapped it. "My mother said I shouldn't scratch."

I looked more closely. The bite was now an angry red

splotch trimmed in yellow. "That kind of looks infected. Better leave it alone."

She stared at it again and gave it another slap.

I walked through my front door to the sound of the telephone ringing, so I picked up the receiver and said hello.

"Sophia." It was a statement, not a question.

"Yes?"

"This is Nathan. May I speak to Lily?"

I put the receiver down and went in search of her. She was no longer on the lounge chair in the backyard. She wasn't in our room. I finally found her in the den, on the couch, feet curled under her, watching TV.

"Nathan wants to speak with you," I said.

Her eyes widened. "Who?"

"Nathan. He's on the telephone. He wants to speak to you."

She reached for the telephone on the end table beside her. I saw her swallow. She put her hand over the mouthpiece of the receiver and said, "Go hang up the other phone. And you'd better hang it up." She squinted up at me. "I'll know if you don't."

I didn't listen in. I had more important things to do.

I had to memorize Olivia's lines. And I'd decided to memorize everyone else's lines, as well. But I needed a book on acting. I needed to get back to the library.

CHAPTER 13
Suspicion

LILY IMMEDIATELY STARTED sneaking around with Mrs. Baylor's son. It was the backdrop to my days— watching how she did it. I figured her methods might one day come in handy for me. He'd tap on our bedroom window at night, after we'd gone to bed, and I'd peek from under my covers to see her get up, already dressed, quietly tiptoe to the bedroom window, tug it open, and, after glancing back at me (I managed to close my eyes just in time), climb out.

That first time, I got up and settled on the window seat to see what they were up to. They sat shoulder to shoulder at the top of the small hillside behind our house. The moon was full, and my sister and Nathan were a vision under its light.

I could hear them murmuring back and forth, back and forth. Occasionally I heard Lily's giggle mingled with his laugh, and I thought, that's what I want to do when I fall in love—just sit on a hillside, shoulder to shoulder, and talk and laugh into the night.

I pretended to be asleep when she climbed back in. She said nothing about it when she awakened with a stretch the next morning. I said nothing about it, also.

Then there was the telephone. How many times did she drag it into the bathroom to murmur and giggle for hours? Not the giggles of girlfriend to girlfriend. Giggles with a different quality to them altogether.

And then there were the times she called home to announce that she'd be spending the night at Lydia's. That's where he must have picked her up for their dates, I decided.

Finally, I asked her outright: "Lily, are you seeing Mrs. Baylor's son?" She was trying on several work outfits, deciding what to wear with her new tan.

Her eyes met mine in the mirror, and her whole face assumed a kind of slyness: squinted eyes, pursed lips. "He has a name."

"Are you seeing Nathan?"

"What makes you ask that?"

I didn't want to reveal my observations because they might make her craftier, so I said, "I was just wondering."

"So you think it's your business?"

"Mom's going to be mad. If she finds out."

"She'll just have to be mad, then."

CHAPTER 14
China Cup

S OMETHING HAPPENED THAT took my mind off Lily's business. Something I'd never tell Jennifer. She had a perfect family, and I'd be embarrassed to have her know what was going on in mine.

It was the usual way bad things happen: you're always in the middle of other stuff. I should have known that what my father was doing wouldn't just dangle there in our lives and go unnoticed, or that if I didn't think about it, it would go away. That wasn't going to happen. It was going to be a big interruption. It was going to have *consequences*.

I was beginning to realize that there was a difference between my mother's public face and what she thought her world was and what was *really* going on. I was amazed over and over when I passed her room and saw her sitting at her desk shuffling her important papers around or reading them, looking so confident and assured about her life, that she chose not to see inconvenient things.

So first, there was this happy, peaceful lull: me studying my lines, since I was going to be Olivia by being better than everyone else; Lily pretending she was not seeing Mrs. Baylor's son; my mother pretending that her life was perfect and she had everything figured out; days going by without one cutting remark from Mrs. Baylor about my lack of friends, and specifically colored friends.

Then, one evening, it happened. Or the beginning of it happened. I'd put the script aside and was sitting at my desk painting the kitchen scene from *Anne of Green Gables* in my diorama. I liked what I had done so far, having made sure that I'd penciled it in first so all mistakes could be erased before I painted it. I looked forward to showing my creation to Jennifer and seeing the expression on her face.

Lily was sitting on her bed with her back to the wall, reading.

The telephone rang and part of me listened to see who it was going to be for and kind of hoped it wouldn't be Jennifer calling, because I was busy and didn't want to be interrupted.

Soon I heard my mother stomping up the three stairs that led up to our den. And that didn't sound good. My heart began to beat fast. Apparently, she was looking for my father.

She must have found him because she screamed so loudly that even the Bakers down the street probably could have heard her. "Please do not have your *whore* call this house!"

Lily closed her book and we hurried out to the hall. I could hear my mother's hysteria and my father's deafening silence. She repeated her command, but this time with a space between each carefully articulated word: "Do. Not. Have. Your. Whore. Call. This. House!" My mother did not care that we could hear her. She did not care if Mrs. Baylor could hear her. She did not care if all the neighbors on Montego Drive could hear her. She did not want Daddy's whore calling the house. Period.

I said to Lily, who was now standing behind me with her hands on my shoulders, "Daddy has a whore?" I knew who the whore was but I was pretending I didn't know that lady—who didn't look like what I thought a whore would look like—was my daddy's whore. She looked regular. She wasn't prettier than my mother, who still had her Dorothy Dandridge kind of beauty. But she was younger.

Lily didn't answer me. "You don't need to worry about it," she said quietly. "Don't think about it."

But I did think about it. If that woman I saw was my father's whore, this meant he could start to like her so much, he might just fall in love with her and then marry her and then we would have a whore for a stepmother. I stood there conjuring up new worries.

The voices quieted and then there was silence. Lily and I went back to what we'd been doing.

For the next few days my mother and father acted as if the other were invisible. My mother was busier than ever. My father was absent as much as possible.

By the following Saturday things were nearly normal again. Or so I thought. I'd forgotten that trouble always comes unexpectedly. We'd just sat down at the breakfast table together. And that was promising, as far as I could see. The whole house seemed to be breathing a sigh of relief. Mrs. Baylor had just gone out the door and climbed into Nathan's car to begin her weekend. She'd be returning Monday morning. Nathan had been picking her up those days. And standing on our porch, craning his neck to catch sight of Lily.

On that particular day my mother was lingering at home and it was a nice change from her running out with briefcase in hand. She'd just set a plate of pancakes in the middle of the table when Mrs. Baylor came back into the house with a stack of mail.

"This was in the mailbox," she said, setting it on the sideboard before heading back out.

"Thank you, Mrs. Baylor," my mother replied. She reached for the stack and placed it next to her. Our father glanced at it without much interest and then proceeded to douse his pancakes with maple syrup. Lily used honey these days, rebelling against a product pretending to be maple syrup without a speck of the real thing in it. That was when I began to think she was easing under Nathan's influence. Before Nathan, she'd never scrutinized labels on food packaging. But he probably did.

"You know that stuff is fake, right?" she told me as our father passed the bottle my way. They were both looking at me to see what I was going to do. I poured the syrup on my pancakes and smiled at my lying, cheating father. Why did I still want to please him? Maybe so he wouldn't leave us—for his whore.

I began to feel a shift in the air. Something dark settling over our breakfast table. My mother had been sifting through the mail and placing envelopes on the table next to her after she glanced at them. Then she stopped. She pushed the stack out of the way with her elbow and quickly opened the envelope in her hand. She unfolded the contents and sat there, slowly scanning each page, setting it aside once she'd scrutinized it. She glanced at my father and there was something in that brief look that unnerved me. I felt a storm brewing. I noticed the rise and fall of my chest. A tiny thread of fear began to wind through me. My mother stacked the pages, folded them in thirds, business style, and slipped them back into the envelope.

With her voice cutting through the fragile air, she said very calmly, "What I want to know is why the hell we're getting a copy of a bill from the Red Lion Hotel and the carbon from your credit card. The bill is for Mr. and *Mrs.* Robert LaBranche," she hissed through clenched teeth. My breath quickened. My heart began to pound in my ears.

Lily looked down at her lap, though her eyes were shifting back and forth.

My father, with his silly comb-over, glanced up quickly. He raised his eyebrows as if to pooh-pooh it. "It's gotta be a mistake," he said, as if his pronouncement alone should make us all get on board with his lie.

"You think so?" my mother said, slapping the envelope on the edge of the kitchen table. "You think they got your name and credit card by"—she paused and shrugged dramatically—"*accident?* Is that what you're telling me?"

He drew his mouth down at the corners, as if puzzled. He shook his head. "It's a mistake. Somehow it's a mistake."

"You've said that three times now, and each time you've told a barefaced lie."

"Nobody's lying here. I don't know how that hotel got my name and credit card."

Our mother slapped the credit card slip on the table in front of him. "Well, let me ask you this, *you lying sack of mule shit.* How in the world did they get your signature?" She angled the credit card carbon so he could see. "And that *is* your signature."

Tears began to fill my eyes. This was going to be bad. Even Lily seemed to be sitting on the edge of her chair.

Our father took the carbon from her hand and squinted at it as if there could be some other explanation that had nothing to do with him.

My mother opened her mouth, but no words came out. She looked down at her cup of coffee. She'd just about finished it. She picked it up, drank the last few sips, then stood up and took aim. She hurled the cup toward the sink with a baseball player's fast, hard pitch.

It shattered, sending china shards all over the sink and floor. That seemed to calm her, I noticed. Though her face was still wild and red and her chignon was not quite holding. Sitting there in her satin robe with her hair uncoiling, she looked like a woman in excruciating pain. She got up and walked out of the room, her robe billowing behind her as if she could open the front door and float away, never to be seen again.

Lily and I stared at the mess on the floor. I started to cry, and Lily was saying, "Sh, sh, sh." Mrs. Baylor was gone. We'd have to clean it up ourselves. Our father wasn't going to have anything to do with it. He was already coolly getting up from the kitchen table, as if he was the saner of the two of them, gathering the morning paper, and heading to his home office. His steps were soft and measured, deliberately calm. We heard him open the office door and step inside, and then the awful sound of the click as he turned the lock. It was as loud as thunder.

"Don't worry. Don't worry," Lily said. "It's going to be okay." She tugged at my braid and put her forefinger over my trembling mouth. "Let's clean this up."

She stooped to pick up the bigger pieces and drop them in the waste can beneath the sink. I got the broom and dustpan from the back porch and proceeded to sweep the fine china pieces into it. When I turned it over into the wastebasket, the small heap sparkled like diamond dust. I stared at it and thought, *This is like our family — broken, shattered into dust.*

Soon we heard our mother in the hall. I held my breath at the sound of her approach. In one hand she carried her luggage and in the other she already had her car keys. She came to the kitchen door and set the suitcase down. I glanced at it and my bottom lip began to tremble again.

She looked at us, first one, then the other — for what seemed minutes. We waited. I could barely breathe. "I'm going to Aunt Rose in Elsinore," she said calmly. "I'm not sure for how long." She turned to me. "You make sure you practice 'Für Elise' for your recital next week, and Lily, take care of your sister."

She must not have known about Nathan. Otherwise she would have added, *And you leave Mrs. Baylor's son alone.*

With that, she was gone. I sat back down at the table. What were we going to do? Lily put away the milk and juice, loaded the dishwasher, and wiped the counters and table.

I watched until she looked over at me. "Go practice your piano."

I started to get up, then I sat back down and crossed my arms. "I've decided that I don't want to be in the recital."

"And I've decided you do."

"Mom's gone. Daddy doesn't care. He probably doesn't even know I take piano lessons."

"What are you talking about?"

"And I think you should not go to Spelman. I think you should stay here so you can be with Nathan."

She shook her head. "I don't know where you get your crazy ideas. We're just friends. That's all it is. Why does everyone want to make it more than that? Anyway, he's going back up to Berkeley."

"Can't you go to that school, too? You got in." I pictured

going there by train and her picking me up and taking me sight-seeing. A new sight every month—or maybe every other month.

"Too late," she said.

"Anyway, there won't be anyone at the recital," I said, getting back to the subject. "Daddy will probably just drop me off and pick me up."

"Nonsense. I'll get Nathan to take us."

The best part about "Für Elise" was the two dots above the *u*. It made it look extra-interesting and complicated, which made me seem smart. The beginning was easy. I could sail through it. It was after the change that it began to get hard, and Mrs. Virgil would curl her lip slowly as if there was a bad smell in the air. She'd blink and her nostrils would widen. Then she'd close her eyes and hold her head in a way that made it seem as if she was trying to listen for a mysterious sound, something coming up through the carpeted floor beneath the piano, maybe.

Then she'd start slowly shaking her head. "Go back to the change," she'd say, as if one round of torture wasn't enough. She was listening for something, listening for exactly where I'd started to go wrong.

I would have to ready myself for when she'd hold up her hand and say, "Right there. Stop right there." I'd sit in fear, knowing that any minute she would start spraying, and there would be the risk of her spittle landing on my cheek. Piano lessons with Mrs. Virgil were always full of small fears.

"Have you been practicing?" she would ask at some point, and look over her glasses, ready to catch me in a lie.

"Kind of," I usually said, trying to remember when I'd practiced last.

"What does that mean?"

"I could practice more."

"Precisely," she'd say, and I quickly regretted the *c* and the *s* in that word.

So I needed to practice before my last lesson before the recital. The recital my mother planned to miss. And I still needed to memorize my lines for the tryouts. Because I *was* going to be Olivia. There was no doubt in my mind. I wanted it very badly and I figured that should help me get it. Besides, I was going to be the best. I was sure I would be the only one who would not have to read lines from the script—the only one who could actually act them out from memory.

Later, Jennifer and I sat on the grass in Jennifer's backyard under her Chinese elm with our scripts on our laps and me pretending that nothing was going on in my house and everything was just fine. We were doing the scene where Julie and her "best friend," Sandy, are in the cafeteria ragging on just about everyone.

Julie: *Did you see that sweater Marcia had on this morning? I happen to know she rescued it from one of those bargain tables at Dillard's. I saw it Saturday. It had been marked down twice. I picked it up as a joke, thinking,* who would buy this rag?

Julie and Sandy together: *Marcia!*

Olivia: *Did I mention that Julie Jenson talks about everyone behind her back? Yes, even her best friend, Sandy. She told Evie Parks, who told Linda Merkin, who told Iris Jamison, who told me that Sandy's brother had been picked up for drunk driving and the whole family is just a bunch of drunks. She said this about her own best friend. Talk about two-faced!*

Jennifer stopped me. "You're saying, 'Talk about *two-faced!*' I think you should say, '*Talk* about two-faced!'"

I thought about this. "That doesn't make sense to me."

"Just try it."

But the words wouldn't come out. My mind drifted and then I forgot what I was supposed to do. It felt like I was going to cry—right there in Jennifer's backyard.

"What's wrong?" she asked, looking at me closely.

"Nothing," I told her. "Nothing at all."

CHAPTER 15
Recital

I DON'T HAVE ANYTHING to wear," I said to Lily the day before the recital. "And my hair is ugly."

She looked up from *The House of Mirth*. "We'll get some money from Daddy. When he's feeling guilty, he just hands it over."

Lily said we'd take Daddy's car and go down to May Company or Broadway Department Store later that day, then she'd take me to the beauty school to get my hair washed and straightened. Because it was long and thick and bushy, they would charge a dollar more. When my mother didn't feel like doing it herself, that's where we went.

. . .

It was easier shopping with my sister. She didn't have to stop at the makeup counter and get powder mixed. She didn't even wear face powder. Nor did she have to slip her hand into samples of hosiery to choose just the right color. We went straight to the juniors' department on the second floor of Broadway Department Store, where she scanned the racks to see what was there before sliding clothes along them one after another.

"This is cute," I said, holding up a red velvet drop waist.

"Oh, for Pete's sake, Sophie. You can't wear that in July."

"Why?"

"It's velvet and red and they're probably just trying to get rid of it because they couldn't sell it at the end of last winter when they were making room for the spring stuff."

"Oh." I put it back, realizing it had lost some of its luster. Then I saw the same style in lime-green cotton with tiny white polka dots. "How about this?"

"Hold it up to yourself," Lily said.

I did as she said. She studied it for a few seconds. "That'll do." She took it out of my hand and headed for the register. Daddy had given her twelve dollars to buy me a new dress, and the lime green one was eleven.

Soon we were on to the beauty school to get my hair washed and pressed. I was looking forward to two things. The first was laying my head back in the special sink with the curve for my neck. That was so much better than kneeling on a chair at the kitchen sink, where shampoo would almost always get in my eyes. And while the beauty school lady was straightening my hair, I got to look at the big bank of mirrors and watch it transform from kinky to straight. Like my mother, she used a pressing cloth, and when she was finished, my hair was as straight as a white person's. I got to see other people's hair go from nappy to straight, too. Some had hair that was thick and bushy, others, short and hardly there. After my hair was straightened, I had curls put in with a hot curler.

The curls had to cool or they wouldn't stay. Ladies with rows of sausage curls sat side by side in chairs flipping through old *Ebony* and *Jet* magazines while their hair cooled. I *loved* going to the beauty school.

Lily went off somewhere but returned just as the lady was combing my newly straightened and curled hair into a style. As we were walking out the door, Lily studied my new hairdo— which was half up in a barrette, with the rest hanging down my back.

"You're going to have to be careful," she said, leading the way back to Daddy's car. "No running around and sweating it out, and tonight I have to roll it up for you. I'll use sponge rollers so you can sleep on them."

"Has Mom called?" I asked as we slid into the front seat.

I'd rehearsed the question so I wouldn't sound like I was about to cry. The night before, I'd expected her to call. To see how we were doing. I'd waited the whole evening for the telephone to ring, and now I held my breath for Lily's answer.

"I didn't go home," Lily said with a closed expression that let me know not to question her about where'd she been for the last two hours. "Don't expect her to call, though. She's making a point." She started the car and pulled away from the curb.

But I *had* expected her to call and reassure me and tell me things like, "I'm only going to be gone for a little while—just until I feel better."

"What's Daddy doing?" I asked.

"Daddy's not home. Someone picked him up before we left."

"His whore?"

"Don't use that word," Lily said. She turned the car up Forty-Eighth, using only one hand to steer the wheel in a cool way like on television. I liked to see Lily drive. She made it seem casual and easy. "No. One of his poker buddies."

"They're probably all in it together," I said.

"In what?"

"Having whores."

"I told you not to use that word."

• • •

Nathan picked us up the next day. It was strange seeing Mrs. Baylor's son not in his painting clothes but in an actual suit, and Lily acting as if she'd known him all her life. It was all upside down. I kept looking from one to the other from my place in the middle of the back seat.

Before he started the car, he turned around and peered at me for a moment. I half dissolved under his handsome gaze. "So who else is in this recital?"

"Mrs. Virgil's students and Miss Miller's."

"So which one is your teacher?"

"Mrs. Virgil."

"Do you know all of the students of both teachers?"

"Yeah," I said slowly. "Kinda."

"Come on, Nathan," Lily said.

He looked at my sister and smiled as if he loved her. "Hold on," he said. "Now—out of all the students, which one is the best?"

"This girl who lives down the street. Jilly Baker," I mumbled, hating to admit it.

"Wow," he said. "I know all about the Bakers." He laughed and Lily poked him in the ribs. He turned to my sister. "Yeah, you terrorized that little Baker girl. Which one was that? I'ma have to call the po-leese on you."

"Then I'ma have to tell the *po-leese* you been smokin' weed,"

Lily stated, and they both laughed and laughed. Lily looked over her shoulder at me. "You know I'm kidding, right?"

I frowned. Wasn't weed marijuana? And didn't it lead to more serious drugs? Lily had already told me about the film they'd shown all the twelfth graders about how one puff could make you break open a glass Coca-Cola bottle and drink from the jagged edge, not even caring about cutting your mouth.

"Okay, so this Jilly has your teacher?" Nathan went on.

"No, she has Miss Miller, the white teacher."

"Yeah, that figures." He nodded slowly with mischief in his eyes. I loved it.

"What are you going to do?" Lily asked.

Nathan smiled and shrugged. "I'm just going to make faces at her when they introduce her—throw her off her game."

"People will see you," Lily said.

"No, they'll be looking at her."

My sister was silent for a few moments. Then she said, "You can't do that."

Nathan looked at her, seemingly surprised. "I can't?"

They glanced at each other sideways and smiled. And that's when I realized that I'd settle for nothing less. I wanted someone who would look at me like that and accept my wishes with a smile on his face.

. . .

When we reached the school auditorium and got out of the car, Nathan said, "Hey, Sophie, do you want me to teach you the Ghanaian handshake for good luck?"

"Yes," I said eagerly.

"Well, it's not really for good luck," he said. "But it might give you confidence."

"What's Ghanaian?"

"Anything and anyone from Ghana."

"What's Ghana?" I asked puzzled.

He laughed. "It's a country in West Africa."

Lily had stopped to take out her compact and reapply her orange ice lipstick as if she'd already heard all about West Africa and Ghana and people from Ghana.

"I lived there for a school year," Nathan said. "When I was a junior at Cal."

"You lived in Africa?"

"Right."

"They'd kill me if I went to Africa."

"Huh?" Nathan and Lily said at the same time.

I was almost too embarrassed to explain—especially to Nathan, who, because he was very, very dark skinned, never had to worry about Africans killing him.

"Because I'm light skinned and they don't like light-skinned Negroes there."

"What?" he said. "Where on earth did you get that?"

"Your mother told me."

He gave a quick snort and rolled his eyes. "It's not true," he said. "You know what they'd really think?"

"What?"

"They'd know you were American and they'd think you were *rich*."

I thought about this.

"Hold out your hand," he said.

I held it out.

"Shake once, slide your palm just a little bit back and snap."

I did as he said and giggled on the snap.

"Want to do it again?"

I nodded. We did it again and I still giggled on the snap.

"Now you know how to do the Ghanaian handshake. It's a man's handshake, actually," he added. "But you can use it for good luck."

My sister hung back a bit and whispered in my ear, "Nathan knows *everything*." I thought she was joking, but her expression seemed serious.

I had to add that to my list. I wanted someone who smiled when I disagreed with him and I wanted him to know *everything*.

. . .

Those who'd be playing first had to sit away from their families, in the front row. Both classes sat mixed together. Mrs. Virgil had only three students who'd be performing. That's why she was having this recital with Miss Miller. It was supposed to work out fine, with us playing one after the other, no matter who our teacher was. I looked at the program we'd gotten at the door and was dismayed to see Jilly scheduled to precede me — and she was playing "Für Elise," as well. My heart sank and I began to get the jitters. I looked back to see Nathan and Lily in the second row across the aisle.

Then I saw my mother. She was tiptoeing down the aisle, her eyes searching the faces in the auditorium. My heart began to race. I felt a weight in my stomach. I looked down at my hands. Then I looked back again and she spotted me and waved. My mother.

I didn't even know that she'd remembered. What did this mean? Was she coming back home? She pointed to a seat in the middle of the row and started making her way to it. She was five rows behind Nathan and Lily. I saw her catch sight of them and stop to stare. She sat down slowly, then glanced at me, as if I was involved in Lily's doings.

I turned around to avoid seeing the look on my mother's face. I wanted to concentrate only on the part just before and after the change in "Für Elise." I began to practice on my lap. I moved my fingers very slightly so no one would know what I was doing. I peered down the front row. Everyone looked as nervous as I felt. Even Jilly Baker was twisting a lock of hair. I'd seen her parents as soon as we'd walked in and wondered again if Deidre had told them yet what Lily had said. I came to the conclusion that she hadn't. Maybe she'd told her sisters, but I didn't think she'd told her parents. They hadn't even looked my way.

Miss Miller was talking. Saying the usual things about how excited and happy she was to see all the parents in the audience and how she loved seeing this kind of support and blah-blah-blah. She wasn't going to leave anything for Mrs. Virgil to say. Then she went on to introduce "a very talented pianist" (said in a funny way) "who promises to delight us—just delight us." And oh yes—after the recital she hoped that members of the audience would help themselves to refreshments at the back of the auditorium. I looked back to see punch and doughnuts on a long table. But even that didn't thrill me. In fact, with the weight in my stomach, just the sight of food made me feel queasy.

Soon, Miss Miller was introducing Jilly. Jilly sprung up out of her seat, as if eager to get to it. She even glanced over her shoulder to give me a little haughty smirk. I looked back at Nathan. He smiled at me and winked. He didn't look like he was going to put his plan into play, and I was a little bit relieved. Lily had her arm looped through his, apparently unaware that our mother was sitting five rows behind them with her eyes on their backs.

Jilly did everything right. She emphasized the sudden B-flat chord in just the right place. She made the first change effortlessly, and she made her face look like a concert pianist—all solemn and stuff. I liked the way she seemed to softly rake the keys at times and at other times made her fingers dance on them. Oh, well. So what if I hadn't acquired those gestures and I was still just trying to get through the piece without messing up?

Mrs. Virgil had been showing me how to do a crescendo to bring the B flat out. The ABACA was easy because it repeats itself, but those changes! I always hesitated, and that made everything so awkward.

Before I knew it, Jilly was rising from the bench and bowing to applause. She glanced at me again and gave me the faintest hint of a smile. It was not a friendly smile. It was a smile that said, "Your turn."

Mrs. Virgil was already up at the mic introducing me. I didn't know what she was saying exactly, but I knew I was standing and walking on shaky legs to the piano.

"And we're in for a treat because we get to hear 'Für Elise' again with Sophie LaBranche."

There might have been clapping, but I could hear only my thumping heart.

I sat down on the piano bench and moved it forward. I positioned my fingers on the keys. I put my feet on the pedals and then I chanced a look at my audience. Everyone was gazing at me with expectation. I smiled and avoided looking at Jilly Baker, who probably thought I wouldn't be any good because I was colored.

I began.

It felt as if I was crawling, even through the easy beginning. My heart pounded at every change. I could have done the crescendo better. Mrs. Virgil was probably making a mental note of that and I was sure to hear about it. Finally, with every change a struggle, I crawled to the end. I sat there for a couple of seconds after I played the last note. I had to steady myself before I stood up and managed my bow.

The best part about the whole thing was walking back to my seat and watching all the other kids go through their own special torment. One by one. I turned around to see Lily give me a thumbs-up and Nathan nod slowly. But where was my mother? When I looked for her to see what she thought of my performance, she was gone. She must have left just after I finished.

So in the end, what did anything matter? Other than just getting through it.

CHAPTER 16
Once a Little Girl (and Before That, a Baby)

LILY WAS GOING OFF with Nathan to get together with some of his friends, so I went into the house alone. I could take Oscar out and walk by Anthony Cruz's house. I could see what Jennifer was up to. I could memorize lines. I could read.

But nothing was of the slightest interest to me. At this hour, only the news would be on television. Still, that's what I opted for. I dragged myself into the den, still in my new dress, turned on Channel Seven, and flopped down in front of the TV. I could hear Mrs. Baylor in the kitchen. I thought I smelled meatloaf baking in the oven. I wasn't hungry. Too many doughnuts at the recital. As soon as I had finished "Für Elise" and sat down, my appetite had returned.

I got up at some point, walked to my room, changed into pedal pushers and a T-shirt, and sat on my bed. I had twenty-three more pages of *Footlights for Jean* to read and it was the good part, but I knew the book was going to remain closed on my nightstand. I pulled out the script from under the bed and placed it on my lap. I felt not a bit of inspiration. I thumbed through it, checking for Jennifer's parts. She had lots of lines.

If I was going to be Olivia, I needed to memorize her lines before tryouts in two weeks. *Tomorrow,* I vowed.

I returned to the den and the *Nightly News.* Boring stuff about troop increases in Vietnam. I watched a grainy report and wished I'd gotten home early enough for *General Hospital.* Even though I couldn't understand the appeal of Nurse Jessie Brewer when she always acted so unhappy, talked in a deep monotone, and hardly ever smiled. She was super-serious about everything.

Yet men were always falling in love with her. I didn't get it, but still, I liked to watch—every day in the summer and whenever I could get home from school early enough the rest of the year.

I heard Mrs. Baylor moving around in the kitchen, preparing my dinner. I got off the sofa, crept into my daddy's home office, and eased the door closed behind me. I stood there a moment, looking around. I wanted to see if the letter I'd discovered under the desk organizer from that Paula person had been opened. If it had, I could read it.

I sat down in his chair and resisted the urge to spin around. I couldn't get caught up in silly things. I had to hurry before Mrs. Baylor called me to dinner. I looked at the desk organizer for a moment, then lifted it. Nothing. *Nothing.* The letter was gone—it was probably in my dad's pocket. I was disappointed.

I twirled in his chair just once, then stopped. Maybe he'd put it in one of the drawers. I opened the file drawer and went through the folders. No luck. Then I tried to open the drawer just above. It was stuck. Something was catching. Something was in the way. I hadn't looked in this drawer during my last visit to my father's office.

Now I sighed, tugged on it, and managed to get it open. I reached into the back of the drawer and pulled out an old, bent *Jet* magazine. It was from September 22, 1955. Ten years ago. I could easily imagine my father being annoyed by the drawer but just letting it go. It was probably a drawer he didn't use much, anyway.

I loved *Jet* magazine. It reported all the colored celebrity news and gossip and it was full of interesting pictures. The cover showed a light-skinned girl in a bathing suit. "A pretty Los Angeles City College student," the caption stated. I checked her closely to see if she was all that good-looking. She had a nice smile and a nice figure. I guessed most would think she was pretty.

I turned a page to see a picture of Nat King Cole and "the tall, beautiful Maria Ellington"—whom he was going to marry and make Maria Cole. I stared at her. She was fair skinned, too, with straight hair and light eyes. "Tall and beautiful," the magazine said.

I turned a few more pages, looking for more old celebrity news, and stopped at a small headline: NATION HORRIFIED BY MURDER. I stared. There was a picture of a young boy standing next to his mother. Colored. He was the one who was murdered, I guessed, and it was odd to think of a young boy *murdered.* He looked so alive and happy in the picture, but since his photo was right under the headline, he must have been the murdered one.

The boy and his mother were both dressed up. As if it was Easter or something. And they were smiling. She had her hand on his shoulder and a proud look on her face. The caption said the boy's name was Emmett Till.

I turned the page and let out a cry. I slapped my hand over my mouth. I saw something so horrible, it didn't seem it was meant to be seen. That same boy was in his *casket.* His face was smashed. His head looked like a pumpkin that had been dropped from a second story. He looked like a monster. I couldn't tell where his eyes were.

I quickly turned to the closed office door. I could still hear Mrs. Baylor in the kitchen, cooking my dinner. She'd be calling me soon.

I found myself shaking my head slowly and whispering, "No, no, no."

What had happened to that boy, Emmett Till? "What happened to you?" I said under my breath as my eyes filled with tears. "Who did that to you?"

I tucked the magazine under the elastic waist of my pedal pushers and pulled my shirt over it. I slipped out of my daddy's office and into my room just as Mrs. Baylor was calling me to dinner. I stashed the magazine under my pillow and went to the kitchen.

She'd set one place at the table and dished up the green beans, mashed potatoes, and meatloaf. I stared at the plate of food. She stood there looking at me with a strange expression on her face.

"Help yourself to more if you want," she said as she took off her apron and headed to her room. She glanced back at me over her shoulder as I pulled out the chair and sat down, and a strange look passed over her face. Her lips parted as if she was about to say something but then thought better of it. It wasn't anything mean or curt or critical. Maybe she wanted to ask me how my recital went. Or maybe she wanted to ask me about Nathan and Lily—find out what I knew, what I thought. I would tell her that I thought they loved each other and no one could stop true love. But she turned and went up to her room with slow, heavy steps.

I wasn't hungry. I stared at my plate of food. I felt so tired. And sad, about everything, everywhere. I ate all of my dinner anyway. So Mrs. Baylor would be pleased.

Then I watched all the Friday night TV I wanted, but by the time *Peyton Place* came on, I was too sleepy to continue. I went to my room, got into my pajamas, and walked to the bathroom to brush my teeth (I was trying to be better about that). All that time, I was listening for Nathan's car or my daddy's or my mother's —*someone's!*—to turn the corner and pull up in the driveway or in front of the house. The street was quiet.

I pulled the *Jet* magazine out from under my pillow and read the article and stared at the happy, smiling face of Emmett Till— when he was just being a person, just being fourteen with Bobo for a nickname. There were also pictures of his two cousins. He'd had a last happy day before they did that to him. The report said he'd whistled at a white woman. And that two white men had come for him in the night. Dragged him away from his family. And threatened to pistol-whip his grandmother. His *grandmother.*

Two big white men. What was in their hearts? What was in their souls, that they would pistol-whip an old woman if she tried to stop them from taking her grandson?

Tears streamed down my cheeks. I put my face in my hands and knew exactly why people put their face in their hands. It's because there's nothing else you can do. We didn't live in Mississippi, but hate was under the surface everywhere. Wasn't it? Even if it was a sneaky kind of hate. It made people look at me and automatically think they were superior. It made them think I was a thief or maybe I'd do something to their swimming pool . . . and that white was better.

I lowered my hands and stared at the smiling picture of Emmett Till and thought, *He didn't even know what was coming.* I heard a car and caught my breath. But it went by.

With a fresh and minty mouth, I got on my knees and began my prayers. First the Lord's Prayer, which was more serious than "Now I lay me down to sleep, I pray to God my soul to keep." It was the prayer I said when I needed hope and wasn't in a hurry.

Then I prayed the extra part, that my mother would come home and Lily wouldn't leave me in a few weeks to go off to Georgia (though I wasn't very hopeful about that) and that my father would be true to my mother and that Lily and Nathan would get married and that starving children would get food and that all the soldiers would come home from Vietnam. (While I was on my knees in my clean pajamas and my freshly brushed teeth, I thought I might as well pray for everything I could think of. I did not want God to find me selfish.) And I added Mrs. Baylor. I prayed that one day she would like me because I never ever, ever, *ever* thought that my color was better than anyone else's. *Ever.* I prayed for Emmett Till—and his mother. And his father. And that he was in heaven. (Although there was no picture of his father, he must have had a father.) I prayed for his cousins, too, and his grandparents, whether alive or not.

I heard the floor creak in the hall just as I stood up. I looked around to see Mrs. Baylor standing there with her arms full of folded sheets. I felt my face grow warm. She left the door and went to put the sheets away in the linen closet next to the bathroom. Then she came back.

She stood there in the doorway and looked at me with her head cocked to the side and her eyes squinting.

"Let me tell you something, child," she began.

I braced myself.

"You are a good girl."

I looked at her and began to cry.

She came and sat next to me on the bed. She took my hand. "I should have never said to you that thing I said."

"About the Africans?"

She snorted. "Can I tell you a story?"

She didn't wait for my answer. She just took a deep breath and began.

"This ol' lady here," she said, bringing her finger up to touch her chest, "was once a little girl—just like you." She sighed. "And before that, a baby."

Mrs. Baylor paused, thinking back, I supposed.

I dared to look at her then to find out if I could see the little girl in her. Or the baby. I couldn't quite, but I knew she had to have been one once. She stared down at her hands. "I'ma tell you why I said something so hateful. Though there is no excuse."

More tears welled in my eyes. I think it was all the emotions of the day: getting ready for the recital, feeling nervous, having stage fright, seeing my mother, and discovering what had happened to Emmett Till.

"I know you feel alone," she started.

The tears came. I quickly wiped them away.

"Listen to me. I was born in Jamaica. My mother did not want me because she did not like my father, her husband. She married him because he could give her things. He had a good government job, but she never wanted to have a baby by him. He was a very black man. He looked like an African. But here I came anyway. It was God's will. And a girl. Who took after her father. I looked just like my daddy shrunk down."

I laughed.

"Really," she said. "My mother, on the other hand, was small and delicate, with soft brown skin and with what we call nice features: small nose, lips not too full, thick wavy hair that hung down her back. She was quite proud of that hair. Sometimes she'd let my father brush it. She was a beautiful woman, something like your mother." She looked at me sideways.

I thought of my own hair. "I once heard my mother and father blaming each other for my hair," I said.

"You have a good healthy head of hair. Grows long," Mrs. Baylor said. "Takes a press real good."

"My mother calls it rhiny. She says rhiny hair is usually kinky."

Mrs. Baylor laughed. "I'll braid it up for you sometime."

She was quiet for a moment, so I waited to hear more about this little black baby whose mother didn't want her.

"My mother hired a wet nurse for me. She would not nurse me herself. The wet nurse was Nancy. We did not have her long. My father died and we were soon destitute because there was no will and he had left a lot of debt.

"My mother went to work in a hotel, cleaning rooms. She shipped me off to my father's mother, and that's where I spent the first twelve years of my life. I was happy. My grandmother loved me so. I was the daughter of her most successful child."

I shifted uneasily. *What must it have felt like to be shipped off?* I wondered.

"When I was twelve—just your age—my mother sent for me. I was so happy, thinking she finally wanted me. My grandmother made me a new dress, fixed my hair, and bought me little gold hoops for my ears. These very ones," Mrs. Baylor said, pulling at an ear lobe. "I still wear them after all of these years, for my grandmother."

I imagined Mrs. Baylor all dressed up. I stared at the earrings. It was the first time I'd really noticed them. They'd always just gone with her look. "What happened when you went to live with your mother?" I asked.

A shadow fell over Mrs. Baylor's face then. She gazed out my window at the black night. "My mother didn't want me for *me*. She wanted me so I could take care of her baby."

My eyes widened.

"She'd gotten pregnant by one of the white hotel guests—a married man who'd flattered her, made her think on his short visit to Kingston that he would be her ticket to the States. I think she got pregnant on purpose, not knowing that the white man already had a wife."

"A girl baby or a boy baby?"

"Girl," Mrs. Baylor said simply. "I was pulled out of school —the wonderful school that I adored. Snatched from the love of my grandmother and my teacher, who always praised me as the smartest girl in her class."

"What happened?" I asked.

"My mother lied to my grandmother. Told her she was ready to be a mother to me now, so my grandmother was happy to re-unite us. But my mother turned me into a nursemaid. She did not send me to school. She kept me home to care for my sister while she continued to work in that hotel.

"She was a tiny little thing, my sister, Kate—I think because my mother had had to hide her pregnancy. She would have gotten fired if anyone found out she was getting with the guests. I don't know how she managed to hide it, but she did. Then she told the hotel people that Kate was the child of a sister who couldn't care for her."

I pictured a baby the size of a small doll.

"She was tiny and so pale, you could see the blue veins in her temples. A frail little baby. But I took excellent care of her. I was hoping to earn my mother's favor. As Kate grew, certain fea-tures showed up: blue eyes, dark-blond straight hair; my mother was so proud of those blue eyes and straight hair. Soon Kate went from being a sweet baby to a spoiled little girl who thought she was better because she looked mostly white. She began to mimic our mother by treating me like a servant put on earth just to care for her. I lost years of schooling and fell so far behind, I was never to catch up. Never to return to school."

I felt my throat tighten at the injustice of it. Tears welled in my eyes again. I wiped them away with the back of my hand.

"When I was seventeen my father's sister, my aunt Blanche, who lived in New York, sent for me to go live with her. In secret. I think she guessed what was going on. I sneaked away. I won't say how, but I was able to leave and then live with my lovely Aunt Blanche."

There was a moment of quiet. "Mrs. Baylor?" I said.

"Yes, girl."

"I never think of my color being better than anyone else's. Never." And I was telling the truth.

CHAPTER 17
Beach

MY SISTER WAS in her bed, snoring softly, when I awoke. It took me a few seconds to remember my sad situation. My mother was gone. I sat up and looked at Lily for a moment. I could hear Mrs. Baylor in the kitchen. Daddy must have asked her to stay in light of my mother just up and leaving. I imagined August twenty-sixth, when I would wake up to see a made bed and think of Lily in Atlanta already awake and in the dorm room unpacking her suitcase, deciding where to put stuff.

I considered showing her the *Jet* magazine. But then I thought better of it. She was going to the South. It would make her afraid, and I didn't want her to be afraid. The magazine was on the floor. I leaned down and pushed it farther under the bed.

The snoring stopped and her eyes opened. She lay there staring at nothing. Then she came up on her elbow. "Has Mom called?" she asked.

I shook my head slowly. She flopped back down and closed her eyes as if it was of little importance to her.

"I want to call Aunt Rose," I said. I expected Lily to protest, but she just yawned and said, "Do what you want."

Now I had to be brave and follow through. I had to ask Daddy for the telephone number, then I'd probably see him not care as he scribbled it on a scrap of paper or said with a shrug that he didn't have it.

I decided to dress and eat breakfast before going to find him. If he said he didn't know it or didn't have it, I could go straight to Jennifer's so we could practice our lines for the tryouts.

"I'm off today. You want to go to the beach?" Lily asked me. She was sitting up and looking out the window at the marine layer, frowning slightly. "Mmm, cloudy. I guess the sun's coming out sometime today."

"Yeah! When are we going?"

"Whenever Nathan comes to pick us up."

I felt a flutter of excitement in my stomach. I liked his Volkswagen Beetle. I liked the radio stations he played. I liked that he knew how they shake hands in Ghana.

"Go ask Daddy for Aunt Rose's telephone number."

I made my way to the kitchen to check if Daddy was in there having his coffee. Through the window, I could see Mrs. Baylor hanging up laundry on the clothesline again. Our mother had no plans to buy a clothes dryer. She liked the fragrance of clothes dried in the sun. I pulled back the curtains over the sink and Mrs. Baylor caught my eye and smiled. A really nice smile. I thought of her as a baby with a mother who didn't want her. How could a mother not want her own child?

Daddy was in my parents' bathroom, leaning toward his mirror, shaving. "Mornin'," he said. "How can I help you?"

He hadn't gotten to his comb-over yet and I was thrown a little bit by his shiny, balding head.

"I want Aunt Rose's telephone number," I said, happy to get it out.

"I don't have it."

I had half expected him to say that. So I wasn't surprised. Did this mean I might never talk to my mother again? Then I wondered where my father was going on a Saturday morning.

"See if your mother left her precious datebook behind." He turned toward their room. "It would be in the top nightstand drawer. On her side. I can't see her leaving it, but she was in a big hurry, I guess you could say."

I stood there for a moment. Then, before I could stop myself, I blurted out, "Daddy, are you just going to let her stay gone? Don't you care about Mom?" The vision of him sitting in the café across from that woman and putting his hand on hers came back to me, along with the sick feeling that had lasted the whole rest of the day.

He put his razor under the tap and shook it. He glanced over at me and sighed. "Your mother will be back when she's good and ready. I'm not going to beg her."

"Would you even want to beg her, Daddy?"

He looked at me in the mirror. "The number is in her datebook," he said, and grabbed a hand towel from the rack and patted his face.

I got the datebook and took it to my room. I wasn't going to ask for permission to go to the beach. Lily wasn't asking, so I wouldn't either. She was already in the shower. I'd be able to have some privacy in case I got tongue-tied or started to cry.

I looked at my mother's July calendar. So many things penciled in. How was she doing those things from where she was without her datebook? Maybe she'd decided to take a vacation from all that stuff and left the book there deliberately. I saw my name then, "Sophia's piano recital," penciled into yesterday's square. She'd even drawn a squiggly line around it so it would stand out.

She'd always planned to come. It wasn't a last-minute decision. I flipped ahead to August twenty-fifth. There it was: Lily's flight time and flight number. TWA Flight 624 at nine a.m. Exactly one month away.

I sat down on my bed and dialed Aunt Rose's number. She answered on the third ring. People did that whether they were sitting right next to the phone or not. Nobody wanted to seem too eager.

"Aunt Rose, this is Sophie. Can I speak to my mother?" Oops, I hadn't greeted her first and asked how she was doing. I felt bad because I loved Aunt Rose. She was really affectionate—always free with kisses and hugs. When I was little, she'd called me monkey. She had a birthmark above her right eyebrow. She'd let me reach out to touch it, but when I was about to put my finger on it, she'd yell, "Boo!" making me jump and sending me into giggles.

"Hi, sweetie," she said with a voice full of sympathy. "How are you and Lily doing, darlin'?"

"We're fine," I answered. There was a sudden pain in my throat as if I was going to cry.

"Poor baby," she said. "Hold on, hon. Let me get your mother."

It was almost a minute before my mother got on the

phone. As soon as she said hello, I started bombarding her with questions: "Mommy, are you coming home, ever? How come you didn't stay after the recital? Are you still mad at Daddy?"

There was a long sigh. "Sophia, I'm here because I need time to think. I'm not going to go into it; this only concerns your father and me. Be patient. I'll be back when I'm ready."

"But why didn't you stay after the recital?"

"Because your father was there and I didn't want to talk to him."

"Daddy was at my recital?" I said. "I didn't see him."

"He was sitting way in the back. Behind me, even—off to the side."

"I missed him." Now I felt bad. I'd been blaming him for being selfish and unconcerned all night and all morning.

"I didn't want a scene to occur," she said.

"Oh."

"Listen, Sophia. I just need a little time to think. I'll be back before you know it, and then we'll work everything out." There was a pause where I didn't know what to say.

"Goodbye, Sophia. I'll see you soon." And with that she was gone.

I replaced the receiver just as Lily was coming into the

bedroom in her white fluffy terry cloth robe. "Hey," she said. "So you still want to go to the beach?"

"I saw him, Lily," I said quietly while she searched in the closet for something to wear. I was sitting cross-legged on my bed. And just at that moment, I decided to tell her what had happened.

"Who?"

"Daddy. I saw him with a woman."

Lily pulled out a blue long-sleeved knit top and held it up in front of her. She met my eyes in the mirror. "Where?"

"That café. Prides."

She sighed, then shrugged. "He likes that place," she said.

I felt my face crumble.

She looked out the window. "He's not very discreet."

"You mean you knew? About Daddy?" I asked, my voice cracking.

"I work in the shopping center, remember?"

"You've seen him with her, then?"

Lily nodded.

"What's wrong with him?" I cried. "Why does he act like that?"

"You mean like a man?"

"Nathan would never act like that. I know he wouldn't. He's different."

Lily blushed and looked away. "I take that back. There are a lot of men who wouldn't act like that." She looked at me and said simply, "Go get ready for the beach."

"Where to?" Nathan asked, pulling onto Angeles Vista.

"Zuma, by way of Sunset," Lily said. With our parents too distracted to pay attention to us, it felt like we had a grown-up kind of freedom.

"You are definitely a West Side girl. You ever been to Watts or Compton, or east of Arlington?"

"I've been east of Arlington. A couple of times."

"That's what I thought." He looked over at her and smiled as if that only endeared her to him more.

"Oops. Wait. More than a couple of times. Whenever I go downtown I'm east of Arlington."

Once we got past Doheny and wound through Pacific Palisades, Sunset slid into Pacific Coast Highway and the ocean majestically came into view. We were still under a cool marine layer that was supposed to linger until the late afternoon. But no one planned to go into the ocean above their ankles anyway, so it was okay.

Zuma Beach had swings, and I'd brought a big towel and my script. I was really going to get into my soliloquy about Julie's two-faced behavior behind her best friend's back. I also had a small notepad for ideas concerning my novel, which could occur to me at any moment.

The parking lot was nearly empty. For most people, it wasn't a good beach day. Nathan carried the small picnic basket with bottles of punch and peanut butter and jelly sandwiches that Lily had thrown together at the last minute. I spread out my towel near the swings and settled down with my script. Lily and Nathan walked off like two good friends deep in conversation. I watched them until I got tired of it.

The wind was picking up, so I put on Nathan's windbreaker, which he'd left on top of the basket. Then I dove into my script. There was a family with three small children about ten yards away, so I didn't feel really alone.

Before I knew it Lily and Nathan were back and we were sharing my towel, eating the sandwiches, and watching the waves rolling in and out. Then Lily ran over to the swings. Soon all three of us were on them, seeing who could go the highest and the fastest. Of course I won, because I was lighter and it hadn't been a zillion years since I had gone on a swing. I felt like I was going to fly off and go zooming over the water. Then up, up into the clouds.

Lily laughed, which made me laugh, and then Nathan was laughing, too. And I thought: *This is what I will remember all my life.* Lily would remember Lydia's pool party and all the fun and the music and the cool guys, and I would remember this: laughing and feeling as if I could fly out over the ocean.

When we left the beach it was Lily's idea to drive around the neighborhood in Pacific Palisades, "to see how the other half lives."

"*You* live like the other half lives," Nathan said, grabbing the picnic basket and swinging it onto his shoulder.

"Not even close. You'll see."

"It's all relative," he said. When we got back to the car, he opened the door for her, then for me.

The warmth inside felt cozy and comforting. I settled in a corner of the back seat with my notepad, ready for random thoughts. I looked out the window at the shady streets, the sprawling houses, and the expansive lawns, which seemed more uniformly green than the lawns on my street.

Lily fiddled with the radio until she found a good station that wasn't in the middle of a long run of commercials. "Ooh, this is my *song*," she said. It was half over. "My Girl," by The Temptations.

"I've got sunshine . . ." she sang. "On a cloudy day." Nathan and I joined in, and it was the most beautiful sound I'd ever heard because it made me feel certain that it wouldn't be long before someone would sing that song to me.

But then Nathan's voice dropped out and he peered into the rearview mirror, checking something behind him.

"What the hell," he said under his breath.

We all stopped singing. "What?" Lily asked. She looked behind her. "What's with the police car?"

I looked out the back window and saw its flashing red light. Then I heard a voice that sounded as if it was coming through a megaphone: "Please pull over."

Lily frowned and looked at Nathan. Nathan pulled over to the curb and stopped. He kept his hands on the steering wheel.

"Turn off your ignition," the megaphone voice instructed.

Nathan turned off the car. He put both hands on the steering wheel again and waited. Minutes ticked by.

Lily said under her breath, as if the policeman could hear her, "What does he want?"

Nathan shook his head. He stared straight ahead. I looked back again. The officer was talking into his radio, and though I couldn't see his eyes behind his sunglasses, it felt like he was staring a hole into the back of Nathan's head.

Finally, he slowly got out of his patrol car. He hiked up his pants and sauntered over to the driver's side of Nathan's car. He stood there with his right hand resting on the giant gun on his hip, then tapped on the window and made a rolling motion with his hand.

Nathan rolled down the window.

"I'd like to see your license and registration, please," the police officer said.

Nathan lifted half off the seat to pull his wallet out of his back pocket. He opened it and found his license. He handed it to the policeman. Then he turned to Lily, his expression stony. "Can you look in the glove compartment for my registration?" She quickly retrieved it and passed it to Nathan, who handed it to the cop. Then he put his hands back on the steering wheel. The policeman seemed to study Nathan's documents for a long time. Then he took Nathan's license and registration back to his car. He opened the door and climbed in. He got on his radio again. I heard Nathan sigh. And it was such a sad sigh.

"What's going on, Nathan?" Lily asked.

Nathan shook his head again. "I don't know." In the rearview mirror his face looked tense.

We soon heard the siren of another police car as it pulled up behind the first. A patrolman jumped out as if he'd arrived at a fire. He walked briskly to the first car and leaned in the window, talking to the patrolman. They conferred for a long time.

Finally, they both approached Nathan's car. The second officer leaned in the window with both arms resting on the door. They were covered in a forest of blond hairs. "Could you step out of the car, please?" he said. He glanced at Lily and me, then back at Lily, where his eyes seemed to rest for a moment before he turned his attention to Nathan.

"Excuse me?" Nathan said.

"We don't want any trouble. Just step out of the car."

Nathan opened the door and climbed out. He stood by it with his hands at his sides. The patrolman then grabbed Nathan by the elbow and marched him to the back of the car. He had him lean on it with his arms out and his legs spread. I had a good view out the back window. Lily turned all the way around in her seat to watch. The first policeman squatted and patted down Nathan's legs inside and out. He stood and ran his big sausage fingers around Nathan's waist. He patted all around his raised arms. Then he brought Nathan's arm behind him and put a handcuff on his wrist. He pulled Nathan's other arm behind him and handcuffed his wrists together.

Lily's mouth dropped open. She started to get out of the car, but the first patrolman hurried to her door, rapped on the window, and told her, "Stay inside the car, please."

"What's going on? Why are you doing that to him?" She was trying to keep her voice even, but it was on the edge of anger.

"Just stay in the car, please."

The other cop marched Nathan to the curb and sat him down. Then they both went back to the first cop's car and held another conference. Finally, the second cop came over to Lily in the passenger seat and motioned for her to roll the window down. She did so and waited.

The officer turned his head away and spat. Then he looked back at Lily and frowned. "Let me ask you something," he said. "Just what are you doing with that nigger?"

Lily flinched and my eyes got as big as saucers. I gasped.

"Who is this?" he asked, indicating me.

"My *sister*," Lily said.

He pushed his hat back, squinted at me, then shrugged. "Like I said—your father know you going around with this nigger?"

Lily's mouth dropped open. "What?"

"I think I'm speaking English."

"Can't you see? Do you have eyes? I'm *not* white. And he's not a nigger. What are you, from the Ku Klux Klan?" Though I could see only her profile as she glared at the patrolman, I noticed her lips trembling. She wiped away a tear.

The patrolman studied her for a moment, then glanced back at me. Maybe he was trying to see the nigger in her, too. And maybe the nigger in me.

This is what they did. The two patrolmen chatted and chatted while Nathan sat handcuffed on the curb. They went back to the first patrol car and talked some more on the radio, and after all that, one of them went over to Nathan and helped him stand up.

He removed the handcuffs and said a few words, then they both got in their patrol cars and drove off.

I caught an old woman looking out her living room window at the whole spectacle. Nathan returned to the car, climbed in, and sat there for a few moments, staring straight ahead. Lily seemed to know not to say anything just yet. He started up the car and we drove home in silence.

"By the way," he said, startling us as his voice broke the quiet, "they thought you were a white girl." He looked at her as if he was accusing her of something. She put her hand on his arm, but he pulled away.

I didn't like the way he dropped us off, staying behind the wheel with the motor running while we lugged our stuff out of the car. Then driving off as Lily just stood there watching until he turned down Olympiad. I carried the picnic basket into the kitchen with no help, resting my script and notepad on top.

Lily stomped past me into our room and slammed the door. Which meant it was off-limits to me, at least for the time being. I went into the kitchen to get a glass of water and came upon Mrs. Baylor, peeling potatoes. She looked over her shoulder at me. "Wash your hands before you go in the refrigerator." She stepped aside so I could use the sink. I wondered if I should tell her what had happened, then decided not to. It might upset her. And anyway, it was Nathan's business to tell.

I hung out in the front yard tossing a tennis ball at Oscar for him to slobber all over as he brought it back to me in his wet doggy mouth, waiting until I felt it might be safe to go to my own room. Suddenly Jennifer was coming out of her house burdened with a rolled sleeping bag and duffle that looked stuffed and heavy. She waved. "Bye, Sophie! See you in a couple weeks!" Her father, who'd come out of the house behind her, smiled and waved. He opened the door of the station wagon and helped Jennifer dump her stuff in the back seat. They both got in the car and drove away. I watched them until their car turned down Olympiad. She'd be gone for almost two weeks. I hadn't even had a chance to tell her what happened.

I went back inside and opened the door to our room. Lily was just sitting there on her bed with the phone on her lap. "I can't reach him," she said. "He's not there. Or he's not answering."

CHAPTER 18
Something That Happens

T HAT'S HOW IT went for the next three days. Even when Aunt Rose called to see how we were doing, I could hardly talk to her without Lily pacing and mouthing, *Sophie, get off!*

He was just a friend? I didn't think so. Lily was going around as if she'd been socked in the gut. Sometimes she looked like she was about to tear up and it took all her willpower not to cry.

On Wednesday, my mother returned. She just walked through the door with her suitcase and a box of See's Candies, headed straight to her room, and closed the door behind her. Eventually she came out and called Lily and me into the living room.

When we were seated and giving her our undivided attention, she dove in with "Your father and I have been talking and trying to work things out." My heart started to beat fast with anticipation. Daddy had been gone since early morning. Now I was picturing him walking through the door and sitting down next to my mother to help explain things. I didn't know what to expect from her as she sat there examining her manicure. It looked fresh to me. Her Audrey Hepburn upsweep looked recently done, as well. And she had a new fringe of bangs.

"We think some time apart might be in order." Lily and I looked at each other. "He's staying in a nearby motel right now, but he's going to get a small place of his own. Of course, you'll still see him." She turned to me. "I've arranged for you to be with him every other weekend, Sophia. Once he has his own place. And Lily," she said, turning to her, "I suppose it won't be such a change for you, since you'll be leaving for Atlanta in a few weeks."

Lily glanced at me again and something about that look gave me an odd feeling. She *was* going to Georgia, wasn't she? My mother was sitting there in her blue silk blouse and slim white linen skirt, wearing her pearl earrings and red lipstick and matching nail polish, and she didn't have a clue there was the possibility that my sister wouldn't be doing exactly what she'd planned. After all, she'd had these plans for Lily since she was born.

To all of this, Lily only said, "Can I borrow your car, Mom?"

My mother frowned. "What?"

"I thought I'd take Sophie to a movie—to cheer her up."

They both looked at me and for a second I didn't know if I should put a really sad look on my face or a happy one or what. Lily seemed to give me a silent signal to appear despondent. I did my best.

My mother snorted. "I hope you don't think that we're not going to discuss you attending Sophie's recital with Mrs. Baylor's son."

When Lily had finally come home late that night of the recital, I'd broken the news to her that our mother had been there and had seen her and Nathan. All Lily had done was shrug. Now she folded her arms and dropped her chin.

"What do you think you were doing?"

"We're friends. That's all. Sophie and I needed a ride to the recital. He offered to take us." She rolled her eyes.

"Where was your father?"

Lily hesitated, and I knew she was trying to decide whether she should tell our mother that he hadn't been home. "He wasn't available."

My mother stared at her.

"He wasn't home," Lily said.

"A friend," my mother said, and continued to stare at Lily. "That most assuredly had better be the case."

"Why?" Lily challenged.

"He's not"—she paused—"suitable."

"Why? Why is he not suitable? He's the smartest person I know. He's smarter than Daddy, who knows *nothing* compared to Nathan. *Nothing.* Just law. He doesn't know *history,* he doesn't know the *political* circumstances of black people. Daddy doesn't even *think* about the stuff that Nathan thinks about."

"Of *what* people?"

"*Black* people," Lily repeated evenly.

"And where did you get *that* term from?"

"That's what we are. Why should we just bow down to labels created for us by others? Why? Where is that written?"

My mother was watching Lily with narrowed eyes and then a faint smile crept over her lips. "Seems you've been getting quite an education from this boy."

"He's not a boy."

"Oh, he's a boy."

"Not to *me.*"

They glared at each other with their chests heaving slightly. Tears had sprung into Lily's eyes. I realized then that I'd never seen Lily show that kind of emotion about anything or anyone before.

She took in a deep breath and said, "I didn't want Sophie to have to miss her recital. And there was no other way to get there. He happened to come by for some tool or something he left and I asked him to take us."

I was amazed at the effortless way Lily lied, but she hadn't thought of everything.

"In a suit."

"He was on his way to some event or something."

"Your father was supposed to take her."

"We didn't know that. Daddy never said anything."

My mother dismissed that and got back to the subject at hand. "That boy looked like he was more than a friend. You had your heads together like two thieves."

"He wanted to stay. I couldn't tell him no, could I, after he was being so nice? Anyway we only had one program between us, so we had to share it."

"With your arms looped."

"I was just being friendly . . . gracious."

Amazing.

"I hope I don't find out that the truth is something other than this version," my mother said. "I can always send you down to Atlanta early. One of Dovie's sorority sisters happens to live not far from the campus. I'm sure she would welcome you in a heartbeat and be happy to show you around before your freshman year starts. In fact, now that I think about it, it probably would be better for you to spend a couple of days with one of Dovie's sorority sisters. Yes. I might just arrange that as soon as possible."

I watched my sister grow still. I recognized that pose. She said nothing, but I felt a cool stubbornness. My mother would not be putting Lily on a plane and sending her anywhere early.

"Can I take Sophie to see *Cat Ballou*?" she asked, ignoring our mother's threat. "Just to get her mind off things?"

My mother didn't answer right away. Then she said, "Don't think I'm kidding." She held Lily's eyes for a few seconds. Then she added, "Straight to the movies and then straight home. I'm exhausted. I'm going to go lie down."

Lily wasn't taking me to a movie—at least, not then. I suspected she was going to prowl around looking for Nathan.

She glanced at me in the passenger's seat. "We're going to drive around a bit first," she said as she started up our mother's Grand Prix. Her eyes seemed wild and determined. She looked over her shoulder and backed out of the driveway.

"Where are we going?"

"Just driving around here and there."

We got onto Vernon Boulevard and headed east.

"What street are we looking for?"

"Let's see where Mrs. Baylor lives," she said, ignoring my question. "Aren't you curious?"

"No." But I *was* curious about where Nathan lived.

Eventually we were passing barbershops and barbecue joints and wig shops. Trash-strewn lots and littered sidewalks. "You know how to get there?" I asked.

"You just go east. You keep going east until you get to Avalon. She lives near a hundred and fourteenth."

"How do you know all that?"

"I think she mentioned it once."

That seemed unlikely. "You're not going to stop when you get there, right?"

There was a moment of hesitation, then, "Right."

She was lying.

I looked out the window as Vernon transformed into the ghetto. We passed more liquor stores, storefront churches, and mom-and-pop stores.

"When are you telling Mom? That you might not be going to Spelman?"

She didn't answer right away. Then, "What gives you that impression?"

"I just have a feeling."

"Well, you can quit nagging," she said, checking street signs. She turned to me. "When did you get to be such a nag?"

I noticed she didn't deny it.

"This is Avalon," I said as she was about to go past. She made a right and began checking the numbers.

"We're in the forties," I noted.

She turned on the radio. Commercials. I watched the house numbers until we got to the hundreds.

"Start looking for Nathan's car on your side," she said. "I just want to make sure he's okay, that's all. After what happened."

"Because you're his *friend*."

"Right."

The streets were lined with small clapboard houses. Some had chainlink fences around weeded-over front yards with toys strewn about. One had a car up on blocks right on the front lawn.

"I don't see it," Lily said under her breath. "Where *is* it?"

"Maybe he's out of town."

She turned to look at me with eyes narrowed and accusing. "Why are you being so ridiculous, Sophie? Of course he's not out of town!"

She spoke with an air of desperation. I didn't realize I was being ridiculous. It seemed like a good explanation.

She huffed. "Maybe I'll just park and get out of the car, go up to one of those doors." She nodded at a random house. "Ring the doorbell, and ask whoever answers the door if they know a Nathan Baylor. Or a Nigel Baylor."

"Why are you doing this, Lily?"

"Doing what?" She'd slowed down to a crawl and her eyes were darting from one side of the street to the other.

"Searching for Nathan."

She didn't answer. She just kept her eyes on the passing driveways. Then suddenly she stopped by a house where an older woman stood in front, watering her lawn. Lily got out of the car with a big disarming smile on her face.

The lady aimed the hose out of Lily's path and toward some rosebushes growing along the edge of the lawn as she approached. I couldn't hear them, but I knew Lily was asking her if she knew where Mrs. Baylor lived. My sister was in luck because the woman immediately pointed to the house directly across the street. Lily looked like she wanted to give her a hug.

She hurried across the street, went up to the front door, and rang the bell. She put her head to the door, to listen for approaching footsteps probably. She rang the doorbell again. She waited. Finally, she turned away and came back to the car.

"You got any paper?"

I pulled out the pad I usually carried in my canvas bag. I tore off a sheet, then dug around until I found my pencil.

My sister could be so dramatic. She scribbled a note, folded it, and got out of the car. She crossed the street again and tucked the note in the screen door. She looked back once to make sure it was still there as she returned.

Then she sat behind the wheel, drumming it and thinking.

"Maybe he's at Thirty-One Flavors," I said, trying to be helpful. She seemed to ignore this, until she said, "If you're going to make suggestions, please let them make sense."

Then something happened. Something startling. Right there in my mother's car—in the passenger seat. This thing that happens only to girls. It happened to Jennifer last month. She called me the day after. I knew it was something huge, but she wouldn't tell me what. She just told me to get over there, quick. I put away my green binder and went over there fast. I'd still been writing that stupid *Fleur and Lizeth* book and having the main characters vacation in London. It didn't feel natural. I'd looked up information in the library and in our *Encyclopedia Britannica,* but I still felt I didn't know London well enough. So I was happy to slip the binder under the bed and hurry to Jennifer's.

She met me at the door and gestured for me to follow her up the stairs to her bedroom on the second floor. Jennifer's staircase always made me wish I lived in a two-story house instead of a split-level.

As soon as we crossed the threshold of her bedroom, Jennifer pointed to several items on her bed. There was a sanitary belt, a box of Kotex, and a little pamphlet entitled *When Your Body Changes*. All that was lacking was Jennifer taking a bow.

I was speechless. I didn't get it. I was taller and had just started growing breasts—more than what Jennifer had. How was it that she'd gotten her period before me? I picked up the pamphlet and flipped through the pages. Maybe there was something in it that I didn't know.

In sixth grade, all the girls had been taken to the auditorium for a special film on the subject. When we returned to the classroom, Stanley Harvey, who sat next to me, badgered me about why only the girls had seen the film and what was it about and how come the boys weren't allowed to get out of math drills and go? It wasn't fair.

I wasn't going to tell him. I didn't particularly like Stanley Harvey. He called me touchy just because I'd drawn an eraser line down the middle of the table we shared and asked that he not cross it. Especially when he came in from recess dripping sweat.

I stared at Jennifer. She didn't look any different. "Are you wearing one of those right now?" I asked, gesturing toward the box of Kotex.

She slowly nodded. "Yep," she said.

I must have looked forlorn because she added, "Don't worry —you'll be starting yours soon."

And she was right. I was feeling something strange, right then and there.

"Um, Lily," I said.

"What, what, what?"

"I think I just started my period."

"What?"

"Yeah."

"Okay. We're outta here."

Our mother was napping when we got home. So Lily gave me what I needed, including a little pill in case I got cramps, which I'd heard could be so bad, they could make you faint. Or vomit.

"Unfortunately this pill only helps a little bit. I don't know why they claim it does more." She dropped it into my hand and went to the kitchen to get me a glass of water. I sat down on my bed and waited.

"Should I tell Mom?" I asked when she returned with the water.

"Of course tell Mom. But I wouldn't wake her up to tell her."

Lily reached over and picked up the receiver of our Princess phone. She listened for the dial tone. She was doing this a lot these days—checking to see if the phone was still working. At the sound of the tone, she got a funny look on her face, as if she was trying not to cry. She replaced the receiver, sat down on the end of her bed, and put her face in her hands.

"Lily," I ventured.

She removed her hands and said, "What? What?"

"Are you in love with Mrs. Baylor's son?"

She didn't say anything. It was almost as if she *couldn't* say anything.

The telephone rang and she jumped. She placed her hand on the receiver and waited for it to ring three times, all the while keeping her eyes closed. Then she picked it up and with a cool, calm voice she said, "LaBranche residence." Her shoulders slumped. "I'm sorry. She's not available. May I take a message?" She rolled her eyes at me. "Yes, I have a pencil." There was a pause while Lily closed her eyes again and sighed. "I'll give her the message," she said, and hung up the phone. She hadn't written a thing.

My mother eventually came out of her room. She stood in our doorway and announced that something terrible—absolutely terrible—had happened to the Mansfields.

"I just got off the phone with Dovie." She paused and frowned. "It seems Dale has gone off and gotten himself enlisted —in the *Marines*."

Lily and I looked at each other. He'd done it.

"He's not returning to school. In fact, he's officially dropped out." My mother paused again as if she was trying to take it all in. "He's just gone off—devil may care—and broken his mother's heart." She shook her head. "What's this world coming to? How could he do that to his parents?" She didn't wait for us to answer. She just needed to say these things to reassure herself that we'd never do anything remotely like that—especially Lily.

She clapped her hands once and held them together, sighed a relieved-sounding sigh. "Well. I'm so glad that *I* don't have that problem."

My sister said nothing. She looked at me and got up to leave the room. "Yeah, that's a shame," she said.

"How was the movie?" my mother asked before Lily could get out completely.

"Great," Lily said.

"Yeah, great," I added.

"What was it about?"

"Oh, you know, music," Lily said.

"Music? I thought you were going to see *Cat Ballou*."

Lily didn't miss a beat. "We were, but then Sophie wanted to see *The Sound of Music*."

"Ah. *The Sound of Music*," she said. "Was it good?"

"Spectacular."

CHAPTER 19
Letter

O N SATURDAY, LILY DIDN'T have to be at Marcia
Stevens until noon. They'd be doing inventory after
the store closed. That worked out for her because the
night before she'd gone to a birthday party for one of Lydia's
cousins and she'd gotten back late. Unlike her friends, Lily didn't
like being out late.

"You know what?" she once confided. "Sometimes when
I'm getting ready to go out—like when someone's coming to
pick me up—I look at my bed and the book on the nightstand
and the glow of the lamp and I realize, I'd just rather stay home
and read."

"Really?"

"Yeah, really."

For the past few days she'd been quiet and brooding. I figured out that she was bound to see Nathan again because there was more work my mother needed him to do. Lily'd probably come to this conclusion, as well.

The night before, when Lydia came to pick up Lily, she'd pulled me aside. Lily had run back to our room to get her sweater.

"Don't pester her too much," Lydia advised, her eyes under hoods of bright blue shadow, her hair teased into a chestnut-colored globe surrounding a face that suddenly seemed too small for all that hair. "She's trying to adjust to being dropped."

My mouth fell open. Dropped. She'd been *dropped*.

Now I put the script aside, pulled on yesterday's pedal pushers, and slipped yesterday's T-shirt over my head. I padded to the kitchen barefoot and got the stepladder off the back porch. So far I was feeling fine. No cramps or anything.

I sometimes hid the Frosted Flakes from Daddy at the back of the very top shelf. He loved Frosted Flakes and tended to eat them all up in record time.

As I was climbing down from the stepladder with cereal box in hand, a voice from the breakfast nook said, "Hey, Sophia."

I whipped around, surprised. Nathan was sitting with his back against the wall at the end of the bench. "What are you doing here?" I asked.

"I'm picking up my mother for a dentist appointment before

she goes home for the weekend." I suspected that he'd come inside on purpose. He could have easily waited for her in his car.

I took a bowl down and got the milk from the refrigerator. I didn't know what to say or even if he was expecting me to say something. I heard Lily then, shuffling down the hall on her way to the kitchen, her slippered feet making a swishing sound on the hardwood floor. She was wearing her pajamas and robe, her hair falling down from what was once a neatly twisted French roll. She yawned and opened the refrigerator to see what she felt like eating. It was going to be another long work day. Then she must have seen Nathan in her side vision because she jumped and clutched her robe at her throat.

She looked at him with her face reddening, then quickly looked away. She went about the business of gathering breakfast items, her lips pressed together against saying anything. She got the eggs and juice out of the refrigerator and the bread out of the bread box.

Determined, it seemed, to ignore him, she took in a deep breath and proceeded to crack an egg into a bowl.

"Lily," he said, and his voice sounded odd and sad.

She didn't answer. She began to whip the egg. "You here to pick up your mother?" she asked finally.

"She has a dentist appointment."

"I see." She stooped to get a pan out of a cabinet under the counter, then turned toward the stove. "I think you've been play-ing around with me," she said. She glanced over at me. I'd settled across from Nathan with my bowl of Frosted Flakes, pretending that I wasn't paying attention to anything. Her look told me to find some other place to eat my breakfast.

I got up and moved to the dining room. I was still within earshot.

"You know better than that," Nathan said once I'd left the kitchen.

"I've been waiting for you to call me and explain things and let me know you're all right. And—nothing. You've had me wor-ried about you for days. For you, I think, I was just something . . . different."

"What makes you think you're different?" Nathan asked.

My sister didn't say anything. But I knew what she meant.

"Oh, because you can be mistaken for white? On occasion?"

"That's not what I meant."

"Oh, I get it. Because my mother works for your mother?"

"And maybe you just wanted to play around with me for that reason."

I could hear the tears and hurt in Lily's voice. She thought she was right. She must have been thinking and thinking about this.

He laughed, and that was the wrong thing to do. "You really

believe you're something. Well, I don't live on Avalon anymore. I live in Berkeley *most* of the year, remember? And I'm surrounded by girls who have much more privilege than you, and guess what? They're just now turning to guys like me. Trying to put a little spice in their lives. It's on their list of things to do. You're not special."

"I didn't say I was."

There was silence.

"I left a note on your door."

"I know. Thank you for being concerned."

Mrs. Baylor came into the room. I heard Nathan scoot to the end of the padded bench in the breakfast nook and pull himself up. After a bit, I heard my sister sit down and start in on her breakfast.

And that's the way they broke up—if they'd even been together in the first place. I was glad I'd been there to witness it all. I knew I'd never get anything more from Lily. She turned inward over the next week and acted as if she wasn't bothered about a thing. I couldn't even tell Jennifer about this latest turn of events because she was at sleep-away camp.

On Monday morning Nathan was back on the ladder, putting a second coat of white paint on the window sill next to the front porch. I caught sight of him when my mother sent me out to get the morning paper. He waved and I waved back, feeling a little like a traitor. On Saturday Lily had spent the night at Lydia's. They'd gone to a movie and then Lydia had dropped her back home. I was glad. She could put her mind on other things.

When I went back inside, I looked out the den window and could feel Nathan's watchfulness with every paint stroke. I knew he was hoping to see her. I just knew it. In a way, it was as if he'd broken up with me as well. I thought of the three of us swinging at the beach. Didn't that mean anything to him? How about singing "My Girl" as we drove around Pacific Palisades. Hadn't it been fun—all of us together? I decided to go outside, stand on the curb, and wait on the Helms man and see what Nathan had to say. See if he was going to talk to me. I had two dimes—enough for two doughnuts.

"You waiting on the Helms man?"

"Yeah," I said, feeling a bit disloyal to my sister. After all, he'd *dropped* her. But there was that small part of me that was satisfied he'd spoken first.

Then he was setting his brush on the edge of the paint can balanced on the ladder's little tray and climbing down. He reached in his pocket and took out a quarter. "Can you get me a bear claw?"

I nodded quickly and looked toward the front door. Lily hadn't left for work yet. "Okay," I said.

He sat on the porch after I handed him his pastry and gestured for me to join him. I settled on the top step.

"I have to apologize," he said. "I guess I seemed kind of"— he stopped and sighed—"rude and callous."

"Yes, you did," I said directly.

"I'm sorry. I was just so angry, I had to be alone to . . . *think*. Does that make sense?"

I nodded, though I didn't believe it did—because why did he have to say those mean things to my sister about her thinking she was special?

He glanced my way. "Do you think she'll speak to me?"

I shrugged and stared straight ahead. "I don't know," I said. I could feel him looking at me. He stood up and reached into his back pocket. He pulled out an envelope—sealed. "Will you give her this?" He put it in my hand, and it was as if I was taking it almost against my will.

"I'm counting on you," he said. Then he pulled the bear claw out of the bag and took a big bite.

"Mom up?" Lily asked when I came inside. She'd overslept and now she was hurrying to get into her work outfit and muttering under her breath. "I'll have to call Lydia and see if she can give me a ride." She noticed the pastry bag in my hand. "You got doughnuts?" She uncoiled her hair, ran a brush through it two or three times, and then pulled it up into a ponytail.

"Here," I said, handing her a glazed doughnut.

"Mmm, breakfast."

"Mom's still asleep. I think."

"Don't forget to tell her about your period. Why are you waiting? Go on and get it over with."

I nodded. Why *was* I waiting? Why did I feel embarrassed to tell her?

Lily was now looking in the mirror, putting eyeliner on her lower lid.

Without saying anything, I handed her Nathan's letter.

"What's this?" She frowned at my offering.

"It's from Nathan."

Lily met my eyes in the mirror. She seemed to stop breathing.

She sat down on her bed, held the envelope with both hands, and stared at it on her lap. Then she glanced up at me with a pleading look in her eyes.

I went up into the den to watch morning cartoons. When I heard the door slam, I looked out the window in time to see Lily hurrying toward Lydia's idling car, passing Nathan without a word—not even glancing his way. He noticed this—and I knew he was surprised and disappointed.

When I heard the car drive off, I rushed into our room to search for the letter. I looked in her drawers, under her bed, under the area rug, in her cigarette hiding spot in the bathroom cabinet under the sink . . .

Finally, I gave up. She must have taken it with her to show Lydia.

Then I heard my mother moving around in her room. I knocked on her door.

"Come in," she said.

I entered and stood just inside. She was propped up in her bed, reading a book. The other side of the bed looked still made. I stared at it for a few moments.

"Did you want to talk to me?" my mother asked.

"I have something to tell you."

She patted my father's side of the bed—the made-up side. It felt strange sitting on it.

"Spill it," she said, trying to sound lighthearted, I supposed.

"I started my period a few days ago."

I could tell I'd taken her by surprise because her eyes widened for just a second. Then she was all business. "Do you know what to do?"

"Lily told me."

My mother looked relieved. She wouldn't have to give me instructions about the messiness of it. Lily had told me hygiene was key—especially during that time of the month. And not to flush pads down the toilet, and to soak soiled underwear in cold water. "Make sure it's cold," she had emphasized. And there were pills for cramps, and to expect pain the first few days of every period. Expect it to make you feel like you're going to throw up or faint.

"And you have what you need?"

I nodded.

"Well," my mother said. "I guess everything is all taken care of, then."

I didn't ask Lily about any of her business. I just watched her. Watched her as she came and went. Spied Nathan observing her when she left for work or when Lydia dropped her off from a sleepover. I liked the way Lydia and Lily pulled up with the radio blasting and I liked watching Lily hop out of the car as if she was way past the tears she'd spilled over Nathan—as if she hardly noticed him up on that ladder, putting a second coat on our window sills.

But one day, as she sailed by, he caught her with a straight-forward "You not gonna speak to me?" There was no pretending she didn't see him then. She stopped and looked back at him standing there in the middle of the walkway. "Oh, hello."

"That's better," he said.

I waited in the shadows of our wood-paneled den. But they moved in opposite directions, like two ships sailing to different ports. What had he written in that letter? Whatever it was, it didn't seem to matter to Lily.

I was bored. Jennifer was still at sleep-away camp, and I wasn't in the mood for writing. I'd abandoned Minerva to concentrate on Olivia, and now I felt too blah to think about Olivia. I'd finished reading *Footlights* and I'd finished a diorama of a stage scene.

There was Oscar, but tossing him a ball just did not appeal to me. I could walk to the community center and see if Anthony Cruz was playing Ping-Pong. That idea did seem appealing. I could hang out on the curtained stage and peek through the opening at the cute boys.

But then I thought some more. Could I go there on my own? Actually walk in and go around unnoticed? Lily would do it— and dare anyone to even look at her funny. She had no fear. Not even of that white policeman who called Nathan a nigger. She'd dared ask him if he was in the Ku Klux Klan. If anyone looked at her funny, she was liable to get in their face and tell them, "Why don't you take a picture? It'll last longer." If only I could be like Lily.

I decided if I was going to visit the community center alone, I needed Oscar's support. I put him on his leash, and when I came around the corner of the house, I saw Nathan in the process of moving the ladder. He settled it and took the paintbrush in his hand. He put the can of paint on the ladder's little shelf and raked the brush against the rim. His hair was covered in a kerchief.

Oscar yanked on the leash, ready to go. I looked up the street in the direction of the center, feeling anxious. But Oscar was in charge. He seemed to know where we were headed; he led the way to Angeles Vista—past the Bakers' and the Cruzes', and up Presidio. I was sweating by the time I got there and anticipating the gust of cool air the moment I would walk into the air-conditioned community center. I tied Oscar's leash to the bicycle rack and went in through the glass doors. Immediately, I spotted all three Baker sisters sitting at a round table with several other girls, working on lanyards under the direction of a community center worker. The arts and crafts person, I guessed.

I looked around. Two boys—older—were at the foosball table. Anthony Cruz was not playing Ping-Pong. In fact, he was nowhere to be seen. I suddenly didn't know what to do. I noticed Deidre and Jilly assess me and suddenly go into a huddle.

I glanced at the stage. Looking back over my shoulder at the Baker girls, I headed in its direction. I'd just gotten my foot on the first step when I heard a whistle. It filled the room and seemed to bounce off the four walls. All the kids stopped what they were doing and fell silent. "Excuse me," the counselor called to me. "No getting on the stage." I stepped back down. "Can you come over here please?"

I complied. She stood up and met me in the middle of the room. "Follow me, please."

I could see Deidre and Jilly tittering with excitement.

The counselor led me away from them, out of earshot. She looked down at me kindly. "I want to ask you something." She smiled encouragingly. I waited. "Last week the wallet of one of my co-counselors went missing from her purse, which was kept in an unlocked desk drawer. Do you know anything about that?" She searched my face.

I looked back at Deidre and Jilly and realized they could hear us. They had knowing smirks on their faces. Had she asked them who might have taken the wallet and they had suggested *me?*

I couldn't speak right away. I just shook my head slowly. "I don't know anything about that," I said, and wondered if I sounded like I was telling the truth. Because I *was.*

She put her hand on my shoulder and smiled. "I would like you not to sneak around the center. We have all kinds of fun activities, but the offices and the stage and the kitchen are off-limits. Do you understand what I'm saying?"

I nodded, realizing suddenly that I just wanted to get out

of there—away from a place where people would think I'd *steal*. When I'd never stolen anything in my life. Not even a pencil from school! If Jennifer had been there, she could have vouched for me—and that counselor would believe her, because Jennifer is white.

Something really unsettling crossed my mind, then. What if I had to go through this for the rest of my life? Always, people looking at *me*—with suspicion.

Oscar was really taking his own sweet time, stopping to sniff at every bush, every tossed fast-food wrapper. We'd just turned down Presidio when I heard someone calling my name. I looked back to see Deidre Baker, her two sisters, and another girl I didn't recognize. I kept walking.

"Bet you're not so brave now that you don't have Jennifer to hide behind!" Jilly yelled.

"Or your sister!" Deirdre called out.

Something came over me then. It seemed to rise up from the center of my whole being and take over. I stopped. I turned around and stood there rooted in my spot. They were coming— all four of them—and I suddenly couldn't wait. *Come on, come on.* The words were playing in my mind on a loop. I looked around. I just needed to find a stick on the ground.

Oscar, sensing something, began his low growl. I had an

anger in me that felt as if a volcano were in the center of my chest and was about to explode. I took a step toward them. I looked from one to the other and waited. I was filled with the waiting. *Come on, come on — get here!*

They slowed to a stop, seeming to suddenly sense danger in the situation. Could they have picked up something in the way I stopped, turned to them, and now waited with the growling Oscar on the leash? Deidre called out, "You'd better be glad you have that dog, 'cause if you didn't, you'd sure be sorry."

I stood there and suddenly realized I was breathing hard, but they were turning away from me to take another route home. I wanted to kiss Oscar. "Good dog," I said.

Nathan was packing up when I came around the side of the house to put Oscar in the backyard. "Hey," he said.

"Hey," I answered in a very small voice.

He did a double take as he pulled his tarp off our hibiscus bush. "What's up?" He stooped to pet Oscar.

"Nothing."

"You sound down."

My tears started then and they surprised me. I didn't even know I was going to cry. He stood up and led me to the porch. I sat down and he sat next to me on the steps.

"It's not fair," I blurted out.

"What's not fair?"

"I went to the center just to hang around, since my only friend is at sleep-away camp. Just to . . . I want to be in this play, and I wanted to get on the stage and see how it felt when I said my lines, and I wasn't bothering *anybody*. And this woman, this counselor who teaches crafts . . . She asked me if I knew anything about a wallet getting stolen! And I don't know anything about someone's wallet getting stolen, but I think that was just her way of asking me if I stole it." I paused for air.

Nathan looked off. "Yeah, it was," he said. I thought he was going to say, *No, you're wrong.* He continued. "Yeah, a wallet went missing a week ago and today you happen to walk by."

"It's not *fair!* I've never even stolen a pencil from school."

"That doesn't matter. Don't you know that?"

I took in a deep, shuddery breath. "But why?"

"There's not enough time in the day to tell you why."

"I want to try out for this play and that woman might be one of the judges and she's going to think I'm a thief and not let them pick me."

"Do it anyway," he said simply, but not with the kind of encouragement in his voice that I needed. "Always just do things like that anyway."

I got up and took Oscar around the back. I unbuckled his leash and knelt down beside him to give him extra pets and hugs. He had defended me. My sweet little Oscar.

Days passed. Nathan was now a person Lily was expert at ignoring. When she left for her job, she walked past him, holding her head high and her eyes steady on the street ahead of her. If he spoke, she would respond in the most curt, icily polite way. Eventually the window sills were completely done—two coats—and my mother had Nathan start on the wood railing of our front porch.

Sometimes I watched him out the window and wondered what he had written in that letter.

Then, finally, Jennifer was back. I stood at my den window and watched as her stuff was unloaded from her family's station wagon. I waited a bit, then went across the street to her house. I wanted her to hear me say my parts without my even glancing at the script.

"Hey, what happened to Minerva?" Jennifer said as she dumped the contents of her duffle bag onto her bed. The scent of pine and what I imagined the bottom of a lake would smell like filled the room.

"I don't have time for that right now. I'm trying to be perfect with this part. Tryouts are tomorrow. Can we go over our lines?"

"I don't need to. I memorized everything while I was away at camp."

"But don't you want to go over everything?"

She shrugged and looked shifty somehow. I flopped down on one of her twin beds. Jennifer's parents, anticipating her every possible need (slumber parties, future popularity, and things like that), had given her two beds. I wondered what it was like to be an only child and the center of your parents' world.

We sat facing each other. Finally, she said, "Anyway, Linda Cruz's mother is taking us to the movies. We kind of got to be friends, 'cause, you know, we were at sleep-away camp together."

"A movie?"

"Yeah. She's really kind of nice, actually."

I suddenly felt a little dizzy. It was fear. The kind of fear you have to hide behind a fake smile.

"So now you're friends?"

"Not best friends like us, but—friends."

"Oh."

"I know what you're thinking," Jennifer said. "And I told her that what she said was prejudiced, and I think she understands that now."

I didn't say anything. I just sat there fiddling with some piping on the bedspread. There was a strangeness in the silence that followed, as if it was full of unspoken words. And the words were *you want to go?* Followed by *you can't go with us because it's just Linda Cruz and me going.*

I thought about what Linda had said about her father—that if I came up their walkway, he would just turn me around and send me back home. It made me feel as if someone had slapped me. I told Jennifer I had to go because Lily and her friend Nathan were taking *me* to a movie. Which wasn't true. But it was the only way I could save face on such short notice.

Jennifer quietly walked me to her front porch. "We can practice our lines tomorrow morning," she said. "Right before try-outs." She gave me a little apologetic smile before she closed the door.

"What's Sophia up to today?" Nathan asked.

I was sitting on the top step of the stairs that led down to the backyard's lower level, thinking about the situation with Jennifer. The script was balanced on my knees, but I didn't feel like doing anything with it. I just wanted to sit there and think. "Nothing."

"How's Lily?" he asked next, and that was probably his real question. He had already packed up to go. Now he was squatting by the outdoor faucet, cleaning his brushes.

"She's fine."

"Is she working today?"

"I think so."

"What do you have there?"

"My script for the play."

"Oh yeah, that." He looked off into the distance, considering this. "Just don't let them make you the maid."

That caught me off-guard because the play did have a cafeteria lady, and that was close to being a maid. I smiled, but he'd given me a new worry. *Don't let them make you the maid.*

I went inside to study the script in the den. Halfway through reading everybody's parts as well as my own, I suddenly knew where Lily had stashed the letter. In her jewelry box under the false bottom! Why hadn't I thought of that before?

Lily was gone, my mother was gone, Mrs. Baylor was in the kitchen cooking. I almost had the house to myself. I marched directly to our room and to the jewelry box on Lily's dresser, opened it, poured the jewelry onto the dresser, and pulled up the false bottom. And there it was. She hadn't thrown it away.

Suddenly nervous, I looked around. I put the jewelry back in and positioned the box just the way I'd found it. I hurried to the bathroom, closed the door, found a comfortable position on the edge of the bathtub, and placed the envelope on my knees. I looked at it for a moment, then pulled the folded page out and

spread it on my lap, my heart beating wildly. He had nice hand-
writing.

Lily,

*First, I have to apologize. There's no excuse for the behavior
I exhibited and I don't expect you to forgive me. That was
not the first time I've been stopped. The last time was in
the driveway of a friend from school who happens to live in
Westwood near UCLA. So I don't know why this stop got to
me. Let me move on. You are a very special person and I've
loved being with you, but I fear we come from two different
worlds, and that's going to get in the way. We have two
worldviews. Different goals. And besides, you'll be leaving
soon. I might as well go through the difficulty of that now.
Maybe in a different time and a different place.*

Nathan

Not *Love, Nathan,* I thought. Not *Sincerely, Nathan.* Just *Nathan.*

Why, I'd be cool too in response to such a letter. There was
not very much love on that page. And that was another thing —
such a short letter. What was that about? I didn't blame Lily at
all. *At all!*

I carefully refolded it, slipped the stupid letter back into its envelope, and quickly returned it to its place in the jewelry box. Again, I positioned the jewelry box just so. I picked up my script and settled on my bed. Auditions were a day away. *A day away.*

CHAPTER 20
Auditions

I WOKE UP WITH butterflies in my stomach. This was the day. I'd be Olivia or I wouldn't. I would impress everyone, or they'd just feel sorry for me. I knew my lines backwards and forward. And I didn't sound wooden the way some people who weren't born actresses do, which I suspected I was—along with being born to write. I said my lines with feeling and heart and confidence.

I rolled onto my back and put my hands behind my head. Then I began to go through my opening lines again—and Jennifer's, when Julie sweetly asks Miss Ornsby, her English teacher, if she can write a recommendation for Julie's college application. And I get to say from my place in the attic, "Julie Simmons calls our English teacher Old Slime Mouth. At some point during class, strings of spit are likely to form in the corners of her mouth." (Ew! I could relate to that.) "Though Julie laughs at everyone, she especially likes to laugh at Miss Ornsby and say, 'No wonder Miss Ornsby isn't married. Can you imagine living with that on a daily basis?'"

Lily stirred in her bed. I looked over at her and lowered my voice to a whisper. She was probably dreaming of Nathan.

Auditions were at two. I wondered if Jennifer was going to remember we were supposed to spend the morning running our lines. I planned to wait and see. It would be easy to fill the time until two o'clock if there were no auditions, but waiting for them made every hour leading up to two feel empty and irritating—a means of turning anticipation into torture.

Eventually, Lily came up on her elbow. "What are you doing?"

"Rehearsing for tryouts."

"That's today?"

"Yeah."

She looked at me and then quickly turned away. She said, "Okay, now you know this might have nothing to do with who's the best person for the role. You know that, right?"

"What do you mean?"

"You don't know who your competition is. You're probably the youngest girl trying out for that role."

"I know Deidre Baker and her friend Carla are trying out."

Lily closed her eyes and moaned. Then she went on to remind me that I was black, for one thing. So did I really think they'd make Olivia black? Did I, really?

I'd been noticing Lily using the word *black* these days at every opportunity, as if she liked the feel of it in her mouth, the shock of it and the defiance. I remembered the time this boy in fourth grade got punched in the mouth because he called Stanley Harvey black in front of our white classmates. But when Lily said it, the word had something strong behind it. Something exciting. And I knew she got that from Nathan.

"I think I'll get the part anyway," I said, feeling brave and confident.

"Mmm."

That sure was a downer. I ran that thoughtful "Mmm" through my head over and over. I wished she hadn't said that. It told me there was something behind it that maybe I should pay attention to. Well, that certainly had me quiet as Jennifer and I walked down Angeles Vista toward the community center. She hadn't come over until it was time to head to the center. Just as I'd thought.

Jennifer noticed something. "What's wrong?"

"Nothing."

As soon as we entered the auditorium, we saw that the entire first row was filled with kids sitting according to the role they were trying out for. There were eight girls in the "Julie Section" and six in the "Olivia Section." I signed my name under "Olivia" on the roster that had been placed on a table by the door and sat down behind Carla. She turned around and regarded me with a smile that looked more like a sneer. I wanted to give her the finger, but I didn't. I just stared down at my script and pretended to read. I didn't have to. I'd memorized the whole play—word for word.

I looked around for Anthony Cruz but didn't see him. I wondered if he'd be trying out for a part—but I didn't tell Jennifer what I was wondering.

Marcy Baker craned her neck and peered around the girl next to her to get a good look at me. I didn't know why she was there, since she was too young to try out for anything. Her older sisters were wearing their hair alike. Big teased bubbles. Marcy rolled her eyes and giggled. Jilly and Deidre joined her.

Deidre got up and came over to me. She looked down and said, "There aren't any colored parts in this play. Don't you know that?"

"So?" I said.

"So why are you here?"

"You're here," I said. "And there aren't any parts for bimbos." She had no comeback. She returned to her seat in a huff. I couldn't help smiling at my fast response.

Finally, a middle-aged woman in a blue plaid shirtwaist dress stepped forward. She tapped the mic a few times until she heard an echo. "Good morning, future thespians!" she said with enthusiasm. "My name is Mrs. Milay and I am the director of cultural activities at this center. I am so excited to be involved in our first teen play. I know you're all anxious to get started, so let me introduce you to my assistant, Miss Marburn."

My heart sank as I watched Miss Marburn approach. She was the same person who had nearly accused me of stealing someone's wallet a few days before. Miss Marburn stepped forward and put her mouth too close to the mic. "Hi, everyone!" She scanned the room. She spotted me and her smile seemed to stiffen, but maybe that was just my imagination. She turned back to the mic and said, "So, future thespians, this is how it's going to work: we are going to put you in scenes from the play that include as many roles as possible." There was a ripple of excitement in the air. "That way, the audition should move along quickly and smoothly. At this point you don't know what scene you'll be in, so you just have to be ready for anything."

Some of the kids laughed nervously and looked at each other.

I swallowed.

Carla looked back at me and rolled her eyes.

Miss Marburn continued, "I just want you to have fun! Remember, this is meant to be *fun!*" That's the way she wanted us to think about this audition—each and every one of us, according to her. She stopped and gave us all a special stare. When her eyes alighted on me for the second time, they lingered just a tiny bit, but I caught them. Then she gave me a big, fake, bright-eyed smile. And I thought, *That's what they can do. They can think bad things about you and plaster over it with a big false smile.*

The first scene was in the cafeteria where Julie is asking Chet, her boyfriend, to get her another piece of cake and he's telling her that the last time he did that for her, Miss Brown, the cafeteria lady, caught him and threatened to write him up. Olivia, from her place in the attic, does her soliloquy about how Julie uses the doting Chet and what Julie really thinks of him. Tish, Best Friend Number Two, is also in the scene and, doing Julie's bidding, urges Chet to get the cake. Miss Brown, the cafeteria lady, is standing at the register.

A girl I didn't recognize was called up as Julie, some boy I'd never seen before was Chet, and Carla was Olivia. Carla suddenly didn't look quite so glib. And I didn't feel so glib, either. My mouth felt dry. And was Anthony Cruz going to show up to try out for anything or not?

They all had their scripts in their hands. Even with scripts, the kids playing Julie and Chet had to be prompted several times. What was with them? Had they just heard about auditions this morning and decided to mosey on by? How could people be so casual?

A girl whom I'd seen at the center the first time Jennifer and I had gone there was trying out as Julie's friend Tish. She'd been called up for the scene where Tish asks Julie if she could please take a babysitting job for her so she can go to her grandmother's eightieth birthday celebration, and Julie says she already has to babysit her niece. It's a lie, of course.

Then Deidre was called up for the role of Olivia. I stopped breathing for a few seconds. When Jennifer was called as Julie, I sat up straight and willed her to do great. Two more kids trying out for the roles of Miss Ornsby, the English teacher, and Chet, the boyfriend were called up as well.

I was on the edge of my seat. Deidre gave an absolutely wooden performance. She didn't know her lines. Even when prompted, she couldn't find her place. Miss Marburn had to point it out to her. It was a beautiful thing to watch.

And it was wonderful to see Jennifer give a perfect audition as Julie. She got the scene where she approaches her teacher for the recommendation while Chet waits in the hall. When Miss Marburn attempted to hand Jennifer the script, Jennifer said sweetly, "Oh, I don't need that. I know all of Julie's lines." Miss Marburn stepped back, turned to the assembly, and said, "I'm *impressed.*"

A shiver passed through me. If she was impressed with Jennifer, she was going to be doubly impressed with me because I knew my lines and everyone else's too. I could prompt them each time they stumbled. I sighed and felt a warm sense of satisfaction. I just had to wait.

And wait, because I wasn't being called up. I was watching everyone else get summoned to the stage to audition for the roles they'd signed up for, but I wasn't hearing my name. Then Mrs. Milay was thanking everyone for coming and trying out and that the results would be posted in about a week's time and everybody should be patient and . . . Jennifer looked back at me and frowned. She jumped up and motioned to me to join her. Then she led the way to where Miss Marburn was writing something on a sheet of paper attached to a clipboard.

"Miss Marburn, Sophie didn't get called," Jennifer blurted out.

Miss Marburn looked up. "What, dear?"

Jennifer, her face flushed, and seemingly almost overcome with emotion, said, "You didn't call Sophie. She's trying out for Olivia."

"Oh?"

I couldn't speak. I could only stand there swallowing again and again and breathing fast. I was trying not to cry. Because whatever mean thing she was going to do, she would cover it up with smiles and "dears," and "I'm so sorrys."

Instead, she slapped her forehead and said, "Oh, my mistake!"

I was filled with relief. I watched Miss Marburn look around a bit helplessly. Kids were filing out of every exit door of the auditorium. She turned back to me, shrugged, and widened her eyes as if helpless.

"No, no," Jennifer said hurriedly. "We can do the scene where Julie is trying to decide which outfit to wear to her sister's graduation dinner and Olivia reveals that Julie's always been jealous of her older sister and how she managed to steal her journalism award—an engraved ink pen. We can do that!" Jennifer said with such a look of pleading in her eyes, Miss Marburn shrugged and said, "Okay. I guess we can do that."

She looked over at Mrs. Milay. "We have one more."

It was flawless. I did my own stage direction. I said my lines without a script. My timing was perfect. And all the while only Mrs. Milay was paying attention. Miss Marburn was packing up and noting something on her clipboard that I suspected had nothing to do with me.

Mrs. Milay clapped when I finished. A polite clap. "Well," she said. "You did a good job." Then her voice seemed to wander off as if she was speaking to herself and maybe to us at the same time. "Such a shame you couldn't do a scene with more partici- pants." She sighed. "Well, you do know the results will be posted in a week's time." She smiled. "Check back then and . . ." She held up crossed fingers on both hands. "Fingers crossed!"

I would not cry in front of Jennifer, who kept chattering on and on about how we were going to get the parts and how this was just the beginning because now she knew she wanted to be an actress and wasn't it great that we lived so close to Hollywood and . . . She must have sensed my morose silence because she stopped and looked over at me. "Don't worry, Sophie. We were the best. They have to be fair!"

That was the problem. They didn't have to be fair at all. They could do whatever they wanted.

CHAPTER 21
Peach Preserves

MRS. BAYLOR MUST have noticed me moping around the house over the next few days because she pulled me aside and said, "You didn't get that part you was counting on, did you?"

"The results are going to be posted in four days."

"You thinkin' you not going to get it—aren't you thinkin' that?"

I nodded.

"Well." She put a freshly peeled potato in the colander and picked up another one. "You gonna have to develop a thick skin and don't let nothin' stop you. You keep on pushing and you keep on tryin' and you'll get what you workin' for."

"The role of Olivia?" I asked, a little bit hopeful.

She looked at me and shook her head sadly. "I don't think that's for you, child."

I felt a flash of anger. It was as if her words took the role away from me.

"Now's the time to be grateful for what you do have. Don't look at what other people have. You be grateful for what *you* have. Are you sleeping on the street? You going around hungry?"

"But in this country, nobody's sleeping on the street or going hungry."

"Oh yes," she said. "They just not sleeping on the street or going hungry in this neighborhood. Plenty of hungry people here. And they don't know *where* they gonna get their next meal. You put your mind on that." She rinsed the colander of peeled potatoes and stuck it in the refrigerator.

"Now. We gonna get your mind off that play and I'm gonna teach you how to make peach preserves. It's a sin to let them peaches in your yard go to waste. It's like you've forgotten all about that poor tree down there on the lower level. I think the gardener's been takin' peaches home—so at least they're not all going to waste."

So we were going to make peach preserves. I didn't want to. It felt like it was going to be a lot of work: the picking and the peeling. And I'd have to think of the peaches rather than the bad blow that I'd been dealt. And I might want to go over in my mind the situation with Jennifer. Because she hadn't been dealt a bad blow at all. In fact, soon she was going off somewhere with Linda Cruz. I think Linda's mother was taking kids to the movies again. Jennifer would get to see Anthony Cruz. And maybe she would sit next to Anthony and share popcorn. She and Linda were getting oh-so-tight now that they'd been to the same sleep-away camp.

I had a lot of sulking to do, and this peach project might just get in the way of that.

"I forgot the Mason jars, so listen for the doorbell. Nathan's bringing them this morning."

My ears perked up at the sound of Nathan's name. I looked down the hall toward my room, trying to remember if Lily had to work today or not. In my mind, I was pushing them together.

Mrs. Baylor went out to the yard and then backed through the door with a mound of peaches in her apron a while later. She was careful not to let a single one fall. Nathan hadn't arrived yet. What was taking him so long?

"So many going to waste," she said. "So many on the ground." I hoped that wasn't directed at me. Mrs. Baylor had a knack for preaching under her breath, and you felt ruined if you thought she was preaching about you.

I was eating my Cheerios and reading *The Bobbsey Twins and the County Fair Mystery.* I'd already read it—in sixth grade, I think —but I was desperate. I'd finished *Footlights for Jean* and had found myself without a new book. Mrs. Baylor, usually a stickler for manners ("No books at the kitchen table" and "The kitchen is for eating"), didn't say anything.

She just let the peaches fall from her apron into the sink. We did take our peach tree for granted. I thought of it standing there, all lonely, at the bottom of our small hillside, producing its peaches for nobody. Then I thought of the ficus hedge that bordered our yard, and the distant skyline of Los Angeles. I liked sitting at the top of the hillside on clear days and staring at the high-rises and imagining the hundreds of stories of the people who lived there. I didn't even think of our peach tree.

"Now, you get your mind off that play. What will be will be. I'm going to show you how to make peach preserves on this day. You ready to learn?"

I turned my book face-down and yawned. "Okay," I said.

Then I wondered if she would tell me more about her very interesting life. Maybe she would tell me how she'd met Nathan's father. Or how she got the scar on her wrist, right where a watch would go.

Instead, she said to me out of the blue, "You don't get much mothering, do you?" She stood at the kitchen sink, rinsing, while I stealthily checked the scar she wore on her wrist like a badge. I didn't say anything. It felt like she was arranging her thoughts in her head.

"How are you doing without your father?"

"Fine," I said carefully.

"Uh-huh." She filled a big Dutch oven with hot water and placed it on a burner, seeming to have set aside all personal topics. "Now when the water is boilin', you're going to use this here slotted spoon and dip the peaches one by one into it for ten seconds, and then place them in a bowl of cold water. Get me a big bowl out of the pantry."

When the water was boiling, she showed me how to do it.

"This way, the skin will slide off and then you can slice the peaches off the pit."

We soon had almost all the peaches peeled and sliced.

"See how easy that part was?"

I nodded. I finished the rest of the peaches—slicing them and filling the Dutch oven.

The doorbell rang.

"That must be Nathan with my Mason jars," Mrs. Baylor said. "I don't know why he insisted on bringing them today. I won't need them for a while."

I washed my hands and started for the door just as I heard Lily come out of our room. I hung back on purpose, without even knowing that was what I would do. I got there just in time to see her standing in the doorway, reaching for the box of jars and accidentally touching Nathan's hand. She looked at him for two long seconds, and turned scarlet. I saw his helpless, fragile look. Then she backed away to hand me the jars and I knew that was all it took. Soon they would be back together.

As Mrs. Baylor stood at the sink, washing and rinsing the jars, I brought over the bowl and slotted spoon and stood there waiting, looking at the scar on her wrist—how the light from the kitchen window made it look like new baby skin.

"Mrs. Baylor?"

"Hmm?"

"How did you get that scar? On your wrist?" I wondered if she would tell me.

She didn't hesitate. "I was your age. Maybe a little older." She dried a jar with a towel and set it on the table. "I was taking care of my baby sister and I did a very careless thing."

"What did you do?"

She smiled oddly. "One day I was playing with Kate outside my mother's little cottage behind the hotel where she worked. In that house, I slept on a small pallet on the floor in my baby sister's room."

I did not like to think of Mrs. Baylor sleeping on the floor next to that sister in her nice bed.

"We were playing on the lovely grass in front of the cottage. Kate liked to be swung around and around and I loved the sound of her laughter. I began to swing her by the arms—spinning around in a circle. Luckily, when the accident happened, I wasn't swinging very fast. So when I lost hold of her, it was mainly a drop and a thud on the soft grass. But there was a bit of exposed jagged root, and she cut her chin on it. Not enough to make a scar, but enough to break the skin. And there was blood. Kate lost a baby tooth, as well.

"My mother went crazy, thinking Kate would be marred for life and how would she get a good husband when it was time for that with her face all scarred up. My mother had been ironing one of her work uniforms and was still holding the hot iron. She grabbed my hand and burned me with the pointy part of the iron. She felt I needed to be punished.

"I put a cold, wet cloth on it as soon as I could, but it was destined to make a scar. Always to remind me of my careless-ness."

And that little Kate was her mother's favorite, I thought as she bustled around the kitchen, cleaning up and putting things away. Mrs. Baylor added the sugar and spices and some water. She placed the pot over medium heat.

"We will bring it to a boil," she said. "Then we will let the peaches cool and repeat the process five times over two days. It's something that takes patience."

I had patience, and the thought of the peaches turning into preserves over two days seemed magical. Something I could count on.

The next evening, I sat in the kitchen, admiring the jars of peach preserves, which were neatly lined up on the counter. Mrs. Baylor had labeled them: PEACH JAM AUGUST 8TH 1965. I touched one. It was still warm. She had poured the preserves into the jars hours earlier. Their golden color made them look as though they were full of sunshine and happiness. I wanted a piece of bread with warm peach jam. My mouth watered, not just from imagining the taste but also from knowing how much better I'd feel with warm, sweet jam in my mouth. I needed some sunshine and happiness.

CHAPTER 22
It All Comes Down to This

THE DAY THE RESULTS were to be posted, Jennifer and I decided we wouldn't run over to the community center first thing in the morning. We'd wait until early evening. We didn't want to stand among a bunch of other kids, craning our necks and maybe elbowing people out of the way or being elbowed out by them.

No, we would wait until early evening to see the results. Then we could be alone, together—to be happy or sad. Or maybe we'd wait until the next morning. That way, we'd be even more sure of having privacy.

But then, while I ate my Frosted Flakes in the den and watched *Rocky and His Friends,* I heard a car pull up in front of

Jennifer's house. I looked out the window to see her climbing into the back seat of Linda Cruz's dad's station wagon—with her *beach towel.* Soon, I saw Jennifer and Linda in the back seat with their heads coming together like a heart. Even from where I stood in the shadow of the den, I could see the intimacy between them and the happiness of new friendship.

Linda Cruz's dad—the very one who'd just turn me around and send me on my way if I dared approach their house—backed the car out of the driveway and headed toward Olympiad.

I checked the sky. Yes, it was a good day for the beach. But why hadn't she told me? She could've just told me that she and Linda were going to the beach and that was why she'd suggested putting off walking to the community center. She could've just told me.

Now what was I going to do? Walk over to the center? Take Oscar out? Get back to *The Outside Child*? I could write the scene where Minerva's mother takes Minerva to her real father's house and her father's wife gives her lemonade, but she has to go around the back to get it.

The binder was under my bed. I had to be extra quiet because Lily was still asleep. She was off work today. But as soon as I dropped to my knees to reach for it, she sat up and asked, "Did you get it?"

I pulled out my notebook and shrugged. "I don't know yet. They're posting the cast list today, but I don't want to go look when there are people around. Maybe I'll go early tomorrow morning."

She looked at me closely. "Mmm. I guess. You want to go out to breakfast?"

"I just ate some cereal."

"Lunch?"

I looked at her quizzically. Why was she inviting me to lunch out of the clear blue? I thought of Jennifer at the beach with Linda Cruz. "Okay."

Our mother had a headache and was not going anywhere (she had those more and more since our father had moved out). Lily decided to borrow the car on the pretext of helping her out by doing the grocery shopping.

Our mother hated grocery shopping. It was a chore to her. I liked it, because everything that was put in the cart had a future in our kitchen, and I greeted most of the food with anticipation. Lily bought lemon cake mix—and I planned to bake up a lemon cake. There were Popsicles for the really hot days when everyone ran out to buy ice cream. There was root beer for future floats, and chocolate chips for future chocolate chip cookies. I loved selecting things to pile into the cart.

Lily offering to do the grocery shopping was our ace today for using the car. I knew she planned to drive around a bit first. Just for the thrill of it. We drove down Santa Barbara Avenue until it ran out at Central.

"Let's park and walk around," Lily said.

"You just want to do that because you might run into Nathan."

"I no longer care about him." She turned down Central.

"I think you do."

She lowered her voice. "Well, he no longer cares about me."

"He does. I can tell."

"How do you know?" Her voice was full of caution as she kept her eyes on the car in front of us.

"Because when you leave for work, I watch him out the window."

I could see her struggle against a smile. "What does he do?"

"He looks at you until you get to Olympiad and turn the corner."

She drew in her lips and I could tell she was pleased.

"Does he look at me steadily, or does he paint a bit and then look at me?"

"He looks at you almost steadily. Sometimes he'll paint a bit."

"What's the expression on his face?"

"Sad. Plus he's all the time asking about you," I added.

Lily bit her lip. Her face was full of guarded hope. Then she sighed. "Doesn't matter. We're finished."

"I thought you were just friends, anyway."

"We're finished as friends." She squinted as if determined to strengthen her resolve about this. She had an *Anne of Green Gables* kind of grit. "So he watches me until I'm out of sight?"

"Yes."

We'd have to eat lunch first, and then do the grocery shopping. As if it had been her intention all along, she pulled up into the parking lot in front of Prides. I glanced at Lily and she looked like she knew what she was doing. "Daddy's stomping ground," Lily said. "His watering hole."

"No. The Flying Fox is his watering hole," I said. "I don't want to go in if he's there."

"He's not. I heard Mom tell her friend Mabel he's in court this morning."

"How does Mom know?"

"They talk on the phone almost every day. Anyway, he'll be back."

"Why do you say that?"

"Because it's way more fun to sneak around than to be out in the open in a cheap apartment."

"Mom shouldn't take him back," I said.

"And yet she probably will." I looked at Lily quickly to see the expression on her face. I wanted to know what she thought about this. But her face was unreadable. She just got out of the car and led the way to Prides.

"Daddy's girlfriend, or ex-girlfriend, sometimes eats lunch here. She works in the dentist's office on Stocker—in the building where Daddy has his office."

"So that's how they met, probably."

"Uh-huh."

The hostess led us to a booth next to the window that looked out onto the parking lot. We were settling in, examining our menus (I knew I wanted French toast even though we were there for lunch), when Lily said, "Here she comes." We both looked out the window to see.

The bell over the door chimed and the woman—tall, casually dressed in a straight navy skirt and white blouse—pushed through it. She looked like a stewardess without the jaunty little cap. She went directly to the booth across from us and slid into it as if it belonged to her. That was her—the woman I'd seen. That Paula person.

"Hey, Paula," the hostess called out to her. "Coffee, right?"

"And a grilled cheese, please."

"Coming up."

We stared. Then Lily went back to her menu, but I couldn't tear my eyes away. The woman looked confident, sophisticated. Fair skinned with straight jet-black hair pulled into a tight, severe bun. I thought of the word *chic*.

I didn't like her. She looked hard and it seemed to me she was trying to cover it up with a lot of smiling. She pulled a pack of cigarettes from her purse and shook one out. Then she lit it and took in a long drag and looked around. Her eyes landed on us and slid right off.

She checked us again, and this time she frowned as if trying to place us. Maybe my daddy had shown her a picture of Lily and me. Maybe a family photo sat on his desk.

I saw something dawn on her suddenly, and then felt her sneaking a second look. I buried my head in the big glossy menu and nudged Lily under the table with my foot. She ignored me.

Lily took the bottle of ketchup off the table and placed it on the seat beside her. Then she got up and walked right over to *Paula*.

"I'm sorry," Lily said. "Are you going to be needing that ketchup?"

Paula looked down at the little collection of condiments and said, "No, honey, it's all yours."

She was so different from our mother. Pretty, but with an edge—like maybe she didn't have a very nice background.

Maybe she'd grown up in an orphanage. Or in a foster home. I couldn't see what my daddy saw in her. Our mother was prettier and didn't look like she'd grown up in an orphanage.

Paula plucked a wad of gum out of her mouth and mashed it into the ashtray. She took in another drag and gazed out the window.

"You think she's waiting on Daddy?" I whispered to Lily.

"He told Mom they were finished."

"How do you know?"

"I have my ways."

I couldn't imagine what they were, but I believed her. I looked over at Paula again. My mother was way better.

We ate, shopped, then headed home with the groceries. "You want to go by the community center and check the results?" Lily asked.

"Without Jennifer?"

"Do you need Jennifer to check the results?"

So we drove to the community center, where I expected the list to be posted on the glass-encased message board in the foyer. I pulled the heavy door open, stepped inside, and looked around. The facility seemed deserted. But soon I heard voices coming from the multipurpose room.

I needed to hurry up before someone saw me. I looked back

at Lily in the idling car. She made a motion with her hand, urging me to get on with it. I studied the message board and soon found what I had come to see. There was no need to run my finger slowly down the cast list. I could see that my name was not on it. My name, Sophie LaBranche, was absent. I knew then that I had never even been considered. The role of Olivia—an important role, central to the play—was *never* mine. All that work, all that memorizing and patting myself on the back for having memorized not only my own lines but also the lines of everyone else, turned out to be for *nothing*. I had thought that would be my ace, my ticket to getting the part. My ticket for sailing right over all the competition, or passing them until they were just a dot in my rearview mirror. I'd been certain, even though I knew I had the disadvantage of being colored—being *black*. I'd fooled myself into thinking that if I was outstanding enough, it would make up for everything.

I was wrong.

Lily could see it. When I returned to the car, she didn't even have to ask. I climbed in and leaned my head against the window. There was a charged silence between us. She slowly shook her head. "Oh, what I would like to do to those people," she said. "Let me at 'em."

"Jennifer got the role of Julie," I said.

Lily looked over at me but said nothing more.

"Carla is Olivia. And she didn't even know her lines," I added.

I saw Lily's jaw clench.

CHAPTER 23
Watts Rebellion

I WAS AT THE PIANO, practicing the rough patches of "Für Elise." My mother had fresh criticism after watching me stumble through it at the recital.

Now she sat on the sofa in her khaki slacks, her legs stretched out in front of her, crossed at the ankles. She was thumbing through a *Harper's Bazaar*—looking as cool without my father as she had when she was with him. She was an expert in looking cool and sophisticated. Occasionally she stopped and squinted and aimed her ear at the piano as if this helped her to listen better. Then she said, "Do that part again. It doesn't flow. You don't sound confident—like that other little girl. That little white girl from down the street."

I looked at my mother but didn't say anything. I'd heard

Mrs. Baylor tell her that I didn't get the part in the play I'd tried out for, and I'd heard my mother say, "There'll be other plays." She didn't think beyond that. She didn't think of what it was like for me when Jennifer came bounding over after she got back from the beach so we could go to the community center to check the cast list. And my mother didn't think about how it felt when I told Jennifer I'd already seen the results and that I wasn't cast but that she got the part of Julie, and how it felt to see Jennifer's guarded happiness about getting something she'd *planned* to get.

It was almost time to watch *Gidget* on television, so I was hoping this practicing torture would end soon and I could take my misery to the den. Unfortunately, my mother looked comfortable there on the sofa, as if she was settling in for a long evening of critiquing.

Our telephone rang. We both glanced at it. Lately when the phone rang I immediately recalled the words *Do. Not. Have. Your. Whore. Call. This. House!* And I felt funny, a little skittish about answering it. What if it was someone who just wanted to hear my mother's voice? Like Paula Morrisy, who wouldn't say anything —but would just listen.

Mrs. Baylor picked up the phone in the kitchen and the call turned out to be for her.

We could hear her side of the conversation. She was talking to her neighbor Miss Cissy, who was calling to tell her about something happening right down the street from Mrs. Baylor's house. A big commotion, with police and everything.

Eventually she got off the phone and came in to tell us what Miss Cissy had said.

It seemed someone they all knew from the neighborhood, Marquette Frye, had been pulled over for drunk driving. Miss Cissy claimed he *wasn't* driving while drunk. He was just making his car swerve to the beat of "Quicksand" by Martha and the Vandellas. Kids were all the time doing that. The song was real popular.

"Marquette Frye was just feeling happy. That's all," Mrs. Baylor said. "His brother, who was in the car, had gotten out of the Air Force and wouldn't be going to Vietnam—something to be happy about. Right? Any fool could see that."

While we listened, my mother slowly shook her head and rolled her eyes as though it was much ado about nothing (one of her favorite phrases). But according to Miss Cissy, when the officer had Marquette get out of the car, that boy had no problem walking a straight line. He showed the officer that he was *not* drunk. But the officer was determined. He just wanted someone to arrest.

So he was going to arrest him anyway and have the car towed. He'd made up his mind. Just because he could. On general principle.

"Probably not a bad idea," my mother said under her breath, and I looked at her sharply. Why did she say things like that? Things critical of colored people? Like when she said, "Negroes and flies. The more she was around Negroes, the more she liked flies." How could she say that? How could she even think it?

I looked away and continued to listen to Mrs. Baylor, but I imagined Miss Cissy giving her account in a really dramatic way:

So someone ran to get Marquette's mother so she could take the car. But the police wouldn't let her. Then this big argument started up. A big argument. And people who were gathering around and seeing these things were saying, "Just let his brother go. He wasn't driving!" And "Why can't he take the car?" They know it's gonna be hard to get that car out of impound. All the fees adding up and stuff. Soon more people were standing around and looking and voicing their opinions—to the police. "It's a damn free country!" someone shouted. "Itn't it?"

I could hear that person shouting, "*Itn't it?*" I felt a small thrill saying those words under my breath.

Mrs. Baylor paused from her reporting to say, "Wonder if Nathan's home." I looked at my mother. She was checking her nails. Mrs. Baylor shook her head and continued with Miss Cissy's account.

"Then someone's mother got manhandled," Mrs. Baylor reported. "Someone's mother! Cissy's thinkin' she seen it was that boy, Marquette's, mother. Maybe the police thought she was gettin' too close. You know how afraid they are of colored people. Yes, sir—that's why they always killing us. That's why the LAPD recruits their officers from the Ku Klux Klan—or some other Nazi group. You know that's the truth." Lily came in from work and listened quietly to the rest of Mrs. Baylor's secondhand account.

She glanced at Lily and went on. "Cissy said that the people who'd gathered around didn't like how that woman got manhandled and they began to shout things. Things they been holding inside themselves—for a long time, I believe. The police started getting scared and hurried to call for more backup on their radios.

"Oh . . . it was just brewing. Brewing and spilling over. Miss Cissy and me, we both been thinkin' that. Someone threw something—a rock, I think, at one of the police. They were shouting curses at those ofays. And Cissy says the police—their faces were so red. Then, some fool set a car on fire. Why'd he wanna go and do something like that? Makin' people think they could just set fires and stuff. Whoa! That just started everything. People just thinkin', I might as well tear everything down. That's what Cissy told me."

By now Mrs. Baylor was breathing fast. This was happening close to her house. "So the cops called for the fire truck—and more police." Mrs. Baylor took a hankie out of her dress pocket and wiped her face.

I couldn't believe all of this was happening right down the

street from where Mrs. Baylor lived. Lily didn't say anything, but she disappeared into her room, probably to get on the phone with Lydia. Maybe even to try to get in touch with Nathan—if they were back together.

"Do you think you need to go home, Mrs. Baylor?" my mother asked. "I can drive you. I'm not afraid of them folks." I didn't know if she was talking about the colored people or the police.

Mrs. Baylor shook her head. "No, no. It's best that I stay here until things calm down."

My mother shrugged and turned to me. "Start from the beginning," she said, and the piano-playing critique resumed.

Later, after I was finally released from "Für Elise," I headed to my bedroom and my mother headed to hers. From behind her door, I could hear the Johnny Carson theme song and the audience's laughter, as if they were at a party, having a grand time. They were not even thinking about what was going on at 116th and Avalon.

I looked over at Lily's empty bed. She was in the bathroom —on the phone.

I couldn't go to sleep. I wandered into the den and turned on the television just to see if the networks were reporting anything about what was going on. There was nothing but regular television. It was as if the news hadn't caught up with the events.

"Cissy said she thinks there's about six hundred people in the street now just milling around," Mrs. Baylor said behind me. She'd come up to check the TV coverage as well. "Things are really getting out of hand over there. Some of them folks broke some store windows and started takin' stuff."

And yet, nothing on the news.

When Lily finally got off the phone, there were more reports from Miss Cissy via Mrs. Baylor: The looting continued. Someone threw a Molotov cocktail into one of the mom-and-pop stores and Cissy said the firemen were probably going to use those powerful hoses on the people like they used on Dr. Martin Luther King.

Mrs. Baylor paused to say she didn't think the hoses were ever used on Dr. Martin Luther King, though. But Cissy had said yes, she believed they were. Miss Cissy declared that the dogs would be coming, soon. But the people were ready! They were ready for the po-leese!

Mrs. Baylor and I stood there at the den window, looking out toward Avalon. Lily joined us and said quietly that she knew Nathan hadn't gone home. In fact, he was with a friend in Leimert Park. I looked at her. So they *were* back together. I figured. Mrs. Baylor sighed and looked relieved.

The night wore on, and eventually Miss Cissy stopped calling. We all went to bed to wait for whatever was going to happen to happen.

The next morning I hurried into my robe and peered over at Lily still asleep. Her face was serene. I wanted to get the paper. Surely there were pictures and headlines.

I slipped outside and saw how still Montego Drive looked —quiet as a ghost town, the air hushed and peaceful, the only sound the pulsing rhythm of Mrs. Cantrell's sprinklers. So untouched by the events of the night before. I breathed in the warm air and thought, *Another hot day.*

I picked up the paper off the walkway but waited until I was sitting at the kitchen table to unfold it. There it was on the first page: 1000 RIOTERS! 5-HOUR MELEE IN AN 8-BLOCK SECTION OF LOS ANGELES! By eight o'clock people driving in the area began to report attacks. Cars being stoned. Motorists targeted. The article confirmed that store windows had been broken and merchandise was grabbed. A liquor store on Avalon and 109th had been set on fire.

I felt a stir of dread. I went up into the den, looked out the window toward Avalon, and saw nothing but palm trees and clear blue sky. Then I checked Jennifer's house. Her family was gone. Probably on the trip to Catalina that Jennifer had mentioned a few days before. A ferry trip to Catalina, to go snorkeling. The whole family.

I returned to my bedroom to see Lily sitting cross-legged on her bed and talking on the phone to Nathan. "Stay away from Avalon," she was saying. "Don't go back. Promise me." She looked over as if I was intruding on her, so I retreated to the den to sit on the couch and think.

Miss Cissy had her own theory about what was happening in her neighborhood. Mrs. Baylor told us what she'd said:

The police started this. Plain and simple. They hate colored people. They like stopping them. Especially if they are driving a nice car. They just love throwing them up against that nice car and patting them down.

Plus, they kept Marquette and his mother and his brother at the scene too long. And they manhandled Marquette's mother (seen it with my own eyes) and one hit Marquette with the butt of his rifle for no reason. I was there. I seen that, too. Don't believe me. I don't care. There were plenty of witnesses to that. No reason at all. I'ma see what they going to put in the papers. Watch 'em make it all our fault. And don't you believe them police reports. They lie just as easily as they breathe. Watch 'em make it somethin' that it wasn't. Watch 'em just lie.

I checked Jennifer's driveway all afternoon, thinking they might come back early. I took Oscar out for a walk just to fill the time. Then I staked out the driveway from the porch with my book on my lap until Mrs. Baylor stuck her head out the door.

"Whatcha doing out here?"

"Just reading," I said.

"You waitin' on your little friend to get home, aren't you?"

I didn't say anything.

"She'll be back and she'll be askin' *you* what on earth is goin' on. She'll want you to tell her everything that's goin' on with the colored folks."

"But I don't know anything."

"That's not gonna matter."

I was quiet. After a while, I went inside to get something to eat and to *not wait* for Jennifer to come back.

It wasn't until early evening that I heard their station wagon pull into their driveway. I was sprawled on the den sofa switching from *Gunsmoke* to the televised accounts of all the unrest—the same scene shot from the KTLA News helicopter shown over and over again. I turned off the light and stood at the window, watching Jennifer's family unload their car.

I saw Jennifer jump on her daddy's back while he was weighed down with a giant Eskimo cooler. He almost fell over and they both laughed.

I heard her mother say, "Jennifer!" She was trying to sound

like she was scolding her, but I knew she wasn't. I knew she was happy to see Jennifer so adored by her father. For them, all was happy. All would stay happy. I tried to feel that. I closed my eyes to help me feel what they felt.

But I already knew I was going to go through a rough, lonely patch. Linda Cruz would be taking my place. Jennifer would be Julie. Carla had stolen my role. And Lily would be leaving. How was I supposed to get through all of that?

Jennifer's mother was still pretending to scold. "Your daddy's tired. Let him be." But Jennifer hung on anyway, and her father pretended to try to shake her off, which made her laugh and laugh. He started to trot around the front yard like a horse. Jennifer's mother hauled two grocery bags out of the car and went into the house, ignoring them. She left the door open behind her, revealing a rectangle of welcoming light. Finally, Jennifer's daddy —with Jennifer still clinging to his back—trotted inside.

The unrest was not stopping. It was going on and on and making the country watch and comment and predict and scratch their heads—as far as I could see.

First thing the next morning, I marched across the street and rang the bell. Jennifer opened the door. "Hi, Sophie," she said, and stepped aside so I could enter. Jennifer's mother suddenly appeared. She was putting her hand on my shoulder and looking at me with a face full of sympathy. "Oh, Sophie. How *are* you?"

"I'm . . . fine," I said, a little puzzled.

"Isn't it *terrible* what's going on? I'm in shock."

"Yes," I said. "It's terrible."

"But why? Why are the colored people doing all that . . . *rioting?* I'm trying to understand. Do you know anything? I mean, do you know people over there or maybe have relatives?" She was looking at me closely and with hope—as if I could clear things up for her, tell her the inside story as to why colored people were acting up in this way. She continued to study me behind glasses that seemed to make her eyes big and owlish and full of expectation.

"I don't know anyone from there. Only Mrs. Baylor," I said. "And she doesn't know anything either."

Mrs. Abbott fell silent, and I felt as if I was letting her down, and also letting down Jennifer's grandmother, who was now standing in the kitchen doorway drying a cup. She looked disappointed, too.

Mrs. Abbott shook her head slowly. "Such a shame." She turned to Jennifer. "You certainly won't be going anywhere today."

"Rehearsals start today," Jennifer protested. She shot me

a quick apologetic look, then said, "Can you help me with my lines?"

"Sure," I said, feeling surprisingly grateful that I still possessed some play-related connection to her—that she was allowing me this.

I turned to Mrs. Abbott. "The . . ." I paused before I said the word *riots.* "The riots are far away," I said, as if I had a special duty to calm everyone down. "It's not near here at all."

"Of course, but we can't be sure that this . . . this *rioting* is going to stay far away."

What could I say to that? I didn't like the feeling I had talking to them, that everything was a little bit my responsibility, or that I had some special knowledge about what was going on. Because I had no special knowledge. I was just me.

Finally, Jennifer motioned for me to follow her. "Come upstairs. I got something for you."

That was a thrill. I wasn't forgotten. She retrieved a small white bag from atop her dresser and handed it to me. Inside was a pair of white shell earrings. The tiny shells dangled from a silver chain. But they were for pierced ears and mine weren't pierced. "Thank you. These are really pretty," was all I said.

I saw another small white bag on her dresser. "Who's that for?"

"Oh, that's for Linda."

CHAPTER 24
Where's Nathan?

SOMEONE WAS SHAKING me awake. I felt a breath on my face. "Get up," my sister whispered. "Come out with us. We're going to sit outside and see if we can watch the KTLA helicopter circling over Avalon."

I came up on my elbow. Lily was motioning for me to follow her.

We slipped out the window and joined Nathan on our hillside. He was quietly gazing up at the night sky and the circling helicopter. There was a charred smell in the air, faint but evident, and a light breeze on my arms and face. I was just in my summer pajamas.

We settled next to Nathan. "You know what I'm thinking?" He glanced sideways at Lily and I saw him holding back a smile.

"What?" she asked.

"This is what I'm thinking." He looked at me mischievously, as if we were in on the same joke, then back at Lily. "Now, me. If I was to be driving down the street on Avalon, all I'd have to do is hold three fingers out my car window and yell, 'Blood brother!' and nobody would mess with me. 'Cause I'm a blood brother. Anybody can see." He nudged Lily with his shoulder and they did that back and forth for a bit. "But you, my dear—you better watch out coming to my side of town."

Lily laughed. And I laughed. And then we watched the faint glow of the fires in the distance.

"What happened with your neighbor, Mr. Dawson?" Lily eventually asked Nathan.

"I checked on him this morning. He was actually just getting ready to go to Boys Market on Crenshaw. He was going to drive himself out of the neighborhood—just like that." I knew about Mr. Dawson and that he was white. Lily had already told me about him. He was an elderly man who'd refused to move when the neighborhood started going colored. He'd given Nathan gardening jobs when Nathan was in high school. His wife had died, and he had no children, so there was no one to check on him.

"So what did you do?"

"I got his list and drove over there myself. Before work."

"You're my hero," she said, and they both laughed. She kissed him on the cheek.

Nathan moved on to another topic. "They had a community meeting in Athens Park today."

"How'd it go?"

"Okay, until some guy got up on the stage and started shouting what he and his aces were going to do to the white communities nearby. Then some fool started yelling, 'Burn, baby, burn!' The reporters and cameramen turned their attention to him and *that's* what they decided to put on the television coverage. Over and over."

"Makes for better news," Lily said.

Nathan looked at her in surprise. "Now you're learning," he said.

Lily looked pleased.

"Anyway, he was probably a plant."

"A plant?"

"Yeah, they do that sometimes, the police. To stir things up or shape public opinion."

Lily looked at Nathan with absolute awe.

They were quiet for a while. "I'm going to interview a few people who are afraid to go out of their houses for Cal's student paper. Their stories are going untold."

"Don't," Lily said.

"Why?"

"It's dangerous."

Nathan looked at her as if he was debating whether to counter that. Then he seemed to move on to something else. "So you told your mother?"

Lily didn't answer. She nodded toward me. A small movement, but I saw it.

"We have no secrets from Sophia," he joked.

She shook her head again and the subject was closed.

"Stay in Leimert Park again tonight," Lily said.

"I'm going home. I'll be fine."

First thing the next morning, I went into the den in my pajamas and turned on the *CBS Morning News* while the rest of the house still slept. I knew that later Daddy was coming with money. I never thought about money, so I was surprised when I overheard my mother say to him on the telephone, "The house doesn't pay for itself. The supermarket doesn't give away free food."

The newscaster was calling Friday night the worst evening of the unrest. More looting and burning in the business section of Watts, the neighborhood where Nathan and Mrs. Baylor lived. He listed the events of last night's melee: cars had been stoned on Imperial, a supermarket on Imperial and Success was firebombed, and looters were running off with cases of soda pop and beer. A barbershop had its windows broken out, even though it had a sign that said NEGRO OWNED. The KTLA helicopter had captured all of it on film and sent the images out to the whole country.

I pulled an Oreo out of my robe pocket and twisted it apart. Then I raked off the filling with my two front teeth, as I always did. I heard water in the pipes and knew Mrs. Baylor was up (she had decided to stay the weekend and return home when things died down), so I scooted back to my bedroom before she could start scolding me about sitting in front of the television still in my pajamas and with unbrushed teeth. If she knew I was eating cookies for breakfast, there'd be an even sterner lecture.

I washed and dressed, then headed to the kitchen to sit at the table and eat a bowl of Cheerios.

"I can't reach Nathan," Mrs. Baylor said as she hung up the kitchen phone, more to herself than to me. She seemed fixed to the spot. She looked puzzled.

I saw what looked like an invitation among the stack of mail on the table. The return address was the Mansfields'. Lily was right—we were invited to their big end-of-summer bash. I wondered if it was going to be one of those boring affairs where either there was no one my age to talk to except Robin or she'd have her own friends there to talk to and I'd be ignored.

Mrs. Baylor was still next to the wall phone, looking toward the kitchen window as if lost in thought.

"Is your sister up yet?" she asked.

"I think she might be working today, so she has to get up pretty soon."

Mrs. Baylor crossed the room to the dishwasher and began to unload it, but her movements were kind of mechanical, as if her thoughts were on something else. I supposed she was staying busy to keep her mind off things.

Finally, Lily stumbled into the kitchen in white jeans and a T-shirt, but her hair was a tangled mess. She and Nathan had still been talking on our hillside when I fell asleep.

"I need coffee," she said, taking a mug out of the cabinet. She picked up the percolator and poured a cup.

"Are you getting ready to go to work?" Mrs. Baylor asked.

"No work today. People are a bit skittish about going out shopping, I guess."

"What time did Nathan leave here last night?" Mrs. Baylor asked.

Lily looked surprised that Mrs. Baylor knew Nathan had been there. "Midnight," she said with her head in the refrigerator, looking for the small carton of half and half.

"Did he say he was going straight home?"

"He didn't say, but I assumed he was going home. I asked him to stay with his friend, the one who lives in Leimert Park, but he said he would be fine. I thought he meant he would be fine at home." Lily finished pouring the cream into her coffee. She put a teaspoon of sugar in the cup and stirred. She took a sip. Suddenly, it seemed to dawn on her that Mrs. Baylor was asking all these questions because she was worried.

"Are you trying to reach him?"

Mrs. Baylor didn't answer, but her expression showed her concern. Lily ran her fingers through her hair and sat down at the table. She looked thoughtful as she quietly sipped her coffee. "Maybe he's already left for work. He has a painting job off of Adams today."

Mrs. Baylor went back to unloading the dishwasher, her expression grim.

"I can drive you home," Lily said. "Then you can look around and get some idea where he might be."

I glanced at Lily quickly. Would she really be willing to drive into Watts? Now?

"You can't do that," Mrs. Baylor said.

"I can use my mother's car. She's meeting with my father this morning, so she won't be needing it for a while."

"I don't know." Mrs. Baylor looked doubtful.

"I want to go," I said, happy that I was already dressed.

My sister turned toward me. "You're staying home."

"But I want to see what's going on."

"I can take you a safer way," Mrs. Baylor said to Lily, now warming to the idea.

Lily hurried back to our room for her purse and keys. She'd secretly had extra keys made for our parents' cars ages ago. My sister always thought ahead.

I got up and walked down the hall as if I was going to my room. But then I took a detour. I glanced over my shoulder at the kitchen and quickly eased out the dining room door. The coast was clear.

Once in the yard, I slipped around the side of the house and through the door that led to the garage. Our mother's car was unlocked. I got into the back seat and scrunched down onto the floor. I just had to pray that they wouldn't look back there and catch me.

Soon I heard Lily approaching, shaking the keys in her hand nervously. Mrs. Baylor climbed into the car on the passenger side and placed a floppy, wide-brimmed hat on her lap. I flattened myself on the floor as much as possible. Their doors slammed at the same time.

"My mother is in the shower," Lily said in a low voice, as if she could be easily heard.

She adjusted her sunglasses.

"I'll probably get into trouble for this," Mrs. Baylor said.

"I'll explain."

"Let's switch," Mrs. Baylor said. "As soon as we turn the corner."

"Why?"

"It's not gonna be safe for you. Some people might think you're white."

"Nobody's going to think I'm white. Colored people know light skin from *white*." Lily sounded annoyed.

"That ain't necessarily always the case," Mrs. Baylor said.

Lily pulled over on Angeles Vista. I held my breath and for some reason squeezed my eyes shut. They switched seats, and strangely, the sound of the motor—the turns and rhythm —sounded more confident with Mrs. Baylor behind the wheel.

She reached for the hat. "Put this on," she said to Lily. "And pull it down a bit."

My sister didn't argue. I was sure her nervousness was growing as we drove farther and farther east.

There was no way I wasn't going to look around and see what I could see. When Vernon was about to cross Central, I sat up.

Lily heard me and whipped around. Mrs. Baylor looked at me in the rearview mirror. "Oh, we in for it now," she said.

I didn't know if she was talking about the people in her neighborhood or my mother.

"What the hell," Lily said.

"I wanted to come," I whined.

Lily blew out air and shook her head. "Oh, shit," she said, then looked quickly at Mrs. Baylor. "Sorry."

"What's done is done." Mrs. Baylor began to look around, her mouth dropping open. I followed her gaze and was astounded. I expected to see police cars and newsmen everywhere, but the street looked empty, with a dangerous kind of emptiness. The entire front plate glass window of Pep Boys was blown out. Two kids, not much older than me, were carrying out batteries and car covers. A building that was once a barbershop was burned to the ground—the only thing left was the barber pole. I could see a group of kids milling about in the glass and trash and charred wood that littered the streets. It was like a party among the ruins where they were the only ones still celebrating, but I didn't believe their bravado. Where was the National Guard? I'd heard on the news that they were coming. Maybe there weren't enough soldiers for them to be everywhere.

A car full of young colored men drove slowly by. The guy in the front on the passenger side glanced at Mrs. Baylor without interest. Lily tugged down her hat and I held my breath. All up and down the business section of the neighborhood were burned-up stores. There was a tired feeling lingering in the air. It was the end of a big gala and now everyone was asleep or resting—just waiting for night to return.

Someone sent an empty bottle sailing over the car. Mrs. Baylor looked at Lily to make sure she was still hiding under her hat and behind her sunglasses. She glanced back at me. I had scooted down in the seat as much as possible while still being able to see out the window.

Ahead, the traffic light turned red. Until then we had made it through one green light after another. My heart seemed to beat in my ears as we slowed to a stop and waited. Lily drummed her fingers on the dashboard. I could feel her fear. "Come on, come on, come on," I began to say under my breath.

Suddenly a group of four or five teenage boys, shirtless and laughing and play punching each other, turned the corner. Our car seemed to be the only one on the street just then. No—there were two cars way ahead, beyond the light. One boy pointed at us and started our way, signaling to the others to follow.

Was it Lily? Could he be suspicious of her hat and sunglasses? I looked up at the red light. The boys were coming—getting closer. The one in front began to jog. The others followed his lead. It must have been Lily. I could tell Mrs. Baylor was debating whether or not to drive through the red light. It was too late. They had just about reached our car. But then they ran past. I looked back toward where they were headed. There was an abandoned ice cream truck behind us. An ice cream truck! On this hot August morning, they were running for 50/50s and Dreamscicles and ice cream sandwiches. Drumsticks.

It really *was* like their own private party with their whooping and hollering now behind us. Still, I was relieved when the light turned green and we were on our way.

"You could have gone through the light," Lily said, her voice breaking. "Why didn't you just go?"

"I wasn't going to give the police any reason to crack me over the head."

Lily looked around. There were no police to be seen. Just burned-out buildings and trash in the street and a few people roaming about. "Looks like most folks are still asleep," she said.

"You don't know where the police be hiding out. There were reports of sniper fire on the police from rooftops. Miss Cissy told me she didn't know of anyone bein' on no rooftop. But the police are shootin' first and askin' questions later. According to Cissy, the firefighters are letting buildings burn to the ground. They say they been shot at, too."

"Why's this happening?" Lily said in a near whisper, as if she was asking only herself, not anyone else.

We pulled up in front of Mrs. Baylor's house and Lily started to get out.

"Stay here," Mrs. Baylor ordered.

Nathan's car was not in the driveway. Mrs. Baylor unlocked her front door and stepped inside.

It wasn't long before she was climbing back into the driver's seat. She sat there with her hands on the wheel, breathing heavily. "He hasn't been home," she said quietly. She didn't start the car right away. She just sat there as if she was trying to think of what to do.

Then there was a woman toddling toward us from out of nowhere, it seemed. She was stout and her walk was slowed by her heavy weight. She still had sponge curlers in the front of her hair and when she neared, I could see that her housedress was actually a bathrobe.

"It's Cissy."

So that was Miss Cissy. I gave her a big smile. Mainly because I was always hearing the things she told Mrs. Baylor. Now I got to put a face with the name. She leaned on the driver's side of the car, crossing her forearms on the window sill.

Mrs. Baylor turned to us. "This is my neighbor and dear friend, Cissy. Miss Cissy to you two. This is Sophie." I smiled. "And this here's Lily, the older sister."

Lily smiled and said hello.

Miss Cissy gave us a broad, friendly grin and didn't seem the least bit self-conscious about being out in her robe. "I've heard so much about you all," she said, and I wondered what she had heard. I didn't know if that was good or bad.

She turned to Mrs. Baylor. "You lookin' for Nathan?"

"Yes," Mrs. Baylor said in a breathy way, as if she was about to hear something good or at least have a question answered.

"I hear tell the police got 'im. Think they took him to the Seventy-Seventh Precinct."

"Oh Lord," Mrs. Baylor said. "That's the police station that has a picture of Eleanor Roosevelt on the wall with the words 'Nigger Lover' printed underneath." Could that be true? I wondered. Could they really have those words on their wall for all to see?

"No," Lily said. "Not Eleanor Roosevelt. It's a picture of May Britt and Sammy Davis Jr., posted on their bulletin board, with 'Nigger Lover' written on it. Nathan told me."

"Well, whatever," Mrs. Baylor said. "All I know is that Cissy's brother—he's a cop there, they got a few—they put a noose in his locker. And wherever a colored cop sits during roll call, white cops refuse to sit in that row. There are only seven colored. Cissy's brother was put on desk duty because white cops won't ride with colored."

"If they took him, we're going to get him out," Lily said.

Lonnie Jacquette, one of Nathan's friends from high school,

saw almost the whole thing, Miss Cissy reported. "He stay over there behind Rosco's Chicken and Greens. In that little lean-to he got goin' on. I know that place ain't up to code," she added as if she was going off-track. "Seem like you could just ask him what he know."

Mrs. Baylor sighed deeply. She looked at her watch, then glanced at Lily, who seemed a bit pale with fear. "We have to find out if he's there," Lily said. "We have to."

We drove a few blocks and parked in front of a closed diner. NEGRO OWNED was written across the window in soap. Mrs. Baylor stared at it for a moment, then got out and went around to the back house that sat at the end of a narrow driveway. Lily hid under her hat, and I scrunched down in the seat and watched the street. It was as empty and as dead-looking as a ghost town.

We waited in silence.

Soon Mrs. Baylor was back. Lonnie had given her the details. It seemed Nathan was on his way somewhere when the cops stopped him.

"He had a paint job this morning on Sixth Avenue, off Adams," Lily said quietly.

The police had set up a checkpoint in the street that was nothing but a card table with a sign taped to it. Everyone was supposed to stop there. Nathan probably hadn't realized that it was a checkpoint and drove right past. Everything was so crazy, he must have thought it was just some debris someone had left in the road.

The two policemen sitting in a cruiser nearby turned on their lights and followed close behind for a block before he noticed they were pulling him over. They arrested him and called for a truck to tow his car. Lonnie thought they took him to the Seventy-Seventh.

He saw them pat Nathan down before handcuffing him and shoving him into their car. Even though he didn't have a weapon on him or anything.

Mrs. Baylor looked pained. "Of course he didn't have a weapon on him." She sat there for a moment—stunned. My sister began to cry. I couldn't even remember when I'd last seen Lily cry. Mrs. Baylor reached for her hand.

"We have to get him out," Lily said. "We have to go there right now and get him out."

"I don't think it's going to be that easy," Mrs. Baylor said. "I need to get some money for bail. You know there's going to be bail."

"Daddy can get him out," I blurted. And he could. He could go right down there to that horrible place and get Nathan out of jail.

Lily nodded. "My father will take care of this."

Mrs. Baylor started the car and we headed back to Montego Drive. I reminded Lily that our daddy was coming over to talk about money. We could ask him then to fix things.

We would have gotten away with everything if we hadn't gone in empty-handed—if we'd at least had a bag of groceries. Our mother was sitting at the table drinking a cup of tea and thumbing through a magazine. Our daddy hadn't arrived yet and she was shaking her leg nervously. I could see that she wasn't even staying on a page long enough to read it.

"Where'd you all go?" she asked, looking up.

Mrs. Baylor sat down across from her. I knew she was preparing to tell the truth. I could see it in her face. "We went looking for Nathan, Mrs. LaBranche." She looked over at Lily, who'd taken the seat next to our mother.

"I offered to take her, Mom," Lily explained. "Sophie hid on the floor of the back seat." She nodded at me. I was standing in the doorway. "We didn't even know she was back—"

"Do you know how dangerous that was?" our mother said, cutting her off. "What possessed you?" I noticed my mother had makeup on. She wasn't even going anywhere today, but she'd made up her face and fixed her hair nicely because our father was coming—to talk about money.

"Mrs. Baylor was so worried about Nathan and—"

"And you were, too," our mother finished for her. "Weren't you?"

Lily blushed and looked down. My mother stared at her a long moment, and for the first time I think she understood the feelings Lily had for Nathan.

"He was arrested, Mrs. LaBranche," Mrs. Baylor said. "A friend of his thinks they have him over at the Seventy-Seventh Precinct—in a holding cell. They're charging him with evading a checkpoint or somethin' like that."

My mother frowned. "Is there even such a thing?" She shook her head. "Whatever the case, Mr. LaBranche will be here any minute and you can tell him what's going on. He'll help you."

Mrs. Baylor thanked her, then got up to take a load of wet clothes out to the clothesline. My mother waited until she heard the door close before she turned back to Lily. "Let me tell you something," she said. "You're not going to be with that boy, so get that out of your head."

"Mom."

My mother put her hand up, palm out. "No, Lily. You're going to be leaving soon for Spelman. You're going to be meeting all kinds of suitable young men and—"

"Nathan's suitable."

"He's from a whole different"—she paused—"*culture.*"

I moved to the sink to get a glass of water to sip on.

"You mean his father isn't a doctor or a lawyer or some big shot," Lily said.

"I didn't go through all this, making sure you met the right people and did the right things, for nothing."

"Mom, he's at Berkeley. And that's where I really want to go," she added quietly.

"Oh no, my dear. You're already enrolled at Spelman. You're already in the dorm. You decide to go somewhere else—you're on your own."

Lily's face hardened. She pulled in her mouth defiantly. But then we heard our father coming through the door, using his key as if he still lived with us.

I saw my mother stiffen. She drummed the tabletop with her freshly manicured nails. She sighed and blinked. Lily and I stayed put. He came down the hall, jiggling the change in his pocket. I held my breath. This would be our first time seeing him since he'd moved out.

He stopped at the kitchen door and held on to both door-jambs as if he was holding up the house, showing us the mustache he'd grown. He looked a little like Clark Gable, though not as handsome. He'd lost some weight and his stomach was nearly flat again.

He stood there looking at us. "I'm outnumbered," he joked.

Lily got up and hugged him, but I could tell it was a hug that was barely there. "Hi, Daddy."

"Hey, Plumcake." He hadn't called her that in a long time. Then he looked at me. "What about you, Sweet Pea? You have a hug for your old dad?"

I sat there for a moment, deciding. But then I got up and hugged him loosely. I was still mad at him. We both looked at my mother. She rolled her eyes a little. "Sorry," she said. "I'm just . . . out of hugs."

She turned to me and Lily. "Can you both excuse us?"

"Mommy, don't forget to tell him about Nathan," I said.

She stared at me until I followed Lily out of the kitchen.

As soon as we got to our room, I turned to Lily. "Are you going to UC Berkeley?"

She said nothing at first. Then, "I'm not talking about that right now." She looked out the window. "I'd have to reapply and sit out a year. I don't know if I want to do that."

Maybe not. But I knew she was considering it.

Our father was efficient in getting Nathan out of jail. By that night a curfew was in effect and Nathan had been released from custody. Nathan told Lily later that there was no case. He hadn't done anything wrong. The cops just wanted to arrest folks, to feel like they were doing something. Now there were fees to pay to get his car out of impound. And for nothing. He hadn't done anything wrong.

I wondered if my mother would let my father come home now. Would she think he'd been banned from the house long enough? I'd been imagining him walking through the door with his suitcase in hand so that we all could live happily ever after. Now I pictured him living in a Motel 6, miserable. He was a hero in Mrs. Baylor's eyes, but in my mother's eyes, maybe not so much.

Nathan told Lily more about the people he wanted to write about who were afraid to leave their houses. They didn't want to see the stores that had been looted or burned to the ground and the cars that had been set on fire. They'd been huddled in their homes for four days, hoping they wouldn't run out of milk or bread or need a prescription filled. Nathan still planned to interview them so he could put together an eyewitness account for *The Daily Cal,* UC Berkeley's student paper. He'd decided he wanted to be a journalist.

"Don't go back over there, Nathan," I heard Lily tell him on the phone. "Wait until everything blows over."

Later, Lily and I sat on the den sofa like zombies and watched the news reporting the same stuff over and over. Lily said that's because TV news had only white reporters, and white reporters didn't want to be hit over the head with a Molotov cocktail. We both laughed, picturing it.

The reporting was now all about the curfew and how the National Guard was all over the place. I wondered if—for a lot of people—it was going to feel like the air had been let out of their angry protest, leaving nothing behind but a strange, empty, mocking silence.

CHAPTER 25
Nathan's Words

O N SUNDAY MORNING the news channels were showing a zillion National Guardsmen all over South Central LA. In jeeps and marching in formations. Up and down Crenshaw, protecting the stores and businesses, I supposed.

Suddenly, I wanted to see them in person. "Let's tell Mom we need to go to the store," I said to Lily while we ate our cereal. Mrs. Baylor was up in her room, having a day off at our house. Which was unusual.

"She's not going to let us."

"Let's tell her we need milk and bread and stuff," I said.

"She'll just tell us to do without."

"Tell her you need sanitary pads," I said, and burst out laughing.

"She'll give me some of hers."

Before we could work it out, Jennifer came knocking with her script in hand, asking if I could run lines with her—as if I hadn't been excluded from the beach trip, as if I felt just fine that she'd gotten her role and I didn't have mine.

"I'm going to the store with my sister," I told her. "I'll come over when I get back."

It was the truth, because Lily was suddenly standing in the doorway behind me holding up our mother's keys. "Are you ready or not?"

Ha! I immediately felt better about everything.

"How'd you get her to give you the keys?" I asked after I closed the door.

"I told her we were almost out of food and that I'd do the grocery shopping."

"She's not afraid for us to be out?"

"Nope. For two reasons, I'm thinking. The riots weren't on our side of town and the National Guard are everywhere."

"Let's take Valley Ridge," I suggested.

As we started off down the street, I didn't even glance at Jennifer's house once. I felt a strange sense of independence.

Sure enough, at the bottom of Valley Ridge was one lonely jeep parked by the side of the road. In it were two tired-looking guardsmen wearing helmets that looked like downturned bowls on their heads. Disappointing.

"Draft dodgers," Lily said behind her hand. "They get to stay out of Vietnam."

For a moment I looked at the two guardsmen differently. As if they were cowards instead of big bad soldiers. Then I sort of felt sorry for them, sitting in that open jeep in the hot sun.

One got out with the barrel of his rifle angled down. We were at a stop sign, but he held up his palm anyway, ordering us to stay there. With an air of authority, he sauntered over to us. He leaned his reddened face into the car and cleared his throat.

"Where are you coming from?"

"Our house," Lily said. "On Montego Drive." She scrunched her mouth to the side and looked down. I knew she wanted to laugh.

He gazed up the hill. "And where are you going?"

"Von's Supermarket."

He stared at us for a moment or two. That was probably required—a certain length of time to delay people. "You know there's a curfew in effect," he said.

"Yes. Tonight. Eight p.m.," Lily replied.

He gazed at us for a bit longer, then waved us on. And that was that.

Lily pretended to wipe sweat off her brow. "Did you see that rifle?" she said. "I'm shaking just from being near that thing." Then she laughed.

Jennifer's grandmother answered the door and smiled down at me as if I had just recovered from a long fever. "The girls are in the back," she said. I walked through the living room and the dining room, then through the French doors, toward laughter coming from the side patio. Linda Cruz looked up from the magazine they were twittering over and gave me a small, polite smile. She was wearing the shell earrings.

They had the magazine open to a center spread of Fabian onstage singing before an audience of mostly girls.

"Linda brought over the latest *Teen*. It's got a lot of pictures of Fabian," Jennifer said.

"Oh." I placed the script on the patio table, but something told me not to sit down.

"You want to work on that *now?*" Jennifer asked, glancing at Linda.

I shrugged. "If you want."

"Can we work on it later? Maybe around four or so?"

I was a little bit surprised, but I shrugged dismissively. "If you want," I said again, and it was okay. If Jennifer would rather —at the moment—hang out with Miss "I can't have colored people at my house either. If she came up our walkway, my father would just turn her around and send her on her way," then so be it. I could think of other things to do.

But I knew this wasn't really a dismissal. It was more Jennifer shuffling things around. I noticed the secret pleading in her smile. I saw an apology. "Could we do it later?" she repeated. *Please.*

"Okay. Later, then." I walked back through her house and out the front door. As I crossed the street, I noticed I didn't feel all that bad. There were other things to put my mind on anyway.

Nathan's words were coming out of Lily's mouth more often now. We were having dinner and I was wondering if we'd ever sit together at the table as a family again. Our mother said something about a bunch of fools burning down their own neighborhoods and my sister said "elitist" under her breath (a new word for her, I was sure).

"What did you say?" our mother asked sharply.

"That's elitist commentary," Lily replied.

Our mother frowned. "It's just a fact. It's stupid to destroy your own neighborhood."

"And you're saying that sitting at this table, in this nice house on a hill with nice views of the ocean on one side—on a clear day

—and downtown on the other, with your meals usually prepared by Mrs. Baylor—"

"I've worked hard for everything I have," our mother interrupted. "I couldn't find a respectable job coming out of college, so I did piece-work at a tie factory where I got paid by the number of ties—"

"I've heard all this, Mom. But you were light skinned and, quote unquote, *pretty*, so you got Daddy. And you got to move to this house. You don't see yourself as privileged?"

"If people work hard—"

"Yeah, some will escape being black, but—"

"Why do I keep hearing *black* coming out of your mouth? Where'd you get that word?" our mother asked, shaking her head slowly. "Wait. You don't even need to tell me."

Lily put down her fork and cocked her head to the side, then she poured out this little speech—using Nathan's jargon, I was pretty sure: "You have to understand, Mom, that this is the result of years of frustration and systemic racism and police brutality. *Years.* Everyone in LA knows that when the police stop you, if you're Negro, you keep your hands on the steering wheel and it's 'Yes sir, no sir' all the way." She took a sip of water. "They're just itching to shoot first and ask questions later."

"I've never had that problem."

"That's you."

"Like I said, if people work hard—"

"Didn't Grandma Nanny work hard? And your father, Grandpa Clemons? And didn't that man he sharecropped for cheat him every chance he got? Always making it so he owed and owed and was never able to catch up? You've told us all the stories. And didn't *you* work hard? Walking three miles to school while the white school bus drove past you?"

"And it paid off. I was able to go to college and—"

"You were the exception, Mom. Don't you know that?"

I'd never seen Lily so impassioned. She was *feeling* everything she was saying.

"What does all that have to do with this?" my mother asked. "There's just no excuse. And you can't make me think there is. Destroying your own neighborhood. That's the most ridiculous thing I ever heard of." She shook her head slowly.

Lily sighed. "They were aiming for white-owned businesses that sell inferior goods at inflated prices. There's a study out about how the poor actually pay more for the basic necessities."

That was a dead giveaway. Since when did Lily research stuff or even know about studies? She sat there primly, slipping a forkful of potato into her mouth, then chewing it with a really superior look on her face. I thought, *I must somehow put a scene like this in my novel.* Which reminded me that I had to get back to it. But not then, because it was a good TV night.

And not the next day either because Lily was off work and she and her "friend" Nathan were taking me to the La Brea Tar Pits. It was Nathan's idea. Because we'd all lived in Los Angeles our whole lives and we didn't really know what the tar pits were.

After dinner, my mother seemed to have put the disagreement with Lily behind her. She appeared in the doorway of our room while Lily was writing in her journal and I was working on my novel. I'd changed my mind about watching TV and was outlining the second chapter.

"I've got a surprise," she said to Lily. "From your father. And me." She smiled.

"Follow me." She glanced back. "You too, Sophia."

We followed our mother down the hall to our father's office. The surprise was going to be Daddy. I just knew it. He was going to be sitting behind his desk—or standing. He would try to keep a straight face, even when we rushed into his arms and he had to hug all three of us at once. We were going to be together again, and this time we would act like a family.

Our mother quietly opened the door and stood aside to allow us to go in ahead of her. The room was empty. No Daddy beaming from behind his desk. There was, however, a portable typewriter on the desk, in a little powder-blue case that snapped shut like a piece of luggage. And standing proudly next to the desk like soldiers were three matching powder-blue suitcases.

"We always paid close attention to which girls came with their own typewriter and what their luggage looked like," our mother said, smiling. "This is going to give you the right start —on the right foot." She pulled her eyes away from the suitcases and looked over at Lily to see her reaction.

Lily just stood there staring. She smiled, but it wasn't her happy smile. I wondered if our mother noticed that, too. Lily took in a deep breath and broadened her smile. "It's really nice." She moved over to our mother and gave her a hug. Not a big hug, but a hug.

"This is from your father, too. He got you the luggage and I got you the portable typewriter."

"Thank you, Mom."

"I want you to have a good start at college, Lily. You should have seen the suitcases I brought to Spelman. And they weren't even mine. I had to borrow from relations who were better off. And once I unpacked, my daddy had to haul the suitcases back to them. I couldn't even visit the homes of friends I made because I didn't own a suitcase."

I knew my mother had a whole sad side to her past, but it was always a surprise when I was reminded of it.

So now Lily had her own luggage—*for Spelman.*

CHAPTER 26
The La Brea Tar Pits

F INALLY, MY MOTHER returned to her art gallery in
Leimert Park Village. She had business to take care of, art-
ists to reassure that their work was safe. She was gone by
the time Nathan picked us up.

He had a big grin on his face and a kiss on the cheek for his
mother when she opened the front door. I was ready with my pad
for jotting down random thoughts I could use later in my writing,
just in case the tar pits turned out to be super boring.

I climbed into the back seat and looked out the window at
Jennifer's quiet house. I didn't know how to feel about her. Our
friendship was changing. Then Nathan was saying something to
Lily as he started the car; it was making her stiffen. Even though
he was telling her some "good news."

He'd talked to his roommate's father. It seemed the father had a café next to the bookstore on Bancroft. He was going to need someone in September to replace a waitress whose husband had gotten drafted. The husband had to go down to Camp Pendleton for basic training, so she'd be moving down there with him. Nathan looked at Lily quickly. His eyes went back to the road. But I could tell he was waiting for some kind of response from her.

Lily said nothing. Nathan looked over at her again. "Did you hear what I said?"

"Can we discuss this later?" she asked.

He put his eyes back on the road.

Then he said something that made me realize I'd been right all along about Lily's plans. "So you sit out the year, save money, and start next year. It can be done, and done independently of your parents."

"Can we talk about this *later?*" she said again.

Maybe Lily was thinking of her new powder-blue matching Samsonite. Or the portable typewriter now sitting on her desk, latched shut but all ready to go. *To Spelman.*

I looked out the window and thought how untouched this part of Los Angeles was compared with the streets in Nathan's part of the city. How unaffected. The palm trees along Wilshire were nice and uniform, like soldiers standing at attention, and the medians were landscaped with flowers and low shrubs. The boulevard was manicured and confident and purposeful. What was the word for this contrast? We'd passed a park on La Cienega and kids were playing happily, carefree. The contrast was . . . *amazing.* I just kept looking and looking.

At the tar pits, we wandered around from exhibit to exhibit. Soon I grew bored and wondered why we'd come. I could have stayed home writing. Even when the docent was taking us around the Fossil Lab and then on to the Observation Pit to see the real bones of a saber-toothed cat, Lily and Nathan were lukewarm in their enthusiasm. By the time we saw the Wolf Wall in the Fossil Lab and its four hundred wolf skulls, I was growing weary. I just wanted to go to the museum store to see what I could buy. I had money—Daddy had slipped me a five when he'd come by, and I felt rich. There might be a neat pop-up book, or a dinosaur diorama that I could add to my collection.

As soon as Nathan and Lily found a table on the outdoor patio and sat down to put their heads together for a chat, I told them I was off to find the store.

I drifted around picking up stuff, examining it, and then returning it to the exact same spot. The store lady was watching me, and I didn't want her to think I was trying to steal something. It was so tiresome—people always thinking you might steal.

Nothing was grabbing me. I didn't want a little brown

aragonite figurine of T. rex, with its mouth open and its teeth bared, nor did I want the *Dinosaurs of the Cretaceous Period* poster. I wandered around some more. The saber-tooth earrings looked interesting. I held them up to my ears and checked myself in the mirror on the counter, all the while feeling the clerk still keeping an eye on me. No. The earrings made me look crazy.

I kind of wanted the saber-toothed cat's skull necklace, but then I decided I'd better not. I was going into ninth grade, to a new school. Lily had already told me I should watch my weirdness, keep it in check. I didn't want to make myself more challenged socially than I needed to be.

I held the necklace up to my chest, then put it back on the counter. I wandered around some more. There were T-shirts with dinosaurs and all kinds of mugs. I didn't need a mug until I started drinking tea or coffee, and that wouldn't be until high school or college.

I headed to the book section. I'd been purposely avoiding it because books are what I always fall back on, and I needed to branch out. Immediately one book, face out on the shelf, caught my eye: *The Book of General Cluelessness: What People Don't Know About Scientific Discoveries.* I wanted it. It would make me even more interesting, assuming I already was somewhat interesting. I was pretty sure I would be the only twelve-year-old entering the ninth grade; I wouldn't turn thirteen until the third week of school. I needed to know how to be informed about *something* and not completely clueless.

I carried the book over to the clerk waiting at the cash register. She looked at the title, then looked at me. She rang it up and slipped the book into a bag. I felt I'd made a wise purchase. This book was going to help me navigate my last year of junior high without Lily to set me on the right course. Without anyone to prop me up.

When I returned to the outdoor patio, I could tell that something had happened while I was gone. Something that had Nathan leaning back in his chair with his legs stretched out and his arms crossed, looking off toward Fairfax with a frown on his face. Lily was sitting with her chin in her hand, gazing off in the same direction, but with a wistful expression. Nathan looked down at the ground. They both seemed deep in thought.

"Can we get something to eat at Farmers Market?" I asked. We weren't far from Fairfax and Third Streets. I hadn't been there since sixth grade. I loved all the stalls and the small eateries selling different kinds of food. One shop sold fudge, and behind its plate glass window you could see it being made.

"What'd you buy?" Lily asked, reaching for my bag. "Another book?" I was hoping she wouldn't take it out and read the title—at least not then. She handed the bag back. Something was definitely on her mind. If she hadn't been preoccupied, she would have pulled the book out the bag, read the title, and then challenged me to explain why I had bought it.

We didn't go to Farmers Market. We went home. In silence. Nathan said not a word. When he pulled up in front of the house, he reached across Lily and opened the door for her. Again, I noted that he didn't walk around the front of the car to open the door —and he didn't open the door for me at all.

He said nothing as we got out. Not even goodbye. What had happened while I was in the museum store? What did all this silence mean?

My sister went directly to our room and closed the door. Quietly, this time. It was serious.

But it wasn't long before I heard her on the phone with Mrs. Singer, who was calling to ask Lily if she could fill in for Phyllis. Phyllis was sick. I was allowed back in the room then. Lily looked relieved, actually. I guess she was happy to put her mind on something other than Nathan.

"Is Nathan taking you?" I asked.

"No. Nathan is not taking me." She reached back and zipped up her aqua-colored shift. She slipped on matching aqua flats and grabbed her purse. Then she left. I heard the front door close behind her. She would be walking. Pointing her nose toward Marlton Square and heading that way—with resolve.

CHAPTER 27
Really Over

I WAS REACHING UNDER MY BED for my binder and wondering how to approach the scene where Minerva doesn't get invited to a schoolmate's party, when I heard loud voices coming from the front porch. I tiptoed to the door and stood there, listening. The voices were Nathan's and Lily's. I didn't want Mrs. Baylor to catch me eavesdropping, so I slipped into my parents' room, where the window was open.

I could hear them clearly. Lily was interrupting what Nathan was saying. "Nathan, please! Let me have this one year." She was talking about Spelman.

"Let you have this one year? What does that even mean?" he said.

"I can't just sit out a year and work in some diner."

"Why not? In the long run it's not going to matter. Why are

you so afraid of being on your own? Growing up? Doing a little grunt work."

I peeked out the window. He was pacing back and forth with his palms on his head as if frustrated that he needed to make this speech and, yet, wasn't making himself understood.

"You know I've been working. I know what work is like."

"In a boutique." Then he seemed to skip over that and move onto the gist of the matter. "You love me?"

My heart seemed to stop. He was asking my sister if she *loved* him.

The pause was too long. Even I could figure that out. She was taking too long to answer. Her answer should have been on her tongue as soon as he got the question out. She should have said, "Yes," right away.

"Yes," she said quietly. So she *was* saying yes. My sister was in love with Nathan. She'd said *yes.*

"You want to be with me?"

"Yes," she almost whispered, and I believed her. "But I can't sit out a year. Please understand."

"You know," he said, "you're not that different from your mother. You just imagine you are. But you're falling in line with the bourgeoisie agenda, aren't you?"

"I'm not like my mother. I'm *nothing* like her. I just don't want to disappoint her. I thought I could, but I can't. It means a lot to her—me going to Spelman. She's had this in her head since I was a little girl. She had a rough time there—not really fitting in with all the old colored families of the East Coast and Atlanta. She was smart and got a scholarship and there were her looks, but still she never felt as if she really belonged. And now . . . she's counting on *me* to have this great experience. The one she never had."

He just stood there looking at her.

"She even bought me this beautiful set of Samsonite—powder blue, all matching. Because she'd had to borrow old, broken-down suitcases from relatives, and that made her feel so bad and worthless."

He held up his palm. "Stop. Please." Then he laughed to himself. "You really are that shallow, aren't you?" He let out a short, quick breath. "I *have* been a fool." He turned toward his car, which was parked at a haphazard angle in front of our house.

"Nathan, please," my sister pleaded. Her face crumpled. There was a look of desperation I'd never seen before. She was begging him.

He walked slowly back to her. "I'm going to ask you again. Do you love me?"

This time Lily said nothing.

"What? So you gotta think about that?"

"I said yes already."

"I don't need you to throw me a bone."

"Nathan, I'm not throwing you a bone. It's my *mother*."

"Your mother is not your responsibility."

She just stood there, looking shamed.

I continued to peek out the window. He had his palms on his face as if trying to exercise extreme patience. Then he dragged them down until his arms hung at his sides.

"She told you. She told you a month ago that you were just going to toy with me." His voice was flat, resigned, and I thought, *Had my sister toyed with him? Had she just been entertaining herself?* I couldn't believe that of her. She wouldn't do that.

"You know that's not true." Her voice was suddenly full of tears. "How can you say that to me?"

I felt stunned. Tears came to *my* eyes. This was serious.

He shook his head slowly. "Look at you," he said. "Just skipping off to your little boutique job where they don't even know you're black!"

Lily was crying. "That's not my fault! I never said anything about my race. I just never corrected Mrs. Singer. She just had it in her mind that I was Jewish, and I didn't tell her otherwise. What's wrong with that when you want the job?"

He looked at her for a few moments, then turned and walked to his car. He got in and drove away. Lily stood there in disbelief—that he could leave her that way, that there was a possibility he could just leave her forever. She began to wipe away tears.

I heard her key in the door and I scooted back to our room just in time. She went to the hall phone and called Lydia. "Can you give me a ride to work?" she asked. Lydia said something and Lily listened. After a bit she said quietly, "We broke up."

But it wasn't just her. It was me, too. She was breaking *me* up with Nathan, as well.

Maybe Lily thought Nathan would come back or maybe she thought Mrs. Baylor would say something about him—some little tidbit about his plans or his comings and goings—but over the next few days, she gave Lily *nothing*.

In fact, Mrs. Baylor became extra-polite and extra-careful to withhold any hint of intimacy or special bond. It was as if Nathan and Lily had never been "friends." It was as if my sister had never driven to Mrs. Baylor's house in search of him. As if they'd never cried together in fear when Nathan was arrested, nor experienced relief when my father had gotten him released.

I think that bothered Lily almost as much as Nathan not calling and not coming back. And we both knew there was only one more Saturday to possibly see Nathan before she left for Spelman.

By Tuesday the news channels were reporting that things were largely under control. The TV stations were showing the ruins of Watts's business section and other places in the south central part of the city over and over, making all the colored people in Los Angeles feel bad, as if it was all our fault. Making Linda Cruz and Deidre and Jilly Baker stare at me and whisper behind their hands at the library when I'd gone there to look for a book. I just couldn't continue reading old Bobbsey Twins mysteries.

I'd been browsing the stacks, when suddenly there were Jilly and Deidre following close behind me, talking loudly enough for me to hear, but not loudly enough to be shushed by the librarian.

"How come colored people act like that? Why are they always fighting and burning up stuff?" Jilly was saying to her sister.

"'Cause they like to fight all the time," Deidre said.

I eased away a bit, down the Adult Fiction section. Lily had told me I needed to move on from the kiddie stuff and read something more challenging. Broaden my mind.

"If they don't like this city or this country, they should just go back to where they came from." That was from Jilly.

I looked at the titles on the spines, pretending I was paying no attention to them whatsoever. I stopped at *Two Women.* Lily had seen the movie. She'd liked it a lot. Sophia Loren was in it. I took the book off the shelf and opened it to the first page. That's how I usually decided on a book—by reading just the first page.

Jilly, with her fat tummy showing between her shorts and her top, and Deidre, with her ratted hair and pink lipstick, moved closer. I shut the book and pushed past them, deliberately shoving my shoulder into Deidre, who was just my height. If I was going to have that reputation, I might as well finally earn it. I practically knocked her over. She stumbled into Jilly with her mouth open in protest, but no words came out.

Gosh, that was a wonderful feeling—being colored and liking to fight.

"I'm glad you didn't get that part in the play," Jilly said to my back. "Ha-ha. You thought you were going to get it but you *didn't.* So there!"

Her words stung. But I slowed my pace and pretended I couldn't hear a thing. I pulled a book out from the shelf next to me and flipped through it. Something occurred to me then. I really *could* take care of myself.

Lily's last day at Marcia Stevens would be on Thursday the nineteenth. They hated to see Lily go, but they were happy she was going off to college—though they'd never heard of Spelman, Lily added with a rueful smile on her face. "It's going to be so funny when they find out it's a Negro college," she said, sighing. "They're going to be so confused."

She came home on the evening of that last day with a bouquet of roses, and for a moment I thought maybe Nathan had brought her flowers to celebrate her final day of work. But no. It was from Mrs. Singer and her staff.

"You know what?" Lily said as I took the flowers from her so I could put them in a vase with water.

"What?"

"I told Mrs. Singer I wasn't Jewish, that I was colored."

"What happened?"

"She just laughed and laughed, then asked me why I let her think I was Jewish."

I put the vase on the kitchen table and carefully lowered the flowers into it. I filled the vase with water.

"I told her that I thought if she'd known I was colored, she wouldn't have hired me. She wondered where I got that from, and I told her that's what I'd heard, and she said no wonder no one colored ever applied."

"That's funny," I said.

"Yeah." Lily drifted off in thought. She looked so sad and drained and quiet and stunned. Poor Lily. This was the first time I'd ever seen her not in command, the first time I'd felt disconnected from her, as if I were somewhere on the ceiling looking down at her life.

I'd spent the entire summer dreading August twenty-fifth. All that anticipation, and still it had sneaked up on me so simply, so quietly. My sister was leaving in less than a week. I would be on my own. But I wasn't afraid. I picked up the vase of roses and followed her into our room. She sat on her bed and gazed out the window, but when I put the flowers down on her nightstand, she looked up at me and smiled as if she noticed my small kindness and it gave her a second of pleasure.

Lily finally began her packing. She kept the biggest piece of her Samsonite luggage open on the floor at the foot of her bed and, slowly, she began to fill it. As she thought of stuff she'd need, she just tossed it in the suitcase to be arranged later.

On Friday Lydia came to help her — or mainly to watch her pack. Lydia's parents had pointed her toward Howard University in Washington, DC, and she was due to leave the day after Lily. Now she sat on my bed while I sat crossed-legged on the floor. Lily rolled shirts and pants and skirts into tight tubes and placed them back into her largest case. It was as if the summer had dissolved right under my feet. And now we had to turn our attention to the fall and new beginnings and the mystery of what was to come.

"Do you *want* him to call?" Lydia asked.

Lily's eyes filled with tears. She had explained the breakup to Lydia in detail: the look on Nathan's face, the things he'd said, the way he went to his car and marched back to say more things, accusing her of using him and stuff.

"Yes, I want him to call. I want to explain how I feel."

Lydia picked at her peeling fingernail polish. She was wear-

ing her hair in a perfect flip with a pink headband. Flips and headbands were suddenly popular, I noticed. She had on hip-hugger
pants with suspenders. She could be in *Seventeen* if they had colored people in that magazine. "I think you explained enough.
You're tired of him. He should get that."

"That's not *true,*" Lily said, the tears spilling from her eyes.
"I'm *not* tired of him. I'm just going in a different direction than
the one he planned for me. Just for now. It's just for *now.*"

"You're tired of him," Lydia said blandly. She sighed. "Anyway, what would you say if you saw him?"

"I don't know."

"Precisely."

Then it was Saturday morning and Mrs. Baylor was gathering her
stuff, packing her shopping bags to go home for the weekend.
Lily was milling about, trying to plan it just right so she would
be the one to answer the door when Nathan came to pick up his
mother.

I was certain her mind was still full of Nathan and she was
thinking that this could not be the end. That there might still be a
tap on the window or his voice on the phone.

I knew her calls to him were going unanswered. There was
this look on her face when she replaced the receiver that told me
she'd called him. A look of pure misery. But I was the one who

told her that he wasn't even there. He'd been staying with his friend Jonah, the one who lived in Leimert Park, far from where the police were concentrating their presence, where they were likely to pick him up for nothing at all. I'd gotten this tidbit from Mrs. Baylor.

I saw my sister's face light up with hope. *See?* I wanted to say. *There's a perfectly reasonable explanation for why his phone is going unanswered.*

But this is what I know now—and it's best to learn this early: *You can't force something to happen.* If it's meant to happen, nothing will prevent it. If it's not meant to be, you can try *everything,* but it will be to no avail. She was putting all her hopes on stumbling upon Nathan when he came to pick up his mother and then charming him to take her back.

All she had to do was be there to open the door, to greet him, and . . . She probably hadn't thought beyond that.

But then I wondered about something as I glanced over at my sister sitting cross-legged on the floor, rereading what her friends had written in her yearbook. She was laughing at some, shaking her head at others. This is what I wondered: Were her feelings about Nathan based on love for him or a reaction to being dropped? I studied her as she slowly turned the pages and read some of the comments out loud—as she stopped to laugh again and to explain who had written them.

Soon Lily was making trips to the bathroom to check her reflection in the mirror. She had a special way of angling the mirror on the medicine cabinet door toward the mirror over the vanity so she could check herself from all angles. She returned to our room, stopping at the vanity to pluck at her tendrils and smooth her French roll. She put on more eyeliner. "Do I look okay?" she asked.

Then the doorbell rang. Lily looked at me. We could hear Mrs. Baylor in the kitchen, gathering her bags. Lily hurried to the door to get there before her. I stood in the hall, but out of the way. Lily opened the door.

It wasn't Nathan standing there on the porch. It was Miss Cissy.

I could see the look of disappointment on Lily's face as she said, "Oh, Miss Cissy." She took a small step back to let her through the door.

"Hey, darlins. How you two doin'?" she asked, looking around. "This is *nice*. How long you all been livin' here?"

Lily seemed flustered. "Not that long," she said. "Early spring, I guess."

"Where you all live before?"

"In the Adams district," Lily said.

"Well, that's nice, too." Miss Cissy looked around again. "Yeah, this sure is *nice*." She drew out the word *nice*.

"Thank you," Lily said. She looked down and slowly sighed.

Mrs. Baylor joined them with her arms loaded down with bags. Miss Cissy took two from her. "Well, let's be off," she said, and then they were gone. Leaving no hope for any of the scenarios that my sister had probably concocted in her head.

As soon as Lily had closed the door behind them, she stomped into her room and slammed the door. My book was in there — *Two Women* — and I wanted to read it. Right then. But I knew not to even think about going in our room to get it.

So I marched over to Jennifer's instead. I needed to hear her take on the awful situation that was tearing my sister apart.

Jennifer answered the doorbell with a guarded look on her face. As if she was happy to see me, but was unsure. As if maybe I was there to accuse her of not being a very good friend.

"Hi," I said.

"Hi."

"I have something to tell you."

She seemed to be bracing herself for a scolding.

"I mean, I need your opinion about something."

Jennifer smiled.

We sat down on the top step. She looked over at me expectantly.

"Nathan broke up with Lily."

"He's done that before."

"Not like this," I said. I told her everything while she nodded thoughtfully.

"You have to get them back together," Jennifer said simply. "It's true love."

I nodded. I already knew that.

I started to get up, but Jennifer stopped me. "My mother said I should apologize to you, but I was going to apologize anyway."

"For what?" I said, but I could guess what she meant.

"She said that I was only thinking of myself. And I was. When I was happy that I got the part, and not even thinking about how you must feel. You were the best, and you didn't get the part you wanted because—" She stopped.

"I know why I didn't get it. I'm still really mad but . . ." I let that just sit there unfinished because I didn't have the rest of the words. "I'll help you with your script anyway," I finally said.

She smiled again. "Thanks."

"My mother said there'll be other roles, and if I decide I want to be an actress, I think there will be," I told her. And suddenly I believed it.

CHAPTER 28
Another Sunday

S OMETIMES SOMETHING MAJOR can happen just like that—and with no discussion. With no warning. Daddy moved back on Sunday. I heard his key in the door while I was in the kitchen making a cup of tea for Lily. She wasn't feeling well. She'd been plagued by a headache and sore throat since the night before. Our mother told her she should spend the day in bed so she would be up for traveling in three days. For once there was no argument.

Daddy had his suitcase in his hand. He set it down and gave me a hug, then he walked directly to his bedroom. My mother was just putting on her robe. I saw him kiss her on the cheek, and she sighed and kept her face blank. Eventually she was in the kitchen making pancakes as if nothing had ever happened.

The three of us were soon sitting at the table, passing the syrup around.

"Oh," my mother said. "It seems Dale isn't going back to Dartmouth."

"Did he really flunk out?" my father asked.

"No. He enlisted in the Marines. He's already off to training at Camp Pendleton. Of course, Dovie is beside herself."

"What the hell," Daddy said, and poured more syrup on his pancakes. He always overdid everything. "So they're still having their bash today?"

"Of course."

After breakfast he settled in front of the baseball game. It seemed he just didn't *feel* like putting up with the Mansfields' annual August barbecue. But then my mother stood in the den doorway with her hands on her hips. He got up and turned off the TV, went into the bedroom, and came out dressed in his barbecue clothes (Bermudas and a hideous Hawaiian shirt).

He was obviously on his best behavior. I hoped this meant that he was really finished with that Paula person and she was finished writing him letters and calling our house and that he'd turned over a new leaf.

The barbecue was not as bad as I'd anticipated. Robin was actually cordial, inviting me to her room to sit on the floor and thumb through her 45s and set aside the ones I wanted to listen to. For each song, she told me who her boyfriend was at the time she first heard it and the places they went (their parents drove them) and the fun they had. But mostly the relationships existed on the phone, I gathered. After we got tired of listening to records, we went back downstairs to go outside and sit by the pool.

When Robin got up to take a call from her latest boyfriend, Mrs. Mansfield introduced me to a girl who'd also be going to my school. She'd been eyeing me and I'd been eyeing her. Making assessments about each other, I guessed.

Her name was Charlotte and she was very quirky in a way that you couldn't really put your finger on. You just knew there was quirkiness there. Which was funny, because suddenly it seemed as if I'd let my quirkiness go. I mean, I was still quirky, but it was more of a . . . *subdued quirkiness.*

Charlotte was dark and petite. Her hair was braided in neat cornrows. She had large black eyes and shiny gold hoops in her pierced ears. But I had to do all the talking. I had to ask all the questions. She seemed shy, pensive (my new favorite word).

As soon as she introduced herself, I recognized the English accent. "I was named after Queen Charlotte, in fact," she said. She raised an eyebrow as if daring me not to believe her.

"Who?"

"Charlotte of Mecklenburg-Strelitz, the wife of King George III. She was queen of England and Ireland from 1761 to, oh, I don't remember. It was said she had African blood."

I looked at her, stunned.

"If you don't believe me, you can look up portraits of her. She was fair but her hair was pretty kinky and her lips were pretty thick." Charlotte gave me a tiny smile and went on. "I heard Josephine had African blood as well, being from Martinique and all."

"Who's Josephine?"

"Bonaparte. Napoleon's wife. You know, the one who said, 'A woman laughing is a woman conquered.' Which I agree with wholeheartedly. Don't you like best the boys who make you laugh?" She asked this shyly, as if I might not know what on earth she was talking about.

I didn't know. I didn't remember any boys making me . . . Oh, there was Anthony Cruz when I walked Oscar. I was struggling to remember what he'd said exactly, when Charlotte moved on to another topic.

"Sophie," she said suddenly, "if I tell you something, will you promise not to tell—since you and I will be at the same school?"

I nodded.

She lowered her voice. "I'm only twelve. But going on thirteen. I'll be thirteen in December. December fourth."

"I'm going on thirteen, too," I said. "My birthday is in a couple of weeks."

"I know you're in . . ." She paused. "It's called ninth grade? When you're fourteen."

I nodded. "Most ninth graders are fourteen."

"But school in England is more advanced than here—so they're putting me in the ninth grade. At twelve."

I felt almost giddy about this coincidence. "You, me, and my friend Jennifer are all in the same boat."

She looked a little bit relieved.

"Jennifer goes to a private school. Marlborough. It's very ritzy."

"Oh."

"So why did you move from England?" I'd forgotten what Mrs. Mansfield had told me.

"My father's a surgeon. He got a position at the same hospital as Dr. Mansfield. They're colleagues."

I liked the way she said "colleagues," and I said it over and over in my mind. "My sister's leaving on Wednesday for college. She's going to Spelman. It's a college for Negro women."

"Negro . . ." she repeated.

"For colored women."

"We're called British in the UK or sometimes by one's home country. You know, Nigerian if you're from Nigeria or Ghanaian if you're from Ghana."

"I know how to shake hands like the men do in Ghana."

"Show me," she said.

I demonstrated: shake, slide back palm to palm just a bit, and then snap.

"That's lovely!" she said, her eyes bright.

She lived on Enoro Drive. She could walk to my house easily, so we made plans for her to come over and maybe meet Jennifer, whom I knew she'd like. I suddenly felt as if I was taking the lead instead of just following.

Daddy was glad we got home in time for the preseason football games. He went straight into the den and clicked on the television.

After a little bit, I could hear my mother running a bath.

Our bedroom door was closed, so I knocked on it, not too loudly and not too softly.

"Come in, Sophie. I'm awake."

Lily was sitting up in bed with a magazine on her lap. On top of the magazine were several sheets of writing paper. "I'm writing him a letter," she explained. She tapped it with her pen.

I stood there growing sad because she was sad. I had a question to ask. "Why did you hesitate, Lily?"

"Hesitate? What are you talking about?"

"I heard you guys arguing. Why did you hesitate when he asked you if you loved him?"

"You heard that?" Lily looked miserable remembering. "Because just at that moment, I didn't know if I did or not."

"You should have said yes. That's what did it. That's what turned him off."

"I know that, Sophie. Promise me you'll mail this letter after I'm gone."

"Why don't you just mail it from Atlanta?"

"I don't want it to have an Atlanta postmark. I don't want this to seem like an afterthought. Like I'm throwing him a bone, as he said."

"Then why don't you mail it tomorrow?" I took the letter out of her hand. It had a Berkeley address.

"His roommate will save it for him. Anyway, I want him to know I'm already gone when he gets it. So he'll know I'm not expecting anything. I don't want him to think at all that I'm trying to manipulate him. I just want him to know what's in my heart."

Her eyes welled up on the word *heart*. She plucked a tissue out of the box on her nightstand and wiped her eyes and blew her nose. There were already several wadded-up tissues on the bed. She folded the letter and placed it in the envelope, then sealed it and handed it to me. "Don't forget."

I took the letter from her. I knew something Lily didn't know —because I had eavesdropped. Mrs. Baylor was returning from her weekend early. Our mother needed her first thing Monday morning to box up things for the Salvation Army truck that was due by ten. It was a last-minute task, but my mother (as she explained to Mrs. Baylor) was determined to get it done. She was sick of the clutter. So on Monday, while Lily slept, I went up to the den with a bowl of Cheerios and staked out the front porch.

I saw them pull up. I saw Nathan get out of his car to help his mother with two of her bags and a box. Maybe something to be added to the Salvation Army stuff. I made it to the front door before Mrs. Baylor could ring the doorbell.

She looked surprised when I threw it open. "Mornin', Sweet Pea," she said, using the name my daddy calls me.

I smiled with pleasure. "Morning. Can I speak to Nathan?" I added quickly.

She shrugged. "It's a free country." She moved past me.

Nathan's face was somewhat stony, but it softened when he looked down at me. He held out his hand and we did the Ghanaian handshake. Then I started to cry, which surprised me because I didn't even think I was going to. But it was the kind of cry where tears just come to your eyes and stay there. I handed him the letter. "From Lily."

At least he took it.

"*Promise me* you'll read it."

He didn't promise right away, but he turned it over and looked at what I'd written on the back. He smiled at me and folded it in half. He put it in his pocket. "I promise," he said. He saluted me and walked back to his car. I watched him drive away.

CHAPTER 29
So Long, Lily

THE DAY CAME, just like that. The sun was shining. Someone in the neighborhood was mowing the lawn, and I could hear pigeons cooing. The riots were no longer front-page news. Now, in other sections of the paper, there were articles about *why* it had happened.

The night before, I had gotten on my knees and prayed to God that Lily would be okay. I thanked Him for my new friend, Charlotte, as well. I thanked Him for Nathan taking the letter and for Mrs. Baylor liking me and saying I was a good person. She's a good person, too, and she raised Nathan to be a good person. I almost cried for all the good people in the world.

There was so much goodness, I didn't even care about Linda Cruz or the Baker family—not even a little bit. And I'd put

my writing aside. Just to take a little vacation from it. I'd revisit
Minerva, probably when Charlotte and I got our club going. We
planned to petition the school to have a writers' club. Charlotte
was into poetry. There were probably more students who needed
the company of other writers, as well. So we had our plans.

Lily's luggage was beside the front door. I wondered how she'd
manage with it. Then my mother explained that the skycap would
be at the curb ready to take care of her bags, and when Lily arrived in Atlanta, Dovie's sorority sister would be there to pick
her up and take her to the campus. And there were always some
Morehouse students ready to lend a hand for a pretty girl. That
was the men's college across the street. For Negro men.

Lily was wearing the navy sailor outfit she knew our mother
liked. "Why not make her happy," Lily had explained to me.
"Sometimes you have to do that because she means well. You
know?"

I nodded. I knew exactly what she meant. Then I thought
about her bed. I planned to meet more people and have slumber
parties when I started going to high school in another year. Tenth
grade would be here before I knew it. Her bed was going to come
in handy.

I had such plans!

We lived so close to the airport in Inglewood, we were there in no time. Lily was quiet during the entire ride, whereas my mother chatted nervously, giving advice about curfews and the procedure for receiving a gentleman caller and housemothers and vespers on Wednesdays. And how to get along with a roommate. And how to behave if you should visit a roommate's family. Lily just quietly listened with her head turned toward the window, watching the passing scenery.

"Nina, Nina, Nina," our father finally said. "Don't overwhelm the girl. She'll learn as she goes."

Our mother stopped, looked at our father with a tiny smile on her lips, and then pressed them together to keep more chatter from spilling out.

We parked in the garage, then walked like ducklings in a row into the terminal and all the way to the gate. We'd stopped to check Lily's baggage with the skycap, leaving us free of the Samsonite at last. We found seats next to each other at the gate, which was lucky because everyone seemed to be flying to Atlanta on that day at the same time. We were quiet, and it felt like we were in a hospital waiting room and the doctor was going to come out any minute to tell us something important. Lily sat ramrod straight, looking neither to the left nor to the right. I could tell she'd resigned herself to never seeing Nathan again. I'd resigned myself to never seeing him again until maybe his winter break. Mrs. Baylor mentioned he'd be going back up to Berkeley in the next day or so.

I looked at my parents. They were huddled together, deep in conversation.

Then there was the stewardess in her smart blue uniform and jaunty hat, with the microphone in her hand, announcing Lily's flight and that the passengers could board the plane. Lily got up. She gave me a long hug. "Branch out," she said in my ear. She gave our mother a long hug, too, but she gave my father the longest hug of all, as if to say, *You'd better treat my mother right. You'll be old one day and looking to her to feed you your applesauce.* At least that's what I thought the hug meant.

We turned toward the escalator. I looked back to see Lily before she boarded, and suddenly there was Nathan—standing near the entrance of the gangway. Nathan, really *there.* And it was not my imagination—or Lily's. Her knees actually buckled a bit. Then she was walking toward him and taking his hand and talking to him fast and desperate.

My mother glanced back to get a last look at Lily. She stopped and pulled on my father's arm. But I scooted to her side. "Mom, she's going. She's going to Atlanta. Nathan's just saying goodbye. That's all." I had to make it so my mother would let

them say goodbye. *Goodbye*. Being able to say goodbye is important—for everyone.

I wondered what Lily would say if she knew what I had
done—that I'd put the flight information on the back of the envelope that held her letter, as well as the phone number of her
dorm. I'd gotten it out of my mother's datebook. Nathan had
smiled when he saw that number, and that had given me hope.
Could I ever tell her? Yes, I could. I wanted credit—for whatever
was going to happen, because I believed it was going to be good.
Before we reached the escalator, I looked back again to see Nathan moving away and Lily searching the crowd. She found me
and waved goodbye.